Class No. _FC(IR)_ Acc No. _C/151047_

Author: _Corkery, D._ Loc: ~~8 JUL 2000~~

LEABHARLANN
CHONDAE AN CHABHAIN

_____

_____

_____

1. **This book may be kept three weeks. It is to be returned on / before the last date stamped below.**
2. **A fine of 25c will be charged for every week or part of week a book is overdue.**

The publishers gratefully acknowledge the financial assistance
of the Arts Council/An Chomhairle Ealaíon

First published in 2003 by Mercier Press
Douglas Village, Cork
Email: books@mercierpress.ie
Website: www.mercierpress.ie

Trade enquiries to CMD Distribution
55A Spruce Avenue
Stillorgan Industrial Park
Blackrock, County Dublin
Tel: (01) 294 2560; Fax: (01) 294 2564
E-mail: cmd@columba.ie

© Estate of Daniel Corkery 2003
Selection © Paul Delaney
ISBN 1 85635 419 9
10 9 8 7 6 5 4 3 2 1

A CIP record for this title is available
from the British Library

Cover design by mercier vision

Printed in Ireland by ColourBooks,
Baldoyle Industrial Estate, Dublin 13

Daniel Corkery

The Stones and other stories

edited by Paul Delaney

Mercier Press

CONTENTS

INTRODUCTION

For many years Daniel Corkery has occupied a controversial position in the history of Irish literature. This is largely a result of comments which were included in his critical study, *Synge and Anglo-Irish Literature* (1931). In the opening chapter of that book, Corkery dismissed the entire tradition of Anglo-Irish literature as neither national nor natural, remarking that, 'Ireland has not yet learned to express its own life through the medium of the English language'. Corkery also argued that unless writers are absorbed in the forces of Nationalism, Religion (that is to say, Catholicism), and the Land, their work should not be considered Irish. Through the application of these criteria, many writers found themselves rejected from his literary canon. Some writers were dismissed because they didn't engage with the right issues, while others were disallowed because of their ancestry and religion; others still were discarded because they lived too long abroad (the so-called 'wild geese of the pen'), or because they wrote primarily for an overseas audience.

For these reasons, Corkery has often been remembered as a rather doctrinaire figure and his name has been invoked to signify an intolerant and insular mode of defining ideas of Ireland and 'Irishness'. However, while there is plenty of evidence to substantiate these claims – especially as Corkery became increasingly didactic in his later years – there is nonetheless also a sense that this is only a part of his larger significance. His biographer, Patrick Maume, for example, has drawn a fuller portrait of a more complicated and less self-assured individual, and has chronicled the ways in which Corkery changed in the early decades of the twentieth century, from being a sensitive provincial intellectual to becoming an exclusionary critical figure. It is important, therefore, that any reading of Corkery should begin with a consideration of his cultural and political context.

Daniel Corkery was born in Cork in 1878, and died in the same city in 1964. He travelled little in his lifetime, but nonetheless exerted a considerable influence as a writer, a cultural nationalist, and a teacher. He was shy, slightly lame, and a bachelor. He was actively involved in the Gaelic League, and was a prominent member of the Irish Ireland movement; he also played a part in the establishment of a number of local cultural organisations, like the Cork Dramatic Society. Corkery was an Irish-language enthusiast (although not a native speaker), and was republican in politics. He was a close friend of Tomás MacCurtain and Terence MacSwiney (successive Lord Mayors of Cork), and was shocked by the brutal manner of their deaths during the War of Independence; he was also profoundly disturbed by the Civil War. It has been suggested that these events contributed to a shift in his thinking in the 1920s, and that this led to a narrowing of his interests and concerns in the post-Treaty years.

Aside from his involvement in polemics and politics, however, Corkery was also an accomplished water-colourist, and for much of his life served as a mentor to younger generations of artists and writers. Perhaps his most celebrated protégés were Frank O'Connor and Seán O'Faoláin. (His influence on the early work of both writers is recorded in their autobiographies, *An Only Child* and *Vive Moi!*) After many years in education, Corkery was appointed Professor of English at University College Cork in 1931; in later years, he served in the Seanad and on the Arts Council. In addition to these activities – and notwithstanding his reservations about Irish literature in English – Corkery was quite a prolific writer. His published works include the acclaimed study, *The Hidden Ireland* (a study of eighteenth century Munster Gaelic poetry) and *Synge and Anglo-Irish Literature*. He also wrote a novel, a few plays (including an Irish-language play, *An Doras Dúnta*), several pamphlets, some poetry, scores of articles and essays, and four collections of short stories.

Corkery's non-fiction – with the possible exception of sections of *The Hidden Ireland* – has been regularly criticised for being parochial or unsophisticated. This criticism has been principally directed against his exclusion of 'non-native' writers, and his representation and romanticisation of the Irish peasantry. In contrast, many of his stories have been praised for providing a controlled and complex depiction of Irish society (particularly Irish rural life) in the process of transition and change. Many of his stories are austere, unsettling and intricate, and are memorable for their evocation of atmosphere and their use of silence and understatement.

Corkery's first collection of short stories, *A Munster Twilight* (1916), provides evidence of this. It consists of a dozen stories and a loose sequence of tales entitled 'The Cobbler's Den'. Approximately half the stories in this collection are set in the back lanes and dilapidated tenements of Cork city, while the rest of the stories range across the hidden glens and fields of the surrounding countryside. *A Munster Twilight* has a strong local flavour (a characteristic of Corkery's fiction), and references places throughout County Cork and neighbouring Kerry. It sketches communities and a landscape which are unlike anything depicted by the writers of the Celtic Twilight movement. Corkery's cast

8

of characters are largely unromantic (those in 'Solace' are perhaps the exception, with their talk of 'the pride of the Gael'), and include the slum-dwellers of 'The Cobbler's Den', and the inarticulate, traumatised peasantry of 'Storm-Struck' and 'The Ploughing of Leaca-na-Naomh'. The stories in this collection gain verisimilitude through their use of language, and make use of realist literary techniques. They also draw upon the conventions which govern traditional forms of oral storytelling. Corkery draws on these conventions but infuses them with a sense of originality. An early review of *A Munster Twilight* for the *Times Literary Supplement* noted as much, when it remarked that 'Mr Corkery's stories read as if he had heard them from old Irish peasants and set them down in his own way ... so that the endings of his tales come with a queer, unexpected, epigrammatic turn'.

A number of stories in *A Munster Twilight* are narrated by outside figures who act as interpreters or cultural commentators – the narrator of 'Leaca-na-Naomh' is an obvious example, as are the American tourist in 'The Cry' and the English traveller at the close of 'Solace'. In the course of each of these tales, these figures are confronted by strange experiences, and struggle to make sense of unfamiliar customs and ancient pieties. A biographical reading is available, which suggests that the situations which confront each of these characters are similar to the problems which faced Corkery as a writer – it will be recalled that Corkery was city-born, and that in his early years he was unfamiliar with country life or the Irish language. Indeed, in his notebooks, Corkery agonised over his ignorance of rural Ireland, and remarked (in terms reminiscent of Synge on the Aran Islands) that 'our peasants have not got into print – I know nothing of them'. As Corkery became more proficient in Irish, however, and as he journeyed into the remote areas of West Cork, he came to see himself increasingly in the role of a collector or intermediary – mediating between different cultures (oral and literary), and working across different languages. Declan Kiberd has argued that there is a sense in which Corkery presented himself 'as a collector of folklore' in these stories, as his narrators record a trove of anecdotes and tales, and reflect on the ways in which these tales are told.

Many of the stories in *A Munster Twilight* fuse traditional oral techniques with modern literary conventions. Some of the stories make use of residual oral practices and are told in an almost conversational mode, while other stories are written in a more orthodox literary form, but retain an oral echo. Corkery offers a link between these traditional practices and the 'hidden world' of the Irish language. Significantly, while all of his stories are written in English, many of them have an Irish-language resonance – his stories repeatedly draw upon Irish idioms, phrases, prayers, and placenames, and these are sometimes left untranslated by the narrator as if to suggest the sense of a different cultural order. At the same time, it is ironic that while many of his stories display traces of orality, most of the characters in his stories are extraordinarily reticent or quiet. It often appears as if these characters lack an adequate linguistic register to express their innermost thoughts and feelings. Corkery seems to suggest that this is a result of their having endured private anxieties and disappointments (such as heartbreak, loneliness and frustrated ambition) as well as communal traumas, like exile and the crossing over from one language to another. This emphasis on silence and inarticulacy is a characteristic of Corkery's fiction.

Corkery's characters, and his rural characters especially, are typically in tune with their surroundings; they are sensitive to changes in the atmosphere, the elements, and the environment. (In this regard, he is once again reminiscent of Synge.) Indeed, there is often a virtual correspondence between his characters and the places that they inhabit. 'With which shall I begin – man or place?' asks the narrator of 'Leaca-na-Naomh'. This stress on the significance of place, and the attendant emphasis on the power of the land, is a further characteristic of Corkery's writing. It is central to stories like 'Leaca-na-Naomh' and 'The Spancelled', and it gives added significance to those displaced characters in 'Solace' and 'Storm-Struck'.

A Munster Twilight was published to critical acclaim in 1916; it was followed in 1920 by the controversial collection *The Hounds of Banba*. Dedicated 'to the young men of Ireland', this book is often dismissed, perhaps unfairly, as crude nationalist propaganda. It is certainly Corkery's weakest volume of stories. *The Hounds of Banba* comprises six interlinked stories, which describe the experiences of a Volunteer on the run in the period between the Easter Rising and the War of Independence. It also includes three separate stories which take place after the ambush at Soloheadbeg. In its representation of the Volunteers, and its depiction of feats of heroism and sacrifice, Corkery's collection is reductively idealist. The portraits of the Volunteers are often two-dimensional (there are the grim-faced republicans in 'Cowards?' for instance, and the dignified Sinn Féin prisoners in 'Colonel Mac Gillicuddy Goes Home'), and these images are repeatedly set against the agents of a drunken and indiscriminate British army. Moreover, the stories in *The Hounds of Banba* refuse to countenance any sense of individuality, and resist consideration of the human costs of violence. 'Colonel Mac Gillicuddy Goes Home' is the exception, and tells a nightmarish tale of trauma, guilt and narcosis.

By avoiding any reference to loss or suffering, *The Hounds of Banba* differs from other celebrated pieces of contemporary literature, which also engaged with the energies and the anxieties of this stressed period in Irish history – pieces like Sean O'Casey's Dublin trilogy, Yeats' *The Tower*, and Frank O'Connor's *Guests of the Nation*. Seán O'Faoláin succinctly made this point, in an article on his former mentor in *Dublin Magazine* in 1936. By this time, O'Faoláin and O'Connor had both grown apart from Corkery, and were critical of his ideas and his influence. Looking back on the reception of *The Hounds of Banba*, O'Faoláin recalled how he and his fellow Volunteers had enjoyed the stories for 'as long as we were elated by being young revolutionaries'. However, 'the more we saw of revolution', he added, 'the less we liked Corkery's lyric, romantic idea'.

If *The Hounds of Banba* is Corkery's weakest volume of stories, *The Stormy Hills* (1929) is probably his finest. The stories in this collection rehearse themes and concerns which were explored in *A Munster Twilight*. Once again, the focus is on the power of land and place, and the key words for Corkery are silence, restraint and hidden. Unlike his earlier volume, however, only two of the stories are set in the city, and one of these ('A Looter of the Hills') depicts characters regressing into memories of the countryside. Several of the stories employ a seascape to represent a life of adventure and chance; however, the majority of the stories deal with the relationship between people and place, and portray characters struggling against rock-strewn hills and unyielding fields. As Colbert Kearney has noted, the outcome of each of these struggles varies according to the attitude of the characters who are involved – 'those who break the taboo against absolute mastery' over the land 'suffer for their impiety', but 'those who respect the sanctity of the soil achieve a precarious happiness'. For all the talk of sanctity and impiety, however, the stories refuse to lapse into any kind of easy sentiment. The peasants and the farmers are never romanticised by Corkery (the land hunger to which they are prey, in stories like 'The Priest' and 'Carrig-an-Afrinn', remains a sinister force), and a sense of austerity dominates the collection.

There is also a strong sense of loss in this collection, and Corkery repeatedly makes use of the figure of an elderly individual who can't fully understand the world in which he or she now lives. Tadhg Kinnane, John Redney, Mrs Donaghy, Father Reen – these are just some of the many ageing characters who are forced to realise that things have changed in their world. Old customs have died away, and local values and traditions have not been passed on. Thus, when the Colonial begins to dance in 'Nightfall', he becomes an object of instant derision. The gathered crowd comment on 'how limited his steps were', and the narrator remarks that 'to them who had often seen prize dancers from Cork city or Limerick … his style seemed old-fashioned and slow'. Not only have local customs fallen out of favour in these places, the people in these places have lost the ability to interpret or make sense of their surroundings. 'The Stones' is set in an area called Kilclaw, and the reader is told that that placename might mean Stony Wood or the Stone Church. However, it would appear that 'nobody now knows which'. The sense of loss and dislocation is reiterated throughout many of the other stories in this collection. It finds its most poignant expression in 'Carrig-an-Afrinn', where Corkery recounts the tale of another old man, Michael Hodnett, who has grown increasingly obsessed by the memory of a farm he once worked.

Alongside the many instances of loss and dislocation, there are also moments of inheritance and continuity in *The Stormy Hills*. In 'The Awakening', the issue of inheritance is made manifest when Ivor comes into possession of his father's boat, and promises to keep up the traditional work practices which he has learned from his paternal predecessors. And in 'A Looter of the Hills', continuity is provided by the land, or rather by the smells and the tastes of the land, which allow Mrs Donaghy to project back into the memories of her childhood. In Corkery's later work, especially, the city is an unfamiliar place, whereas the land is a repository of memory and identity. Kinship with the land secures a sense of identity; it provides a link between the past and the present through the presence of communities, locations, and placenames (even if the meaning of some names has been lost). At the same time, the relationship between people and place is harsh and sometimes disfiguring, and communities are often made up of broken and ungenerous people. In 'The Priest', for instance, Father Reen speculates on 'the little stony fields that only centuries of labour had salvaged'; these fields demand 'unremitting toil', but only provide a 'poor return'. Moreover, these fields participate in the brutalisation of the people who work them – to the point where the inhabitants of Kilmony are only concerned with price and possession, and are blind to other values and principles.

The most forceful expression of this relationship is provided in 'The Stones' – a haunting story which turns on the belief that the stones of Kilclaw can assume the appearance of local people who are going to die. This suggests an almost elemental proximity between people and place, and the story draws on elements of black magic, pagan ritual, and oral superstition. The narrator is sceptical of this belief, and his scepticism is apparently borne out in the closing lines of the story, when John Redney sees his own image in the stones, but continues to live on, albeit in fear and 'tongue-tied silence'. Despite the narrator's disbelief, however, other characters have been clearly impressed by the legend. Jack Lambert, for example, who is initially described as a worldly type 'who has long since outgrown the beliefs of the hillside', reassesses his opinions before the story's end. So, too, do the village's youths. There is a strong sense of ambiguity in this story, and there is also a sense that information has been deliberately withheld. There is the suggestion, for instance, that Redney's knowledge of the stones is somehow linked to his marginal status and his impoverished condition; however, this is never really developed. Instead, the story is riddled with gaps and echoes, and the atmosphere is charged with a mysteriously unspoken significance. It is perhaps Corkery's finest achievement as a short story writer.

Corkery's final volume of short stories, *Earth out of Earth*, was published ten years after *The Stormy Hills*, in 1939. In many ways it is his forgotten text. Ironically, Corkery himself thought that it contained much of his best writing – when he was asked to compile a selection of his stories for publication in the United States in 1950, a number of the stories came from this collection. Few readers have concurred, and the popular consensus is that the stories in *Earth out of Earth* are outdated and rather uneven. Michael McLaverty, the storyteller, however, has argued otherwise. Indeed, McLaverty claimed that *Earth out of Earth* is Corkery's greatest collection, and singled out the story 'Vision' as 'a little masterpiece'.

'Vision' is one of several stories in *Earth out of Earth* which are written from the perspective of a child. It records the observations of a young boy who travels to a country fair with his father. The story is, in effect, a prose poem, and the young boy's pride in his father acts as a refrain to the story line – time and again he cites the belief that his father is 'a good judge, none better'. The boy's belief in his father's abilities is supported by most of the other male characters in the story. Significantly, it is set against the opinions of the boy's mother, who sounds a more pragmatic note at the story's end. On their return home, the mother rebukes her husband for settling for a poor price at the fair ('Only twelve pounds for the lot?'). Her rebuke, although only partially heard, is significant insofar as it contrasts with the behaviour of most of the other women characters in these stories. Apart from the feisty Maggie Maw in 'The Cobbler's Den', Corkery's female characters are generally invisible and are seldom heard to speak. In 'The Priest', for instance, Father Reen has difficulty identifying the women because their faces are 'so deeply hidden within the hoods of their cloaks'; in 'Refuge', the unnamed daughter remains silent, and 'in the background', for the duration of the tale; and in 'The Forgiveness', Hettie is described as being 'quiet and silent', and Theig's estranged wife moans but barely speaks. Although silence is also expressed by many of the men in these stories, it is intensified when it is directed by or towards women. Evidently, a gender dynamic is at work which suggests different modulations of silence, and which adds a further inflection to instances of speech.

As this brief introduction has indicated, certain issues pre-occupied Corkery in his short fiction. Many of his stories revolve around the relationship between people and place, and provide a meditation on the limits of silence and speech. Moreover, many of his stories explore the significance of traditional customs and practices in a modernising society. Given his persistent interest in these issues – together with his focus on the Munster landscape, and his attention to the residual significance of the Irish language – it could be argued that Corkery was an obsessional writer. Time and again in his later stories, he returned to ideas and incidents which he had already expressed in his fiction. 'Death of the Runner' is but one example, and bears obvious traces of 'The Ploughing of Leaca-na-Naomh'. Regardless of whether the stories were written early or late in his career, however, all of Corkery's best stories share a sense of things unspoken or understated. There is a sense of mystery in his work, and scrupulous attention is paid to the idioms of rural Ireland and the cadences of the speaking voice. His best stories rank amongst the finest in the history of Irish literature.

The twenty stories in this selection are arranged in order of publication. The first six are from A *Munster Twilight* ('The Ploughing of Leaca-na-Naomh', 'Storm-Struck', 'The Cry', 'The Spancelled', 'Solace' and 'The Cobbler's Den' sequence). The next two are from *The Hounds of Banba* ('Cowards?' and 'Colonel Mac Gillicuddy Goes Home'). Nine stories are from *The Stormy Hills* ('Nightfall', 'The Awakening', 'The Emptied Sack', 'Carrig-an-Afrinn', 'The Stones', 'A Looter of the Hills', 'The Priest', 'The Eyes of the Dead' and 'The Ruining of Dromacurrig'). Finally, three are from *Earth out of Earth* ('Refuge', 'Death of the Runner' and 'Vision').

For the benefit of interested readers, a critical bibliography has been included at the end of the book. This contains full references to the critics cited in the preceding pages; it also lists essays, articles, and books which have been written about Daniel Corkery. For readers approaching Corkery, the temptation has often been to focus on his non-fiction or to dismiss him out-of-hand as an exclusivist and intolerant figure. This has often resulted in simplified critical readings, and has meant that his achievements as a short story writer have not always got the attention they deserve. This selection should go some way towards redressing this imbalance, and will help to provide a fuller image of a more complicated – and also a more talented – individual. It will also introduce, or perhaps reintroduce, readers to some extraordinary short stories which have been long out of print. Corkery's original – and sometimes slightly erratic – use of grammar and punctuation has been preserved in the stories that follow.

THE PLOUGHING OF LEACA-NA-NAOMH

With which shall I begin – man or place? Perhaps I had better first tell
of the man; of him the incident left so withered that no sooner had I
laid eyes on him than I said: Here is one whose blood at some terrible
moment of his life stood still, stood still and never afterwards regained
its quiet, old-time ebb-and-flow. A word or two then about the place
– a sculped-out shell in the Kerry mountains, an evil-looking place,
green-glaring like a sea when a storm has passed. To connect man and
place together, even as they worked one with the other to bring the
tragedy about, ought not then to be so difficult.

I had gone into those desolate treeless hills searching after the
traces of an old-time Gaelic family that once were lords of them. But
in the mountainy glen I forgot my purpose almost as soon as I entered
it.

In that round-ended valley – they call such a valley a coom – there
was but one farmhouse, and Considine was the name of the householder – Shawn Considine, the man whose features were white with
despair; his haggard appearance reminded me of what one so often
sees in war-ravaged Munster – a ruined castle-wall hanging out above
the woods, a grey spectre. He made me welcome, speaking slowly, as
if he was not used to such amenities. At once I began to explain my
quest. I soon stumbled; I felt that his thoughts were far away. I started
again. A daughter of his looked at me – Nora was her name – looked
at me with meaning; I could not read her look aright. Haphazardly I
went through old family names and recalled old-world incidents; but
with no more success. He then made to speak; I could catch only broken phrases, repeated again and again. 'In the presence of God.' 'In
the Kingdom of God.' 'All gone for ever.' 'Let them rest in peace' – (I
translate from the Irish). Others, too, there were of which I could
make nothing. Suddenly I went silent. His eyes had begun to change.
They were not becoming fiery or angry – that would have emboldened

me, I would have blown on his anger; a little passion, even an outburst of bitter temper would have troubled me but little if in its sudden revelation I came on some new fact or even a new name in the broken story of that ruined family. But no; not fiery but cold and terror-stricken were his eyes becoming. Fear was rising in them like dank water. I withdrew my gaze, and his daughter ventured on speech: 'If you speak of the cattle, noble person, or of the land, or of the new laws, my father will converse with you; but he is dark about what happened long ago.' Her eyes were even more earnest than her tongue – they implored the pity of silence.

So much for the man. A word now about the place where his large but neglected farmhouse stood against a bluff of rock. To enter that evil-looking green-mountained glen was like entering the jaws of some slimy, cold-blooded animal. You felt yourself leaving the sun, you shrunk together, you hunched yourself as if to bear an ugly pressure. In the far-back part of it was what is called in the Irish language a *leaca* – a slope of land, a lift of land, a bracket of land jutting out from the side of a mountain. This leaca, which the daughter explained was called Leaca-na-Naomh – the Leaca of the Saints – was very remarkable. It shone like a gem. It held the sunshine as a field holds its crop of golden wheat. On three sides it was pedestalled by the sheerest rock. On the fourth side it curved up to join the parent mountain-flank. Huge and high it was, yet height and size took some time to estimate, for there were mountains all around it. When you had been looking at it for some time you said aloud: 'That leaca is high!' When you had stared for a longer time you said: 'That leaca is immensely high – and huge!' Still the most remarkable thing about it was the way it held the sunshine. When all the valley had gone into the gloom of twilight – and this happened in the early afternoon – the leaca was still at mid-day. When the valley was dark with night and the lamps had been long a-light in the farmhouse, the leaca had still the red gleam of sunset on it. It hung above the misty valley like a velarium – as they used to call that awning-cloth which hung above the emperor's seat in the amphitheatre.

'What is it called, do you say?' I asked again.

'Leaca-na-Naomh,' she replied.

'Saints used to live on it?'

'The Hermits,' she answered, and sighed deeply.

Her trouble told me that that leaca had to do with the fear that was burrowing like a mole in her father's heart. I would test it. Soon afterwards the old man came by, his eyes on the ground, his lips moving.

'That leaca,' I said, 'what do you call it?'

He looked up with a startled expression. He was very white; he couldn't abide my steady gaze.

'Nora,' he cried, raising his voice suddenly and angrily, '*cas isteach iad, cas isteach iad!*' He almost roared at the gentle girl.

'Turn in – what?' I said, roughly, 'the cattle are in long ago.'

''Tis right they should,' he answered, leaving me.

Yes, this leaca and this man had between them moulded out a tragedy, as between two hands.

Though the sun had gone still I sat staring at it. It was far off, but whatever light remained in the sky had gathered to it. I was wondering at its clear definition among all the vague and misty mountain-shapes when a voice, quivering with age, high and untuneful, addressed me: ''Twould be right for you to see it when there's snow on it.'

'Ah!'

''Tis blinding!' The voice had changed so much as his inner vision strengthened that I gazed up quickly at him. He was a very old man, somewhat fairy-like in appearance, but he had the eyes of a boy! These eyes told me he was one who had lived imaginatively. Therefore I almost gripped him lest he should escape; from him would I learn of Leaca-na-Naomh. Shall I speak of him as a vassal of the house, or as a tatter of the family, or as a spall of the rough landscape? He was native to all three. His homespun was patched with patches as large and as straight-cut as those you'd see on a fisherman's sail. He was, clothes and all, the same colour as the aged lichen of the rocks; but his eyes were as fresh as dew.

Gripping him, as I have said, I searched his face, as one searches a poem for a hidden meaning.

'When did it happen, this dreadful thing?' I said.

He was taken off his guard. I could imagine, I could almost feel his mind struggling, summoning up an energy sufficient to express his idea of how as well as when the thing happened. At last he spoke deliberately.

'When the master' – I knew he meant the householder – 'was at his best, his swiftest and strongest in health, in riches, in force and spirit.' He hammered every word.

'Ah!' I said; and I noticed the night had begun to thicken, fitly I thought, for my mind was already making mad leaps into the darkness of conjecture. He began to speak a more simple language: 'In those days he was without burden or ailment – unless maybe every little biteen of land between the rocks that he had not as yet brought under the plough was a burden. This, that, yonder, all those fine fields that have gone back again into heather and furze, it was he made them. There's sweat in them! But while he bent over them in the little dark days of November, dropping his sweat, he would raise up his eyes and fix them on the leaca. *That* would be worth all of them, and worth more than double all of them if it was brought under the plough.'

'And why not?' I said.

'Plough the bed of the saints?'

'I had forgotten.'

'You are not a Gael of the Gaels maybe?'

'I had forgotten; continue; it grows chilly.'

'He had a serving-man; he was a fool; they were common in the country then; they had not been as yet herded into asylums. He was a fool; but a true Gael. That he never forgot; except once.'

'Continue.'

'He had also a sire horse, Griosach he called him, he was so strong, so high and princely.'

'A plough horse?'

'He had never been harnessed. He was his master's pride and boast. The people gathered on the hillsides when he rode him to Mass. You looked at the master; you looked at the horse; the horse knew the hillsides were looking at him. He made music with his hoofs, he kept his eyes to himself, he was so proud.'

'What of the fool?'

'Have I spoken of the fool?'

'Yes, a true Gael.'

''Tis true, that word. He was as strong as Griosach. He was what no one else was: he was a match for Griosach. The master petted the horse. The horse petted the master. Both of them knew they went well together. But Griosach the sire horse feared Liam Ruadh the fool; and Liam Ruadh the fool feared Griosach the sire horse. For neither had as yet found out that he was stronger than the other. They would play together like two strong boys, equally matched in strength and daring. They would wrestle and throw each other. Then they would leave off; and begin again when they had recovered their breath.'

'Yes,' I said, 'the master, the horse Griosach, the fool Liam – now, the Leaca, the Leaca.'

'I have brought in the Leaca. It will come in again, now! The master was one day standing at a gap for a long time; there was no one near him. Liam Ruadh came near him. "It is not lucky to be so silent as that," he said. The master raised his head and answered: "'The Leaca for wheat."

'The fool nearly fell down in a sprawling heap. No one had ever heard of anything like that.

'"No," he said like a child.

'"The Leaca for wheat," the master said again, as if there was someone inside him speaking.

'The fool was getting hot and angry.

'"The Leaca for prayer!" he said.

'"The Leaca for wheat," said the master, a third time.

'When the fool heard him he gathered himself up and roared – a loud "O-oh!" it went around the hills like sudden thunder; in the little breath he had left he said: "The Leaca for prayer!"

'The master went away from him; who could tell what might have happened?

'The next day the fool was washing a sheep's diseased foot – he had the struggling animal held firm in his arms when the master slipped behind him and whispered in his ear: "'The Leaca for wheat."

'Before the fool could free the animal the master was gone. He was a wild, swift man that day. He laughed. It was that self-same night he went into the shed where Liam slept and stood a moment looking at the large face of the fool working in his dreams. He watched him like that a minute. Then he flashed the lantern quite close into the fool's eyes so as to dazzle him, and he cried out harshly, "The Leaca for wheat", making his voice appear far off, like a trumpet-call, and before the fool could understand where he was, or whether he was asleep or awake, the light was gone and the master was gone.

'Day after day the master put the same thought into the fool's ear. And Liam was becoming sullen and dark. Then one night long after we were all in our sleep we heard a wild crash. The fool had gone to the master's room. He found the door bolted. He put his shoulder to it. The door went in about the room, and the arch above it fell in pieces around the fool's head – all in the still night.

'"Who's there? What is it?" cried the master, starting up in his bed.

'"Griosach for the plough!" said the fool.

'No one could think of Griosach being hitched to a plough. The master gave him no answer. He lay down in his bed and covered his face. The fool went back to his straw. Whenever the master now said "The Leaca for wheat" the fool would answer "Griosach for the plough".

'The tree turns the wind aside, yet the wind at last twists the tree. Like wind and tree master and fool played against each other, until at last they each of them had spent their force.

'"I will take Griosach and Niamh and plough the leaca," said the fool; it was a hard November day.

'"As you wish," said the master. Many a storm finishes with a little sob of wind. Their voices were now like a little wind.

'The next night a pair of smiths were brought into the coom all the way from Aunascawl. The day after that the mountains were ringing with their blows as the ploughing-gear was overhauled. Without rest or laughter or chatter the work went on, for Liam was at their shoulders, and he hardly gave them time to wipe their sweaty hair. One began to sing: '"'Tis my grief on Monday now," but Liam struck him one blow and stretched him. He returned to his work quiet enough after that. We saw the fool's anger rising. We made way for him; and he was going back and forth the whole day long; in the evening his mouth began to froth and his tongue to blab. We drew away from him; wondering what he was thinking of. The master himself began to grow timid; he hadn't a word in him; but he kept looking up at us from under his brow as if he feared we would turn against him. Sure we wouldn't; wasn't he our master – even what he did?

'When the smiths had mounted their horses that night to return to Aunascawl one of them stooped down to the master's ear and whispered: "Watch him, he's in a fever."

'"Who?"

'"The fool." That was a true word.

'Some of us rode down with the smiths to the mouth of the pass, and as we did so, snow began to fall silently and thickly. We were glad; we thought it might put back the dreadful business of the ploughing. When we returned towards the house we were talking. But a boy checked us.

'"Whisht!" he said.

'We listened. We crept beneath the thatch of the stables. Within we heard the fool talking to the horses. We knew he was putting his arms around their necks. When he came out, he was quiet and happy-looking. We crouched aside to let him pass. Then we told the master.

'"Go to your beds," he said, coldly enough.

'We played no cards that night; we sang no songs; we thought it too long until we were in our dark beds. The last thing we thought of was the snow falling, falling, falling on Leaca-na-Naomh and on all the mountains. There was not a stir or a sigh in the house. Everyone feared to hear his own bed creak. And at last we slept.

'What awoke me? I could hear voices whispering. There was fright in them. Before I could distinguish one word from another I felt my neck creeping. I shook myself. I leaped up. I looked out. The light was blinding. The moon was shining on the slopes of new snow. There was none falling now; a light, thin wind was blowing out of the lovely stars.

'Beneath my window I saw five persons standing in a little group, all clutching one another like people standing in a flooded river. They were very still; they would not move even when they whispered. As I wondered to see them so fearfully clutching one another a voice spoke in my room: "For God's sake, Stephen, get ready and come down."

'"Man, what's the matter with ye?"

'"For God's sake come down."

'"Tell me, tell me!"

'"How can I? Come down!"

'I tried to be calm; I went out and made for that little group, putting my hand against my eyes, the new snow was so blinding.

'"Where's the master?" I said.

'"There!" They did not seem to care whether or not I looked at the master.

'He was a little apart; he was clutching a jut of rock as if the land was slipping from his feet. His cowardice made me afraid. I was hard put to control my breath.

'"What are ye, are ye all staring at?" I said.

'"Leaca-na –" – the voice seemed to come from over a mile away, yet it was the man beside me had spoken.

'I looked. The leaca was a dazzling blaze, it was true, but I had often before seen it as bright and wonderful. I was puzzled.

'"Is it the leaca ye're all staring –" I began; but several of them silently lifted up a hand and pointed towards it. I could have stared at them instead; whether or not it was the white moonlight that was on them, they looked like men half-frozen, too chilled to speak. But I looked where those outstretched hands silently bade me. Then I, too, was struck dumb and became one of that icy group, for I saw a little white cloud moving across the Leaca, a feathery cloud, and from the heart of it there came every now and then a little flash of fire, a spark. Sometimes, too, the little cloud would grow thin, as if it were scattering away, at which times it was a moving shadow we saw. As I blinked at it I felt my hand groping about to catch something, to catch someone, to make sure of myself; for the appearance of everything, the whiteness, the stillness, and then that moving cloud whiter than everything else, whiter than anything in the world, and so like an angel's wing moving along the leaca, frightened me until I felt like fainting away. To make things worse, straight from the little cloud came down a whisper, a long, thin, clear, silvery cry: "Griosach! Ho-o-o-oh! Ho-o-o-oh!" a ploughing cry. We did not move; we kept our silence: everyone knew that that cry was going through everyone else as through himself, a stroke of coldness. Then I understood why the master was hanging on to a rock; he must have heard the cry before anyone else. It was terrible, made so thin and silvery by the distance; and yet it was a cry of joy – the fool had conquered Griosach!

'I do not know what wild thoughts had begun to come into my head when one man in the group gasped out "Now!" and then another, and yet another. Their voices were breath, not sound. Then they all said "Ah!" and I understood the fear that had moved their tongues. I saw the little cloud pause a moment on the edge of the leaca, almost hang over the edge, and then begin to draw back from it. The fool had turned his team on the verge and was now ploughing up against the hill.

'"O-o-h," said the master, in the first moment of relief; it was more like a cry of agony. He looked round at us with ghastly eyes; and our eyeballs turned towards his, just as cold and fixed. Again that silvery cry floated down to us "Griosach! Ho-o-o-oh!" And again the lash of coldness passed through every one of us. The cry began to come more frequently, more triumphantly, for now again the little cloud was ploughing down the slope, and its pace had quickened. It was making once more for that edge beneath which was a sheer fall of hundreds of feet.

'Behind us, suddenly, from the direction of the thatched stables came a loud and high whinny – a call to a mate. It was so unexpected, and we were all so rapt up in what was before our eyes, that it shook us, making us spring from one another. I was the first to recover.

'"My God," I said, "that's Niamh, that's Niamh!"

'The whinny came again; it was Niamh surely.

'"What is he ploughing with, then? What has he with Griosach?"

'A man came running from the stables; he was trying to cry out: he could hardly be heard: '"Griosach and Lugh! Griosach and Lugh!"

'Lugh was another sire horse; and the two sires would eat each other; they always had ill-will for each other. The master was staring at us.

'"Tisn't Lugh?" he said, with a gurgle in his voice.

'No one could answer him. We were thinking if the mare's cry reached the sires their anger would blaze up and no one could hold them; but why should Liam have yoked such a team?

'"Hush! hush!" said a woman's voice.

'We at once heard a new cry; it came down from the leaca: '"Griosach, Back! Back!" It was almost inaudible, but we could feel the swiftness and terror in it. "Back! Back!" came down again. "Back, Griosach, back!"

'"They're fighting, they're fighting – the sires!" one of our horseboys yelled out – the first sound above a breath that had come from any of us, for he was fonder of Lugh than of the favourite Griosach, and had forgotten everything else. And we saw that the little cloud was almost at a stand-still; yet that it was disturbed; sparks were flying from it; and we heard little clanking sounds, very faint, coming from it. They might mean great leaps and rearings.

'Suddenly we saw the master spring from that rock to which he had been clinging as limp as a leaf in autumn, spring from it with great life and roar up towards the leaca: '"Liam! Liam! Liam Ruadh!" He turned to us, "Shout, boys, and break his fever," he cried, "Shout, shout!"

'We were glad of that.

'"Liam! Liam! Liam Ruadh!" we roared.

'"My God! My God!" we heard as we finished. It was the master's voice; he then fell down. At once we raised our voices again; it would keep us from seeing or hearing what was happening on the leaca.

'"Liam! Liam! Liam Ruadh!"

'There was wild confusion.

'"Liam! Liam! Liam! Ruadh! Ruadh! Ruadh!" the mountains were singing back to us, making the confusion worse. We were twisted about – one man staring at the ground, one at the rock in front of his face, another at the sky high over the leaca, and one had his hand stretched out like a sign-post on a hilltop, I remember him best; none of us were looking at the leaca itself. But we were listening and listening, and at last they died, the echoes, and there was a cold silence, cold, cold. Then we heard old Diarmuid's passionless voice begin to pray: '"*Abhaile ar an sioruidheacht go raibh a anam.*" "At home in Eternity may his soul – ." We turned round, one by one, without speaking a word, and stared at the leaca. It was bare! The little cloud was still in the air – a white dust, ascending. Along the leaca we saw two thin shadowy lines – they looked as if they had been drawn in very watery ink on its dazzling surface. Of horses, plough, and fool there wasn't a trace. They had gone over the edge while we roared.

'Noble person, as they went over I'm sure Liam Ruadh had one fist at Lugh's bridle, and the other at Griosach's, and that he was swinging high in the air between them. Our roaring didn't break his fever, say that it didn't, noble person? But don't question the master about it. I have told you all!'

'I will leave this place tonight,' I said.

'It is late, noble person.'

'I will leave it now, bring me my horse.'

That is why I made no further inquiries in that valley as to the fate of that old Gaelic family that were once lords of those hills. I gave up the quest. Sometimes a thought comes to me that Liam Ruadh might have been the last of an immemorial line, no scion of which, if God had left him his senses, would have ploughed the Leaca of the Saints, no, not even if it were to save him from begging at fairs and in public-houses.

STORM-STRUCK

I

On an August afternoon the fishing village of Cuandor on the west Cork coast is like a dream-village; it is so still. Its rocky street is then a strip of sunshine, a strip of shadow; and not a soul crosses from the one to the other: the men are far on the sea, they have sailed in their nobbies and ketches for the Manx fishing-grounds; and the women are at work in their gardens, bent over the violets they grow in ridges, like potatoes, for the London markets.

On such a day John Donovan arrived home from Butte City, Montana. It looked as if he had stolen home. Even so, the news was not long spreading from hedge to hedge – an empty story.

Nightfall brought no relief. Instead of his coming into Lavelle's public-house, there came Jack Kiniry from Ringogreine. On his way he had passed the Donovans' house, and his tale was that the place was dark and silent. And as he said so, his questioners saw it in vision – a windy, stony place, just where the good land ended and the cliffs began. Because it was so poor, the boy, John Donovan, had sailed six years before for America.

The following day was Sunday. The church bell had tolled for Mass; yet still, as was customary, the dark-cloaked women and the sun-tanned men from the hills lingered in groups. They whispered in low voices that the boy of the Donovans had come home – a blinded man. But when, at the end of the rocky street, the group they had waited for appeared, the blind man and his aged father, the peasants moved silently into the church, where already the priest was praying on the altar.

As the old man, bent almost double from years and the slavery of his toil, led his son over the uneven ground, he looked up from under his brows, to right, to left, and spoke no word. He looked like one who had done something wrong. But his son was more than erect, his head

27

flung nervously up in that sorry posture common to blind men and dreamers, his blank eyes sweeping equally landscape and sky and sea.

This had Butte City, Montana, done for him. A flash of light in the gloom of a copper mine, a rumble, a tremor; then, silence. Afterwards, amid a whispering of nun-like voices, the gradual return of consciousness in a bed of snow-white sheets, snow-white to judge by the feel of them. 'I want to go home,' he whined, like a boy who fails halfway in an adventure. Then recalling the explosion, he fainted again, and, as he did so, he heard someone whisper that his sight was gone.

The first night at home he scarcely spoke a word. His father and mother in their lonely house had lived more or less always in silence; and he, since his loss, had become acquainted with it. Perhaps, this first night, he was listening to the loud ticking of the weight-clock or to the crying seagulls. But after a long pause he blurted out: 'Where's Kitty Regan now?'

The old man and woman looked at each other, neither quite ready to answer; they knew what Kitty Regan had meant to him before his departure to America; they knew why there he had chosen the slavery of the copper mines and had hoarded his earnings. The father thought it better to speak carelessly, as if it now was all an old story: 'Oh, she married into Kilvonane parish.'

'I thought so,' said the blind man.

And in spite of his effort at control a quiver crossed his face, such as might happen in a dream. It went through his mother like a sword. She rose, putting an arm around his shoulder, laying her hand on his: 'Don't mind, boy,' she said; 'maybe 'tis she wasn't worthy of you – and look at the man she got; God help us, 'tis a hard life she has.' And the mother pressed the son to her breast.

He sprang to his feet.

'What's this? Bless me! We're not going to have scenes, sure we're not.'

And forgetting himself, he flung forward from her hands and fell on the chair she had risen from. Steadying himself, he cursed several times in a voice that was hard and strange to them; it was his Butte City voice.

At first he took to sitting outside the door in the sunshine, and by dint of short and bitter answers soon rid himself of the gossips of the place. It seemed he could satisfy himself for ever with listening to the seagulls and rooks. However, after some weeks, he made friends with a boy named Conny Maher, and the two of them would go for long rambles on the cliff-tops. One day they got as far as Fylenashouk, the most windy, the highest of all the cliffs; and ever afterwards this was his favourite resting-place. It stands sheer above the sea: eastwards there is the long promontory running out to the Galley Head, in summer time a strip of gold terminating in a white point; westwards the coast is fringed with groups of rocky islets, pearly in the sun. Perhaps he remembered west and east in the touch of the wind.

One day in the late autumn, sitting there alone, he felt the sun darken; then a large rain-drop stabbed the back of his hand. In a second the whole shower was pelting on him. He bent his head waiting for it to pass; but the whole face of the day had changed – afar off he heard the dull rolling of thunder. He began to fidget. Carefully he stood up, crouching his back to the rain. He must not move, he might walk over the cliff; besides, Conny would soon come seeking him. But, as if it had leaped through a great distance of space, the thunder suddenly crashed about him. 'My God!' he said, listening to its rolling off. 'Conny, Conny,' he then cried out, and anger and anxiety struggled in his throat. Again and again he started, feeling that lightnings were playing about him. And 'Conny, Conny,' he screamed between the thunderclaps.

Unexpectedly a hand, wet with rain, caught his, and a coarse voice, yet a woman's voice, said 'Come'. Hastily they made forward over the rough ground, so hastily indeed that soon his breath went from him, and in spite of the rain he grew hot and sweaty. 'Stop a moment,' he gasped; 'I'm bate out, 'tis long since I went so fast.' He made to smile, but it flickered out at once, for he thought that he might be staring at a rock or tree. His hand had been dropped, and the stranger's silence stung him. 'Do you see a little boy anywhere? Dan Maher's little boy, Conny Maher?'

'No,' was the sullen answer.

'We'll go on,' he said, bitterly; his blindness had never so come home to him. The stranger again gripped his hand firmly, almost fiercely, and in the same headlong haste they made on through the pouring rain. 'Oh, oh,' he said, whenever the thunder burst; but his helpmate kept her silence. And so he stumbled on, until his limbs were staggering and his heart thumping.

'If there's e'er a shelter anywhere, I could wait; Conny will be coming – .'

'Where's the shelter?'

Drooping, he stood fetching short breaths: 'You'll be all wet,' he said.

'Where's the harrum in it?'

'I'm all right now,' he said, and stretched out his useless hand once more.

When he found himself being dragged through some bushes he knew where he was.

'The road?' he said.

'Yes,' came a gasping reply.

More swiftly now they stumbled down the hill. He was gaining hope, reckoning that his house could not be far off, when his hand was suddenly flung down, seized, and dropped again, and 'Oh!' the voice cried, as if in terror, 'there's someone coming,' and the woman rushed from him. 'Kitty, Kitty Regan, for God's sake – ' he cried, all in a breath, his voice wild and high with surprise and despair, his hand glauming at nothing. Only with her last word had her own voice broken from her, letting him know whose hand had led him. Too late; there he stood, his empty hand stretched out, the rain drenching it. His father came panting up to him. 'In the name of God, Shawn,' he said, 'how did 'oo come so far?'

'Whisht,' said the blind man, struggling with his thought.

''Tis a miracle from God, 'tis so,' said the old man, and 'Whisht, I'm telling ye,' was again the son's savage reply.

II

That night John Donovan sat like a dazed man in the kitchen; and outside the rain poured and winds went by howling. His presence imposed silence on the room. Twice had the old man raised his head and whispered: 'God pity them that's on the sea this night', and twice his son had scowled at him. At last the old people went off, leaving him alone. He lingered for a few minutes, then taking a pine-splinter, and lighting it at the turves, he went into the little back room, lit a candle, as if he could see by its light, pulled the curtain down from the window, and sat wearily on the edge of the bed. He struggled to keep calm, but hot sweat came out all over him. Then he went cold and shivered. Worn out from stress of emotion, he would yawn in sheer exhaustion, would endeavour to calm himself, to sit still, to smile. But he could not. He rose and moved about; sat down and rose again, while the storm grabbed at his little house as if it would sweep it bodily over the cliffs; and every other moment he would stretch his ear towards the window, listening, jerking his head quickly about like a bird's. At last, muttering, he removed his boots, and was standing upright when, as if he had heard a noise outside his window, he sprang forward, quenched the light with one quick slap, flung open the window, and thrust his head, his blind head, out into the storm, whispering wild and yearning words of invitation and love. But the night was empty of companionship.

Chilled and angry, he drew back and threw himself along the bed, and grabbed at his bedclothes, rocking himself to and fro, sobbing out the one word – No! No! – over and over again, unwilling to confess defeat, unwilling to face the blank, loveless future. Yet in the end his words died away; self-pity clothed him all over with the warmth of tears; his passion ebbed, he slept.

The woman's sleep was different. Her they found next day, bedraggled, muddied, soaked, lying in a gully far back in the hills between Cuandor and Kilvonane, where her husband lived. She had been visiting her parents, had set off across the hills; the storm had overtaken her, had waylaid her. Her hands were torn, and she bled from the brow; she must have stumbled blindly on for many a mile in fright and fear. Perhaps she *had* skulked about John Donovan's house; this, anyway, was what he meant to suggest when in the crowd of gossips that gathered in Lavelle's public-house discussing the event, he began to jest about the storm-birds that seek shelter from the storm at the lighthouse-keeper's window, how they do not have the courage to enter when the window is opened to them. The gossips could not understand; they stared in wonder at his bitter lips, his stony eyes.

The Cry

If Jack Creedon did not get to where the road from Carrignadoura crosses the road to Aharas in time to catch up the mail car – well, he would have to walk the whole long ten miles into Raheen, to walk them every step instead of sitting, neighbour-like, on the car chatting to Larry O' the driver. With him Jack Creedon loved to chat – that is when Larry could be got to speak at all; for the most part he spoke only to his horse.

It had been raining all day. Now, however, the sun had scattered the heavy rain-clouds, and there, behind them, lay a mass of shredded, tumbled, thin-drawn filaments and veils of vapour in which the coming sunset had already begun to heighten the tints. That brightness in the west was beautiful, indeed, after the dull day. Yet Jack Creedon gave it never a thought, unless perhaps to hope that it might have had an enlivening effect on Larry's crusty spirits.

And so he tramped and tramped the mountainy road; and where the water-courses had made their own of its surface he splashed and splashed. All the time, however, he made up and up towards the crossing of the main roads on the ridge.

Above an edge of the hill he presently saw the tail-board of Larry's car; the car was not moving, a thing that made him wonder. And soon he saw Larry himself, a little away from his horse, stamping about on the watery road. His hands were deep in his pockets, his whip was gripped under his elbow, and his face was looking more crusty than ever. There he was stamping about on the mountain-top, impatience itself. A twinkle came into Jack Creedon's eye. He could make no guess at what was causing Larry to delay in so windy a spot after driving through miles of rain; he did not try to guess; the vision before him was sufficient, he enjoyed it, and he knew he would treasure it up in his memory. He raised his voice: 'Eh!' he cried, 'is it taking the air ye are?'

Old Larry turned: 'The air!' he snarled.

'Ye might be civil!'

'Civil!'

'Is it anyone ye're waiting for?'

'Him!' Without taking his hands from his pockets Larry twisted himself until his whip pointed towards a series of step-like rocks that rose to a fine view-point. There Jack Creedon saw a well-dressed stranger staring intently over the steaming valley into the sunset. Its glare had caused him to put his hand above his eyes.

'Who is he?' whispered Jack.

'One of them tourists – lave me alone!'

Then Jack made a motion towards the car; would he mount? Larry surlily nodded; and without causing the crazy old thing to creak in a joint or spring, Jack Creedon got up on it and bided his time. Meanwhile old Larry stamped on the wet rocks.

The sunset soon parted with its glory; the sky grew cold and livid, the clouds became the colour and shape of dusky wings. Turning from it, the American silently made for his seat in the car. He took in the new passenger with a soft glance and slow nod.

Dusk thickened; night fell as they swung along the slopes of the interminable hills. They would climb slowly up a long rise, the stroke of every hoof echoing from the rocks above their heads. Then, a quick change, they swung down the descent at a reckless pace, the car swaying from side to side.

And the darkness added to the mystery of it. Such a progress inebriates; lull and excitement play with the mind and gradually shift it from old cares, old anchorages. Perhaps the mind of the American was undergoing such a change. Perhaps it was for this he crossed the miles of foam. Still he never spoke. But Jack Creedon in his own slow way was putting two and two together. He was saying to himself that this indeed was a very silent traveller, a very queer sort of man to pay his money for so curious a pleasure, standing up on a windy point of rock while the sun set. It did not strike him that the sunset in a mountain valley might seem a very wonderful vision to one who had all his life seen it set amid sky-scrapers and factory chimneys. At the least, however, he understood that one who wishes to see the sun set would also very likely wish to see the moon rise; and it was this thought that opened his mouth. But first it must be said that there are two roads by which you may enter Raheen. One is known as the Old Road, the other they call the Sea Road. The Sea Road is broad and new; over the brows of great cliffs, along the edge of the sea, it winds, giving a succession of mighty views of great headlands and sweeps of sea-water. The Old Road, on the other hand, sneaks, as it were, into the quiet old village. It runs along a little stream; masses of tumbled rocks and slopes of heather are the only scenery to be viewed from it. The moon would be high and small before one caught a glimpse of it in such a place; whereas from the Sea Road you might find it rising up like a glory from the heart of the waters.

'Larry,' said Jack, 'the gentleman would like to see the moon rising up beyond the sea.'

Larry either didn't hear, or wouldn't hear. His voice startled the night: 'Whoa, girl!' he cried to his horse. 'Whoa! Whoa!'

'Larry, what about taking the Sea Road tonight?'

'Whoa, girl, whoa!'

They rattled along, and soon the choice must be made; they must turn to the left and enter the darkness of the Old Road, or taking the right presently strike up into the sky. Jack Creedon must try again.

'You'll take the Sea Road tonight, Larry?' he coaxed softly, smiling at his own acting.

'Up! Up! Up, girl! Up! Up!' went Larry's voice, caressing the old horse he could feel but couldn't see at the end of the reins. His voice – there was such softness in it – puzzled Jack. It was not the voice of a man who was brooding on wrongs newly suffered. Had he forgotten that delay on the mountain-top?

'The moon will be rising any minute, and the gentleman here would like to see it; you'll take the Sea Road, Larry?' There was a certain challenging tone in the voice, and a challenge Larry had never shirked.

'I won't then – no, not if 'twas Bonyparty himself was sitting there besides you, my son!' he said.

For the first time the American spoke.

'If it makes the journey longer, or is harder on the horse, I'll take it into consideration.' It was a stately little speech.

'Whoa! Ha-ick! Ha-ick!' cried Larry; he almost stopped the clatter of the hoofs; then he turned round towards the speaker and answered with equal deliberation: 'Tonight is no different from any other night. Boy and man, I'm coming this journey for over fifty years, and 'tisn't worth while to change – meaning no offence – go on, girl, go on!' He shook the reins.

Jack Creedon turned with some touch of resentment in his quick movement, but a restraining hand was laid on his arm; at the same moment they came to the divide, and without direction, as it seemed, the horse turned to the left; they were to sneak into Raheen by the Old Road.

The road fell away, down and down; and higher and higher the valley sides rose around them, so that soon they were driving head-long through a black darkness. As will happen in such surroundings they sank, all three, into deep silence. Hour after hour appeared to go by and Raheen seemed no nearer.

The horse suddenly stopped. Not a word had been spoken. Not a word was now spoken. The American heard the driver getting down. What was happening? For a moment he felt some touch of coldness and fear. Then he, too, got down. As he did so, his companion collided with him.

'Oh!' he said, with a start.

'One minute,' he heard Jack Creedon's voice and he felt himself being pushed aside, 'stand there as you are!' and then he knew that Jack Creedon had flung a stone against a great heap of stones that rose like a wall at their side. Then it appeared that the driver had done the same, for again there was the same sound of falling and slipping stones. What did it mean?

'What about yourself, sir?' came Larry's voice, and the stranger felt a fair-sized stone being pushed into his hand.

'Just fling it from you straight ahead and say: "May Eternal Light shine upon him!"'

'Eternal Light on whom? What for?' questioned the American quickly.

'Tell him!' said old Larry, again as cranky as ever.

'You don't know, sir,' said Jack Creedon, 'that you're at the Crop-py's grave – and that 'tis the custom to do what Larry is after saying.'

'Oh!' said the quiet, foreign voice, and he flung his stone upon the cairn.

'Up, boys,' said Larry. He was already up himself. They were swinging along again.

'Who was he? Who's buried there?'

'Who knows? – not man nor mortal could tell you that; the oldest man in the world couldn't tell you, not to mind me; but whoever he was we all give him the stones and the prayers, because our fathers before us gave them; and sure if he didn't deserve them he wouldn't be getting them, and the thing he done must have been a great thing, and his sufferings must have been great sufferings. He lies in a lonely place.'

So spoke Jack Creedon, not witting that old Larry's ear was on the stretch. But he knew of it in a moment, for Larry's voice was in the night: 'Do you hear him? Do you hear him, sir? and he wanting me only a moment ago to take the Sea Road, wanting me to go staring at the moon and its grandeur, and leave the poor Croppy there in his loneliness,' and then as if the thought he had kept so long to himself had at last overwhelmed him, had swept him free of his surroundings, he cried out in a sort of wail that trembled with the earnestness of faith, cried so loud that his voice filled all the lonely darkness: 'But old Larry didn't forget you, me poor Croppy. Larry didn't forget you, though the gold of America was shlipping into his hand.' His voice went far back into the silent hills and caverns before it died. It seemed long until they heard the horse's hoofs again.

The American told me this story himself, as much as he knew, when we were in the middle of a discussion as to the power of great singers and great actors to move you.

'I don't say I was moved,' he said, 'by that cry of faith in the night – I was cleansed.'

The Spancelled

The pair of them, spancelled in two such different ways, met, or rather slipped into acquaintanceship in the most haphazard way in Mike Larrymore's meadowland. As to her: if you saw only her brow and eyes – so shapely, so guileless, open, clear – your heart would pity her because of her burden; but when you marked the shapeless jaw and mouth – the upper lip, long, full, protruding, the lower dragged a little to one side, as by some influence of the retreating chin – you could not but reflect that, after all, the man, her husband, who on his death-bed spancelled her so effectually with a few lines in his will, might have had his own thought in doing so. Upper and lower face so different, the general effect was strange and uncertain – shyness, wildness, passion, seemed to be continually deepening or softening, one into another.

The day her husband, Pat Linehan, was laid in Kilvurrish, they say she smiled. Her six long years of drudgery were over. Henceforth if she stayed up all night to see that the sow didn't smother her young, or if her day's work happened to be in a dripping mountainy field, clearing it of stones, her wages when the task was done would not be the bitter word of a consumptive who, finding life slipping from him, spent his days in gazing with his hopeless eyes on the three children that played about the earthy floor – in gazing on them, thinking what would happen when he was gone. Quiet enough he died, singing old tunes in a sort of stupor that at the end came to comfort him. Then the biteen of land on the steep-down, rock-strewn hillside was hers; and she was still strong, young, and not uncomely. But if she smiled on that wild wintry day while he was being laid in Kilvurrish, the grave-diggers looking quite black and huge in the sombre sunset, she had not then learnt the terms of the will. That same night when she came to know them she flung his relations from the door, bolted it, and standing in the middle of the turf-lit room, looked wildly from one child to another, as if they were the offspring of some other woman;

37

for the will had made it clear that the land would pass to them on her marrying again.

The shock wore off; indeed the time was not long coming when the few neighbours she knew – the Larrymores, for instance – would make many a half-hidden joke about how she was spancelled. Freely they laid snares for her: 'Come in here, Maggie,' Mrs Larrymore would say, 'I have as fine a bit of homespun as ever ye seen,' and instead of the bit of woollen would be a young and unsuspecting labouring-boy, who would blush and cover half his face with his hand. 'Isn't he grand,' they'd say, 'and nothing to hinder him – or you.' Simple traps, yet again and again she fell into them. What did it matter when she knew that the young man would learn the story of her life as soon as her back was turned? Thus her very safeguard became in a manner her temptation.

Now, as to the spancelled man who was to meet this spancelled woman: John Keegan his name was. In a far-off parish he was known far and wide as the grabber's nephew. If he were a grabber's son per-secution would have been so hard and constant against him that he might have grown up a man of will, a powerful man; the tree, they say, is strengthened by the storm. As it was, he grew up in an atmosphere of distrust rather than enmity. Of course this distrust did often pass in-to enmity, often became total boycott; but on the falling of the politi-cal weather-glass he would quickly slip back again into acquaintance-ship with such of the young men as were of a character to feel warm elation in forgiving their country's enemies over a few drinks. Thus he became sly, crafty in his knowledge of human nature: he got into the habit of examining every new face he had to speak with; finally he came to know his own power. He discovered distant public-houses, where he found himself mistaken for relatives of the same name – men of spotless character. And soon, of course, he knew how exactly to set gossip on false scents; and found a certain pleasure in watching the faces of his pot-house companions as they traced curious relationships between himself and his own father, between himself and himself! Lower and lower he sank; yet from all this a good girl would have, at least might have, rescued him if the bit of grabbed land had not stood in the way. From bad to worse it went; derelict, it came at last to hang like a millstone around the grabber's neck; it drove him to drink. Then the nephew became a spalpeen, a roving labourer; but in all his wan-derings he kept as a light in his heart the thought that he would yet be master of Gurteenruadh, would yet be in a position to ask in marriage someone who would not look at a spalpeen. But that day might yet be far off; meantime he was but a spalpeen, an unsettled man. Thus he, too, was in the way of temptation; he was spancelled to a bit of grabbed land in a boggy valley, as the woman was to a bit of rocky soil on a steep-down hillside.

All in two days their intimacy came about. Mike Larrymore had his grass in the inches by the river: his fear was that the water would rise and sweep away his cocks: in years that did not seem any wetter than this it had happened. At last came a day of sunshiny wind and, Sunday though it was, men and horses were sent into the fields to get in the grass. Carts of people returning from Mass upon the road that dipped in festoons midway along the hillside, would pull up, and a man or two would scramble down through the furze, take off their coats, and ask for a fork. The stranger, John Keegan, slid down through the furze-brake in the same uninvited manner and began to work. That night he slept with the other labouring-boys in the barn. Next day he was at work again, the widow by his side, both of them gleaning with long rakes in a far part of the field, and that night he sat in the far-mer's kitchen and took a hand at the cards. Whatever else he could do, he was confident of his skill at cards. His merry, never-resting tongue showed as much. It rattled on and on, and whether he won or lost he had his joke. There was scarcely a card in the pack for which he had not some pet name: 'my little do-een' – that is 'my little two', 'my little ace-een' were expressions they all began presently to use, as also his use of 'old lady' for the queen of hearts. The widow was playing too, in her silent way, uninterested, slow; she lost game after game. They had often to call out to her to play, or to hand her the pack with the one word 'deal'. She was watching the stranger. Other eyes were watch-ing him also, but with far different thoughts. It is a great card-playing district, and they began to resent the stranger's winning of almost every trick. His high spirits vexed them too. He would need to be reminded of his position. Not by the women, however; they took his side in the battle that had not yet declared itself. They saw no reason why a game of cards should be so solemn and quiet: wasn't it for fun they were at them at all? Playing silently, the widow did not seem to care whether or not her brooding on the thought of the stranger's presence was no-ticed. She had much to think about. That day in the field he had poured all the sorrows of his life into her ear, apparently for no pur-pose except to relieve his mind. And only the bare truths of his life he had told her; in a vibrant voice, however, tender and rich. And she was on the point of doing as much herself; but her mouth dried up and she could not speak. Now she was sorry. Never before had she had any thought that such a confession could bring her comfort. Maybe to-morrow she would do what she had failed to do today. And as she watched him she was experiencing the solace of self-accusation; so that the sallies of his wit, which made the others laugh out, some of the men against their will it seemed, were powerless over her; she scarce gathered their meaning. Presently she caught Jack Constantine look-ing at her, making signs to her, nodding and winking, pointing to her cards. Her face was a blank. All she could gather from his signs was that he was suspicious of something in the play. His eyes were hard and fiery, and whenever the stranger played, Jack stretched out his arm and felt the card with his fingers, as if the sense of sight of itself was not sufficient to make out its value. Suddenly he jumped up and lean-ed right across the table, looking down at the stranger. 'Stand up,' he yelled – the voice of one who has been a long time smothering his rage.

'What – what?'

'Stand up, will 'oo?'

'Why? For what? – what are you saying?'

'Stand up when you're tolt.'

Others began to rise up also. 'Sit down, Jack.'

'Take it aisy.' 'Don't spoil sport.' 'What's up with ye at all?' – the voices broke in from right and left, some of them, however, not over-earnest in the peacemaking.

'He's sitting on a card. I'm after seeing it. 'Tisn't fair; we're not fools,' Jack Constantine spluttered out to them, though his eyes seem-ed incapable of swerving for a moment from the man he was watch-ing.

The stranger shuffled and stood up. As he did so, all the cards in his hand fell to the ground. There was no card on his chair.

'That's it,' Jack cried, lying right across the table and pointing to a card on the floor.

''Twas in me hand.'

''Twas not in your hand.'

''Twas.'

''Twasn't.'

'Maybe 'tis cheating I am?'

''Tis.'

'I'm not.'

'You are.'

'You needn't believe me.'

'Who'd believe you – a grabber.' The stranger collapsed.

'All right,' he said, and rose and made for the door.

'You're not going?' said Mike Larrymore, rising also; he was afraid a mistake had been made: Jack Constantine was always a hot-headed man.

'I'm after being insulted.'

''Tis only a bit of temper.'

'I'm no grabber, nor the son of wan.'

'No, only the nephew,' Jack's voice yelled out; he was in the midst of a whirl of inquiries.

They saw how the light of the kitchen lamp caught the stranger's back for a step or two; then he was gone. Mike Larrymore made for the door.

'You should be more careful, Jack,' he said, following the stranger, 'the man has given his labour.'

Then Constantine gave in detail how he had come at the man's history. The widow listened. How strange it was that she should have heard it all before! No circumstance was different. Again there came over her a wave of warm sorrow that she had not told the man her whole history: somehow it would have comforted her to know that he in his homeless wanderings could sometimes think of her. Around her she heard them talking of his story and his relations; and it seemed to her that they had no right to do so, that they did not know him at all.

Mike Larrymore returned. He told them he couldn't get the stranger to stay: 'He's gone wesht,' he said. 'Wan like him,' a woman said, ''tis in his nature to be wandering about.'

'Something like that he's after saying himself; though 'twas hard put I was to make out what he was saying, down in his throat the talking was.'

They made an effort to renew the game; but the women had gathered about the fire; and every now and then one of them would turn to the players with an inquiry: 'Bill, didn't you know Mike Pat Casey, who was an uncle to Dr Casey of Lisheenaglass?' or something like that. All the time the widow's thought was full of a lonely man going west into the heart of the hills.

'Willy, is the moon up?' she asked at last out of her stupor. Willy laughed.

'What ails you, Maggie?' he said, ''tis after coming round by this time.'

'I'll be going,' she said. The moon would take her safely across the stepping-stones.

When she reached the other side of the river, had entered, as it were, her own lonely land, she stood still for a moment in utter confusion, the very landscape seemed unfamiliar. 'Oh! Oh! Oh!' she moaned, and drew her black shawl close about her and swayed to and fro. Then a sort of calmness suddenly fell on her, and almost without a thought in her head she went up the zig-zag path. Presently she came on her little patch of oats, and then above her she could see her little house: in the moonlight the long, low, white-washed wall, seen through the slender birch and rowan trunks, might have been a line of clothes. Suddenly she noticed that the lamp was not in its usual place; she knew as much by the dullness of the window. In these houses the lamps always shine out exactly at the same angle. She hastened, vague thoughts of her children having risen from their beds chilling her. But the silence reassured her. Before entering she paused, and her eyes were towards the west.

Opening the door she saw the stranger, Keegan, half-rising from a stool to meet her.

'Sh!' he said, noting her astonishment, and pointed to the settle. There lay her youngest child, wrapped in a heap of bed-clothes. ''Twas crying,' he whispered. She gave no heed to the words. She stared at him with frightened eyes: in her brain a lonely figure was still trudging along the roads. To her surprise this man before her had again seated himself, and with no confusion, by the settle, and was now arranging the disordered mass of clothes. She withdrew quickly through the open door. One glance he shot after her; then with a slow smile he bent again upon the infant. A rustle made him look about. She had returned, was crouching as far from him as possible, in her hand a crazy-looking gun held awkwardly.

'Go on out,' she murmured, with no strength in her voice. In a leap his arms were about her, the gun falling with a rattle on the earthen floor. He heard it, half-stooped to seize it; then something made him glance at the woman's face. Her eyes were shut, the mouth wide open and panting; he felt her whole body trembling from head to foot. As if in very pity he kissed her, babbling old-fashioned love-words at her ear.

And so they leaped from their pit of sorrow, as the spancelled will until time be over; in no other way is it possible for them – this is their philosophy – to revenge themselves on fortune, to give scorn for scorn.

SOLACE

Time: The Eighteenth Century
When Eoghan Mor O'Donovan, poet, stooped down and came in over
his threshold he saw in spite of the gloom that his son Diarmuid, who
all day long had been with him leading the cow at the ploughing, had
eaten his evening meal of potatoes and milk, and in his exhaustion had
leant his head down on the deal table and fallen asleep. The boy's unkempt head was almost buried in the potato refuse. No one else the
poet found before him in the cabin; and the only light was the glow
of the broad fire of turf sods. Looking on the weary figure of the boy, in
a flash of thought the poet saw more plainly than when he had stood
in it, the stone-strewn patch of mountain-side they had been trying to
soften up beneath the plough that bitter February day, and he, with
the pride of the Gael in his soul, felt more deeply than ever before the
hopelessness of his position, the slavery and indignity. Yes, there it
was before his eyes: the dark-coloured patch of turfy hillside, with the
weather-bleached rocks that stuck up through its surface, piled with
the stones and shale his bleeding hands had gathered from it winter
after winter. But the vision made his voice gentle, whereas the living
sight of it would have filled him with anger.

'Where's your mother, lad?' he said, laying his earthy, toil-thick-
ened fingers on the boy's shoulder, not without gentleness and warm
love in the touch. Diarmuid struggled with his sleepiness.

'Father?' he said, having failed to catch the question.

'Your mother, lad, where has she gone?'

'As I came in she was crying out angrily at a stranger, and he was
laughing, mocking her, as he went away.'

At the words the weariness fell away from the poet's limbs. He
was again a strong, gaunt peasant, his voice harsh and angry: 'Is it of
Tadhg Smith the Bailiff you are speaking?' he asked, his eyes on fire.

'It is.'

The poet wheeled and made passionately for the door. He stared a moment into the gathering night. Then he returned. And weariness was again in his limbs, making them heavy and awkward. Without a word he seated himself listlessly on the settle, and, a hand on either knee, stared helplessly before him. The sound of waters falling among the rocks outside, the roaring of a far-off bull on a mountain ledge, and, occasionally, the stir of the turf sods as they fell on the flagstone were the only sounds until he spoke: 'We might have left our ploughing till tomorrow – or the day after,' he said.

The boy was blinking at him. The sleep had brought back some fullness to his eyes; but they were still jaded-looking.

'Yes!' he answered, not having caught all the meaning in his father's words, and ''Tis Yes! indeed,' replied the poet, with a return of the gentleness the first glance at the spent little figure had inspired.

The boy's head went slowly down among the refuse again.

'And I might have left my new song till tomorrow or the next day,' the poet added, half to himself.

But though he said the words as if he saw and felt what a foolish thing it was that he should have slipped unknowingly into the making of one more vision-song while this storm was gathering above his weed-tattered roof of scrahs, the power of song was already surging up within him; and a riot of words, golden and flashing with fire and sound and colour, was already taking his brain captive, making it reel for very bliss. But it was not the words of his half-made vision-song were rioting within him now; that song was definitely done with; in the deeper inspiration the bursting of the storm has unloosed, the half-made song seemed but an idle, cold-hearted thing indeed. A new song had leaped within him, leaped with such a strength as made him reckless of the smaller things of life.

His wife entering found him as still as a tree in the evening. She, too, had had time to shed the first madness of despair: she spoke calmly: 'We will be saying farewell to Gortinfliuch,' she said; 'you have ploughed the ground for a stranger.'

He was sensitive; but the song was struggling within him, growing from moment to moment, its promise vast and great: his spirit was on the heights: 'Gortinfliuch!' he said, with earnest scorn – ''tis a poor place for such as you to dwell in.'

She was in the act of shaking Diarmuid from his sleep, fearing some fever was overcoming him; but she paused and looked at Eoghan; though always a wildly-earnest man, it was not often he had spoken in such a strain.

'One would think you were one of those poets who teach school, like Eoghan Ruadh,' she replied, 'wanderers, with whom one place is as good as another.'

'One would think,' he answered, in the same tone of sad earnestness, 'your name had never been put into a song.'

Whatever look was in his face it made her recollect the many songs he and other poets had sung to her name; she guessed that the same phrases of these old songs as were in her brain now, were singing also in his. And so she drew quietly away from the sleeping boy and, her hood still hiding her face and head, seated herself on a sugawn chair before the flameless glow; she turned to speak, but speech failed her, she could see that her husband's thoughts were gone far away.

Through the one dim little pane of glass the poet saw the white stars sparkling in the sky, the night-blue of which appeared deepened and enriched by reason of the red turf-glow with which the cabin was filled. He thought of the clods in the new-ploughed field as crumbling under the touch of the keen frost – a thing that had happened ever since the beginning of the world, that would continue to happen until the end, whatever woe befell the world of the Gael.

'God's will be done' he said aloud out of his thoughts, and bent his head.

'Amen, O Lord,' his wife answered.

They both sank again into themselves; and the silence was again deep, except when the boy would stir or snort in his sleep, but at last the woman began to rock herself, and wail in a low and constrained and unnatural tone that had but little resemblance to human speech. Uch! Uch! Ochone! she would cry at the opening of each phrase of her keening; and the name Gortinfliuch was sure to come into every sentence of it: about that homely word she was gathering up the most intimate memories in traditional phrases of woe. One would think that Gortinfliuch was a pleasant, sunny place, and a soil of good heart, instead of being what it was. And she keened old chieftains of the O'Donovans and old dynasties of the MacCarthys, the MacCarthys who once were overlords of all those bleak uplands, their sunken rivers and hidden woodlands.

To that long-continued wail of sorrow, the poet gave no heed. An odd phrase would strike on his ear and stir memories or flash landscapes on his eye. But just then the keening was of no more moment to him than all the other sorrows of men's life; the keen was a part of that life which his spirit was shaping anew, at its own imperious will.

45

He gave no sign when her voice died away into a long litany of the saints of the Gael, and finished with the name of the Mother of God. There was then a deeper silence than before: the poet was conscious of its breadth, its grandeur. The wheeling of the night's great shield of stars had carried that heart-broken keen away with it, as it had done with a hundred others from the same stricken land; and that great shield of blue and gold had dipped its eastern rim in the western sea before any other sound except the regular breathing of the boy disturbed the fire-lit gloom.

Silent but not asleep as yet, the woman's mind was dulled and tired; her grief had spent itself; her spirit had reached that tranquil shore which lies beyond a flood of tears. Her eyes were wide, cold-lidded, piteous; and the fire of anger was entirely quenched in them. The poet's eyes were different: in them was an ever-increasing glow, but it was the heat of great energy of creation, not of anger. Except for the eyes and the tense brows, the man's tall and haggard frame might have been asleep. All day long his body had lurched and swung to the timber plough, as it skirted the rocks; now his body was having its waking rest, while his mind had taken up the ploughing – ploughing of another sort. And the fierce labour held him until at last the grey dawn touched the beams of the hut with its wan light; at which moment it seemed his song came finally to perfection. The triumphant '*ceangal*' or envoi, his first enraptured line had aspired to was reached just as the last star drew back into the spreading light of the sky. He rose silently up and stretched himself and appeared to notice for the first time the uneasy attitude of his only child, his head resting on the table, the uneasy attitude of his wife, her head fallen low on her breast. Looking at their pathetic figures, for the first time he became conscious of how the night had passed; and conscious too that a new day was come upon the uplands. There was indignity in either thought, a sense of uncomeliness, of fear; and his hut looked miserable in the cold light of morning; the golden song within his brain, however, he soon recollected, was lavish recompense not alone for this night of stormy wailing, this unhappy dawn, but for all the abiding sorrows he and his had ever wrestled with, only to be at last overthrown. It was more than recompense. It was they themselves – these sorrows of his years – crystallised, transfigured, recreated – the same in elements, the self-same, yet a solace instead of a despair, rest instead of worry, triumph instead of defeat! He had often wondered at the miracle of song; the immediate needs of his spirit bade him now not to wonder but to accept. Because he had accepted his face was calm.

Fearing to awaken his little clan, it was on tiptoe he stepped from the room into the haggard. From a brad he took down a huge, clumsy-handled mall. As if still pursued with the fear of awaking the sleepers, he stepped gently towards the tumble-down cow-house where their one beast – their whole wealth – had passed the night. He undid the wooden bolt, stooped his head, and entered the close-smelling, brown-hued darkness in a gush of lovely sunbeams. The cow was lying lazily on her belly, staring up at him with mild eyes that blinked in the sudden glare. This the poet saw. Without a moment's delay, he raised the mall, swung it and struck one swift, crashing blow at the animal's skull above the eyes. The mall sank in a little way. It was withdrawn, swung again, and there was again the sound of crunching bone, less sudden, less loud. A quiver that began at the hind feet travelled through the animal's frame like a wave, another, yet another; then the life went out, and there on the floor was a high mass of bones and flesh. The poet went for his butcher's knife to let the blood run from the veins.

After a short time he re-entered his hut: his wife, his boy still slept. He wondered a moment at the silence. Then in a voice of authority, and speaking the Irish of the Bardic Schools, most classical of tongues, he cried out: 'Maire, the daughter of Kearney, and Diarmuid, the son of Eoghan Mor of the Aislingi, awaken! Awaken and order the house for feasting and revelling – the house of Eoghan Mor of the Vision-songs. Before the coming of night some of them will have gathered at our threshold – the poets of Muskerry and Carbery, Iveleary, and Iveragh and Uibhrathach, of Slieve Luchra and Corkaguiney, of Imokilly and the Deise; and it will not be long until they will all have come. After the feasting I will silence them and recite, so that they may know it for ever, the song I have made in the night that has passed over us.'

The glow of triumph in his appearance was more radiant than his wife had ever seen there before; yet she made bold to answer, speaking with reverence however, and as one who would urge a necessary consideration, and in the common language of the people: 'The feasting will not last for long; the poets will leave us in the end as desolate as we are now in this dawning: when at last it comes to the nailing up of the door there will be few except ourselves to behold it. Have you thought of the days that will follow on the feasting?'

'Woman,' he answered her, 'the sorrow that has made us desolate has this night given birth to a song that will live for ever; because of it my name and your name and our son's name, which are woven into its *amhrán* metre, will not pass: were I given my choice this moment to choose between Gortinfliuch and my song, to which would I reach my hand? This trouble that has come to our doors is as nothing to the rapture in my song!'

That day the poet went east and around by the north; and his son went north and around by the west; and other messengers went in other directions announcing the Bardic Sessions that were to be held at the house of Eoghan Mor O'Donovan, and as they sped, the messengers could not refrain from hinting at a new song that had just been made which was thought to excel even Egan O'Rahilly's '*Gile na Gile*'.

In the eighteenth century a certain traveller, an Englishman, wrote a book of his experiences in the south of Ireland. In one chapter he deals both with Carbery and Iveragh – in neither of which he found much to dwell on. He tells how as he left Carbery and made northwards he came on a curious scene: 'As my servant – the droll-spoken Hibernian I have previously made mention of – and myself rode through the mountain pass we became aware that some gathering must be about to take place farther on towards the west. We overtook and passed several knots of these tatterdemalion figures without which no Irish landscape seems complete; and these little groups – some of the wayfarers curiously excited in appearance, wildly gesticulating, which seems to be a national characteristic – were all making, we observed, in the one direction. Over the mountains we would notice other groups coming to swell the gathering: it was not wonderful therefore that one in whom curiosity is ever alive, as it seems to be in all those who travel much, more especially if their wanderings take them into foreign lands – should set his horse's head in the same path as these turbulent-looking figures. As daylight failed we came on a miserable hut on the fringe of a bleak upland. Several peat-fires, which had been used apparently for the cooking of huge meals, had begun to die: but their relics still encircled the house and set it apart from the one or two others in the same district. The house itself, a miserable cabin, was crowded to the door with wild and picturesque figures. We heard no language but the Gaelic. In the midst of the assembly, as I took trouble to note, a huge gaunt man was reciting what was apparently a very violent poem – to judge by the excitement under which he laboured. I can recall but two lines which run (by the way my guide offered to translate the whole poem into Greek or Latin, as he did not seem satisfied that he could appositely render it in such English as he knew).

> Till through my coffin-wood white blossoms start to grow
> No grace I'll beg from one of Cromwell's crew.

'It was a strange scene to come on in the midst of lonely mountains at the close of the day; but I could not help reflecting that these strong-bodied, though ill-clad peasants, might have found better employment on an evening admirably suited for ploughing. I noticed in a patch of bogland not far from the hut, some ploughing gear lying haphazardly in a half-length of furrow, as if the peasant had flung it down on hearing a call to join the curious throng. But such reflections come into the mind of the observant traveller at every hand's turn in this strange land.'

THE COBBLER'S DEN

I
A Trump of Doom

In every close-knitted nest of lanes you will find a sort of guest-house
– a chosen spot where the gossips meet. It may be a little huxter's
shop, or a little newspaper shop, a barber's shop, or, best of all, a cobbler's workroom.

If you went even casually into John Ahern's little cobbler's shop
– it had once been a shop anyway, for the counter still remained – you
would feel almost at once that you had arrived at one of those belated
guest-houses. First of all, you leant over the counter and he looked up
at you from his stool – a kindly-eyed man, with a head entirely bald,
except for a fuzzy-wuzzy top-knot in front that seemed to announce
somehow the innocence that was in him. But before long you were inside the counter, seated on a crazy stool at the fire, and he had wheeled round his bench to be able to gossip with greater comfort.

The Blind Man would then come in. He spent his days going from
door to door, encumbered with a stick and an accordion. The stick he
never seemed to use, the accordion he never played; yet on a good day
he would bring back eighteen pence. He was a quiet, happy man who
loved his pipe. Although he might have passed the day in the most
noisy part of the city, he would sit quite silent of an evening at John
Ahern's fireside, as if he had only risen from his bed and had not yet
heard the day's news.

And then Maggie Maw would come in. She spoke too much, far too
much; but when she took it too far entirely you could say to her, and
keep on saying it, Maggie Maw, Maggie Maw, and so get her out, raging mad. She was a dealing woman. From wholesale chinaware stores
she would buy for little or nothing chipped ware and odd cups and
saucers, and this merchandise she took from house to house and ex-

changed for soiled or torn clothes which, in turn, she bartered for cash. She was worn to a shadow; but it was not her bartering had worn her away; it was her spirit. This you knew if you saw how she tumbled headlong into whatever argument would be going on at John Ahern's. There was scarcely a night that would not finish by her flinging out of the house with fire in her eyes – victorious or, for the moment, routed.

Very quietly she would come in; she always came in very quietly – passionate people are either dead or blazing. But at her appearance a change would come over us all; John Ahern would begin to talk loud and to hammer on his lap-iron like anything, this was to get up his courage; and the Blind Man's head would begin to move about more jerkily: when he took the pipe from his mouth and held it poised an inch or two away from his lips, the storm had begun.

This night when she came in, the cobbler was in the midst of some old rambling stories he had about the floods that used to rise in the centre of the city in other years. Dead cows, he said, he had seen floating in the streets, as well as great trees and empty boats. And he had seen a hen-coop on one occasion. But the worst flood of all was the one that swept a poor watchman off his feet as he turned a corner, and drowned him.

'Maybe 'twas a big flood,' said Maggie, 'but it wasn't as big a flood as was in me Uncle Din's time.'

''Twas bigger, Maggie,' the shoemaker replied, calmly.

'It couldn't be bigger,' returned Maggie, just as calmly.

''Twas bigger, Maggie, I seen the two of them.'

'How could it be bigger? What was it but a rain flood? Didn't I often hear tell?'

''Twas a tide flood, Maggie, everywan knows that.'

'How could it be a tide flood, in the name of goodness? Catch a watchman not to know if a tide flood wasn't coming – unless he was a country boy, and no wan ever seen a watchman that was a country boy.'

''Twas a rain flood and a tide flood together, I'm telling ye,' said the cobbler, giving the boot-sole a terrible bang.

'Well, that's the best of all,' said Maggie, with that pertinacity of hers which always made us wild, 'a rain flood and tide flood together, and me brave boy of a watchman, born and reared in the Marsh, not to know that neither wan nor the other was coming! – well, Mr Ahern, you must think that we're terrible greenhorns altogether. Of course I'm not saying that we aren't, because we all know what you think of us; but praise be to God 'tisn't to you we'd be coming if 'twas a character we'd be wanting and – '

But a little barefooted boy had come in to see if Mr Field's boots were done, and as Maggie noticed how he was staring up at her, she thought it better to turn away and poke the fire and at last to sit down. The Blind Man put the pipe again into his mouth and leaned back against the wall.

When the little boy had gone out, the cobbler remained bent over his work for quite a long time; but Maggie was busy with her thoughts – even the Blind Man could feel that.

'The flood in me Uncle Din's time, 'twas awful altogether,' she began, quite simply, ''twas how the weirs bursted; and of course no wan was prepared for a thing like that. Maybe the people living near the bridge, although I never heard tell of anywan living there, maybe they heard the roaring of all the water coming down; but not a living soul was thinking of a flood that night. They were all in their beds with the first sleep over them – only for Jim Costello wouldn't there be hundreds and thousands of them drownded – a flood like that rising up unbeknownst!'

The Blind Man took his pipe from his lips – an action that encouraged Maggie more that one might imagine; her brain worked the quicker for it.

'Jim Costello was sleeping on the ground floor, and 'twas a noise again the window he heard that woke him, and he sat up and he said, "Cush, cush" thinking that maybe it was a cat; but, lo and behold you, there it was again, rubbing and leaving; and so he pulled the blind aside, and he saw a light moving, and there were voices speaking to wan another. But the queer thing was he didn't see any water, for what was he doing but looking through the branches of a tree – 'twas a floating tree was rubbing again the glass all the time. All at wanst the tree said Swish! and away it went sailing for itself, and then he could see the lantern shining in the water, and when he put his foot out of the bed, 'twas into cold water he put it. He called out to the people in the boat, and they came over and took him off; but just when he was in it, he said: "Wait a while, now, men; I won't be long," and he went back into his little caboose of a room again, and they waited, thinking 'twas something good he was gone back for; but sure it wasn't; what did he come out with but his connopium.'

'His what?' said the Blind Man.

'His connopium, he was in a band the boys had. Well, they pushed away through the floods, and there wasn't a sign of life anywhere, only blackness and misery all around them, with the houses dark, and all fast asleep. "'Tis right we give them a chance for their lives, anyway," said Jim, and with that he blew into his connopium terrible strong, and, to make it sound like the Last Day, he played up "Arise ye dead and come to Judgment!"'

'My God!' said the Blind Man.

'Yes indeed, sir, "Arise ye dead and come to Judgment!" was what the poor souls heard, and maybe some of them dreaming and some of them sick and sore.'

'But they were all saved?'

'Hundreds and thousands; but sure some of them were never the same afterwards.' She said this rising up from her chair and pulling her shawl about her.

'Never the same, sir,' she repeated.

'They warn't!' said the shoemaker, under his breath.

''Tis to the good man I'm talking, sir,' said Maggie, indicating the inoffensive Blind Man, and she left us, rather more self-satisfied than usual.

After a pause the Blind Man said: 'What's a connopium?'

John Ahern raised up his head and looked bothered for a moment; then enlightenment came into his eyes: 'There's no such thing,' he said, drawing hard at the waxed hemp, saying 'Ha! Ha!' breathily in the dint of exertion. Then there was another pause; and again the Blind Man spoke: 'That tune, "Arise ye dead and come to Judgment", must be grand, but I never heard it?'

'Hard for ye.'

'How so-a?'

'There's no such tune: you couldn't believe daylight from that wan,' said the shoemaker.

II
The Heiress

The shoemaker came in with the light of discovery in his eyes; he was both happy and excited. The Blind Man and myself were waiting for him, and I was now more than glad at not having gone away; for when that light is in a person's countenance it is a cruel thing if he must keep his story all to himself. Besides, a story of something that has just happened is always better than an old story you have heard before. By the way in which he delayed over beginning his tale, we knew he thought much of it. He was evidently very pleased to have us there to listen to him.

'Leave me alone! Leave me alone!' he was saying as he tied on his apron, although we hadn't as yet questioned him about the matter at all. 'Leave me alone!' he said again as he sat down on his bit of a stool; and 'Well! Well!' he muttered, as he looked through his glasses at a pair of boots that had come in since he went out; he didn't see a bit of these two raggy boots he held in his hand, soles up. All this, of course, was acting. At last he had to make a beginning: 'Do you know what I'm after seeing?' he said, looking straight at us.

'We do not,' we said.

'Maggie Maw,' he answered, 'and she arm-in-arm with the Heiress!'

'Go on!' we said, surprised.

'Yes, indeed, on the Grand Parade.'

And then he went into the whole matter. The point of his discovery was that Maggie Maw – we had often heard her – had been the most outspoken and vigorous scorner of all those who had been seen to make up to the Heiress, now that she was an heiress and had ceased to be an apple woman. Old the Heiress was, old and withered, a small little thing, a quiet but not unhappy woman so long as her trade was apple-selling in the open-air market-place. There she used to sit, her apples spread around her in great heaps, and if no one was buying she made the time pass by humming old songs that had been street songs when she was a little girl. We had never known that she had a brother in America until the news came one fine morning that he had died and left his sister heiress to half a brand-new American city. Of course the will was disputed both in the Irish and American law-courts, as such wills always are – and altogether there was a heap of trouble, the days, the months, the years passing on meanwhile, and feeble wits getting older and feebler. Far and wide poor old Judy Brien, honest woman, became known as the Heiress, and her picture appeared in the newspaper; it was no wonder then people had made up to her; and these people were scorned by us who had known poor Judy all our lives, but of course none of us scorned them as Maggie Maw did: fire would come into her eyes as she spoke of them. And now here was Maggie Maw herself making up to the Heiress! The like of it was never known. The shoemaker awaited her with shining eyes; and we waited to see what would happen.

At last she came in; and immediately the shoemaker began: 'Wisha,

Maggie,' he said, 'maybe you could give a poor struggling shoemaker the lend of a ten-pound note?' And he winked at us.

'Maybe 'tis two of them the poor man will be getting, if he waits for it,' she answered, settling herself down, and looking around at us, as if she had said something very clever. There was a little rest then; but the shoemaker began again: 'Mrs Cullinane,' he said to her, 'maybe when you get the chance, you'll recommend a man who you've known all your life to the grand ladies – the grand ladies who'd be able to give him a decent penny for his work?'

She knew then he was up to something. She cried out: 'In the name of goodness, Mr Ahern, tell me what it is ye're driving at, at all, at all?'

'Mrs Cullinane,' he answered, 'I'm driving at nothing, only we're honoured by the grand company we're keeping this holy and blessed night!'

How it would have ended I don't know; but then a very queer thing happened: Just as John Ahern let it out that he had seen her walking arm-in-arm with the Heiress, and just as she cried out, ''Tis a shame for ye; leave the poor creature alone; I tell you I wouldn't swap my own station in life with that poor distracted woman this night,' – just as she said this, in walked the Heiress herself! We hadn't a word in us. Though the courts, it was said, allowed her a few shillings a week until their decision would be made, the poor woman had become quite old-looking and feeble, her hands were crooked and skinny, and her face pinched with the hunger and cold. It was a great pity she ever heard of this American money at all: her mind was going. We made room for her at the fire, and she spread her blue hands out to the heat of it.

She seemed greatly disturbed. There she sat gazing at the heart of the fire, not speaking a word, not understanding a word of what we were saying. It was likely she was thinking of the one thing always. Maggie Maw had said 'Sh!' as soon as she came in the door; then she rose and pinched the Blind Man and told him who the visitor was, and after that we had great trouble in keeping up some sort of conversation.

Yes, not one word of our gossip did the Heiress pay attention to. Maggie Maw, good-hearted soul as she was, would hand her the snuff-box or bid her draw in to the fire – and a fine fire it was, for the Heiress' boots began to steam in front of it – they were sodden from her wanderings in the guttery streets. And generally Maggie treated her as you'd see a mother treating a child that was beginning to get better after a long sickness.

At ten o'clock the Heiress got up and went out as silently as she had come in, our eyes following her to the door.

It took us some time to get back to our joking. At last, however, we saw the shoemaker hold out a little tin box of tacks he had to Maggie Maw, as if it were a box of the best snuff. Without stopping to look at it, she put it away in the middle of whatever she was saying to the Blind Man. Then the cobbler said, mimicking the gentle way in which she had spoken to the Heiress: 'Maybe you'd draw in to the fire, ma'am, you're after travelling a power and all, to judge be the state of your boots.' She got cross with him.

'Mr Ahern,' she said, 'maybe you didn't see the tears running down the cheeks of that poor misfortunate creature?'

'Go on, now, Maggie,' he said, trying to put her off.

''Tis no lie,' she said.

'There were no tears,' he said.

'There was.'

'Was she swinging on her stool, back and forwards?' said the Blind Man.

'She was so-a!' said Maggie.

'The poor thing,' said the Blind Man, 'is it how she's after hearing she's not the real heiress at all?'

''Tis worse than that.'

'In the name of God, how could it be worse?'

'Well, 'tis worse, 'tis far worse!'

'Go 'long, Maggie, go 'long with you!' said the shoemaker, as if he was ashamed of her lies.

''Tis worse I'm telling you,' she repeated.

They kept it up that way, the two of them, until the Blind Man had to put out his stick straight before him: 'Stop now, all of ye, stop! stop! I say, and let us hear what the woman has to say.'

Well, then they stopped, and Maggie after settling her hair began: 'And I coming down the Parade who did I see on before me but herself – '

'Ah!' said the shoemaker, not caring if she stopped again.

'Don't mind your Ah's or your Oh's, if you please, sir, or I'll rise up this minute and walk out that door!'

Not one of us said a word; and Maggie went on: 'There she was, walking on before me, and I hardly knew her, 'cause it wasn't her own natural walk at all she had, but a grand sort of walk, with her head stuck up in the air, like them painted damsels on the stage that you'd see going around with little pug-dogs in their arms – well, there she was walking along like wan of them: "Glory be to God," I says to me-self, "is it how the poor thing is going out of her mind entirely?" and so I followed along through the crowd, and leave me tell you, 'tis around her the crowd was going, for she wouldn't get out of the way for any of them, not she – '

Maggie took breath here, and then she turned towards the Blind Man, touching his arm: 'Would you believe me, sir, I forgot where I was going with following her. God knows I followed her like you'd follow a poor foolish man who would have a drop of drink in him, afraid he'd do some harm to himself – '

'Go on with your story,' said the Blind Man; his poll was back against the wall, and his face was staring at the ceiling.

'Sudden-like she stops; and there was a grand closed-up motor car standing beside the pathway; and over she steps, and in she gets, as quick as lightning, and bangs in the door after her. "Hey!" says one of them news-boys to the driver – he was sitting half-asleep in the front of the car – "Hey!" he says, "look at who's after getting in!" – and just then out of the shop comes the grand lady who owned the motor. Ah, 'tis then there was the confusion, and nobody but meself there to ex-plain the ins and outs of the whole affair, and I trying to talk to three or four people at the one time. If you please, she didn't want to come out! "Who are ye?" she says. "Go 'way," she says, "I don't know wan of ye," she says – '

'Look at that for you!' said the Blind Man.

'"Drive on," she says. Well, sir, it was I got her out, and a hard job I had to keep her out of the hands of the police – '

'And was that the time I saw ye?' said the shoemaker.

'It was then, and though she's an heiress an' all, I'm not one bit sorry for what I done – so there!'

''Tis how she thought she had the money in her fist – oh dear!' said the Blind Man.

'As I'm after saying, I wouldn't swap with her this night,' said Maggie Maw.

'Is there anything worse than being mad?' questioned the Blind Man. We couldn't say.

'There is,' he said, ''tis worse to be half mad.'

'How so-a?' said John Ahern.

'Because 'tis only the people who are half-mad knows they're mad at all – '

57

'That's a fact, anyway.'

'If that poor woman was swinging backwards and forwards on her stool, like Maggie says she was, the tears were running down her face all right – and no wonder.'

'And to think,' says Maggie Maw, 'all the singing she used to have in her and she selling her handful of apples on the Square – '

'That's what herself was thinking of and she sitting there tonight – ' the Blind Man broke in.

'What makes you say that?'

'What else brought her back to the old spot?' he answered.

'Praise be to God,' said Maggie, looking up at his calm face, 'the blind do be very wise,' and then she added, 'well, God leave us the senses anyway, money or no money.'

III
The Wake

'In spite of all,' said Maggie, 'that Hannah Gillane is a proud wan, and the spirit's not broke in her.'

'She was always proud,' said John Ahern.

'She was; but 'tisn't everywan would be proud after suffering such a power and all as she's after suffering.'

'She's after suffering a lot, God knows; there she is now with neither chick nor child – and such a lot of them there one ten years ago.'

We kept still a moment; and then Maggie Maw said: 'Suppose you or me or anywan else in the lane got news home that our last boy was lying dead beyond in America, what would be the first thing we'd do?'

We didn't answer; we knew our ideas wouldn't satisfy Maggie.

'I'll tell you,' she continued, 'ye'd call a neighbour in – thanks be to God, the lane, bad and all as it is, isn't without a kind neighbour yet – well, ye'd call a neighbour in; and then another neighbour, that would be just after hearing the news, would come in, and then ye'd have a good cry over the boy – God between us and all harm – and 'twould do everywan a world of good.'

''Twould that,' said the shoemaker, his head bent on the boot that was caught between his knees.

'But what does she do? – Not a word out of her to man or mortal; but on with her bonnet, and out with her purse, and she fastens the door behind her, and away she goes – business-like to the last – and buys everything that's fitting and decent for a Christian wake – think of that, and the boy lying dead, and maybe buried, beyond in America – thousands upon thousands of miles away!'

At this point, the Blind Man came in, put his stick in a corner, and lighted his pipe. While he was settling himself, Maggie's eyes were bent on the fire, and there was a look of great activity in them.

''Tis of Hannah Gillane we're talking, sir,' she said to the Blind Man when he was settled.

'God help her,' he took the pipe from his mouth, ''tis she have the great sorrow this night.'

'But did ye hear tell what happened at the wake? – maybe ye didn't?'

'What wake?'

'The wake over the boy in America.'

'She hadn't a wake surely?'

'She had then, and a good wake.'

'Oh my!'

'But leave me tell ye.'

We made ourselves comfortable. We had heard whispers in the lane: now we were about to hear the full and all of it; after all there was no one like Maggie: when she told you a story there was no fear you'd hear it better elsewhere; nothing ever escaped her.

'Well, at the beginning, leave me tell ye, 'twas such a terrible lonesome thing to see the four candles lighting on the four cold plates – and lovely plates they were – and the room done up, so spotless and shining you could take your meals off the floor, and the bed laid out, and, God help us! nothing on it! 'Twas the lonesome look of the bed was the worst; as I say, I shivered – '

'No wonder,' said the shoemaker.

'And no real corpse I ever seen made me shiver – isn't that strange?'

'I can believe you.'

'Well, there were four or five market-women sitting in the room, one here and another there, and not a word out of them; and there was herself, with her white, stony face, and her best clothes on her, and she going about, cold and independent, and she saying: "Maybe ye'd rather a drop of wine?"'

'Oh my! Oh my!' said the Blind Man, picturing it all.

'Yes, indeed; you'd think 'twas a heart of stone she had. God knows 'twas as much as I could do to keep without coming away again; but sure that would be a frightful thing to do.'

''Twould indeed.'

'"Whatever'll come of it, I'll take a chair, anyway," I said, and I sat down in a quiet little corner away from anyone. Well, there we were, sitting silent for a long time, and then, little by little, we got to talking of one thing and another; but all the same what was I doing but counting up the hours. Every time I heard Shandon strike, and we were so silent-like, I heard every quarter of it – I'd say: "I'll stay another half-hour, and that's all."'

'It must be terrible on you.'

'"Twas, cold and lonesome and sad, and all on account of that empty bed. But maybe herself had something to do with it, too, for now – 'erra leave me alone, 'tisn't like human nature at all she is – '

'That's true anyway.'

'Is she now? – with her white face, and her slow eyes, and not a tear out of them. No wonder we were afraid to leave the second word out of us for fear we'd say something would offend her. And what happened in the end – well, 'twas all her own fault in a way.'

'How so-a?'

'I'll tell you, then, – because when people are happy and talking they don't drink half as much as they do when they're gloomy and silent – hushed-up-like in themselves, nothing to do but drink the drink that's put before you – and let me tell you, 'twas good drink, too – I'll say that for her.'

'So you may.'

'After a while, when we were getting a little nice in ourselves, we began to find our tongues all right, and then there was talk and plenty of it, and, indeed, maybe too much of it. Anyway, 'twas after getting to be like any ordinary Christian wake – except for the bed, of course – and there was Shandon striking out the hours fine and bold, and not one of us thinking of stirring.'

'But herself?'

'The same as ever, not a word out of her.'

'God help her,' said the Blind Man.

'We were nearly after forgetting her by this. All of a sudden, as will happen at the best of wakes, the talk stopped, and there was no one ready to keep it going; 'twas very awkward, you know, and so at last poor Moll Meany – (she was very salubrious in herself, let me tell you) what does she do but look up towards the bed, and sure I suppose she couldn't see the wall, not to mind the bed; looks up at the bed, and blinks her little eyes at it, and says, like as if it was any ordinary, homely wake: "Isn't it the handsome corpse he is!"'

'She did!' said the Blind Man.

'Would you believe me, we all looked up at the head of the bed before we knew what we were doing! When I thought of what we were after doing, well, I felt I'd go down through the ground with shame.'

'But herself?'

'Up she gets, mad and tearing, and she whiter than ever – "Out with ye," she says, "ye pack of tipplers, ye pack of tipplers, ye pack of dirty tipplers!" 'Twasn't long or lazy we were making for the door – all except poor Moll herself – between us we had to bring her down; and 'twas a job we had with that fierce woman pitching us to the dogs and calling on her dead boy to take her away from us! Wasn't that a terrible thing?'

'A terrible thing, right enough,' said the shoemaker.

''Twas – and do you know I'd be ashamed to meet that woman in the lane now, I couldn't face her, I'd be afraid.'

'You needn't then,' said the Blind Man, ''tisn't of you or Moll Meany that woman is thinking.'

IV
The Forgiveness

There was a sort of hub-bub in the lane, a quiet sort of hub-bub, people going from door to door, and stopping in the street to talk with one another. And it was all on account of what the Night Watchman had said about Theig Gorman, the mason. It wouldn't have mattered in the least if it were about anyone else he had said it; since it was about Theig, however, it filled us with wonder, for he was like no one else in the place. He had been, as long as any of us remembered, living with his sister in a little house in a corner of The Alley. It was the only house in the place that had geraniums in the window, it was the only house that kept no lodgers. Neither he nor she troubled anyone, and no one troubled them: they lived quietly and alone. He was a hard, bitter old man, and she was a quiet, devout woman, who spent much of her time in the Franciscan Church. And so for long periods, he being so hard and forbidding-looking, and she so quiet and silent, you would not hear even their names mentioned, not to mind hearing any news about them. For all that, no boy or girl ever grew up in the lane without coming to know that there was some mystery about the dark, silent man who lived in the nicely-kept house in The Alley, without

coming to know also that the mystery was whether or not Theig Gorman was a married man.

Beyond this the young people never went; they began to grow
old, the question remaining as dark as ever. If he were a married man,
there was no one to say that he had ever seen the wife or knew where
she lived or whether she had not long since died. The little house with
the geraniums in the window kept its secret.

This evening it was the Blind Man began – he said: 'After all the
years I'm going around the lanes, I couldn't swear this moment he's a
married man; maybe he's not, maybe 'tis only a rumour that got out
sometime about him, and that he only laughed at it in the beginning,
and after a while – '

'Don't you know very well that Father Lenihan asked him the
question plump and plain – ?'

'Well, an' if he did, what answer did he get?'

'"Meaning no disrespect, Father," he says, "'tis so long ago I can't
tell" – that's what he said.'

'And what would a person take out of that?'

'That he was married once upon a time, anyway?'

'But how could a man forget whether he was married?'

'Maybe he didn't forget?'

'And the world and all knows that that poor sister of his came
from America to keep house for him, and he still a young man, for
that's forty year ago, if 'tis a day.'

'Very well, and what brought her home? Believe you me there was
something very strange behind all that – a young man to bring his sister home from America to keep house for him, and she earning good
money over there!'

'Wisha! if he was married itself, no blame to anyone for going
away from him, for he was always a sour, crabbed sort of man – ' It was
a stray customer of John Ahern's said this, and the Blind Man didn't
like it.

'But was he always sour and crabbed?'

'Erra, he was, ever and always,' said John himself.

And then Maggie Maw came in, grave, yet shining, a light in her
eyes. The first word she said was: 'I have it all!' And so we made room
for her – our own Maggie.

'Now, for the love of God, don't let one of ye say hum nor haw
out of ye, for 'tis the queer, outlandish thing is after happening in this
lane: last night it happened and we all asleep in our beds!'

Up the shoemaker straightened his back and looked at us: 'I knew I heard something,' he said, staring us all in the face.

'You did not!' said Maggie, and she stared back at him, with fire in her eyes. Soon enough his head went down: 'Maybe I didn't,' he said, beginning again to work silently.

'Theig Gorman is a married man,' said Maggie, after a while.

'Go on!' we said, all of a heap. The Blind Man took his pipe from his lips, John Ahern nodded his head as if to say 'I knew it, I knew it.'

'Married in Tralee town, forty years ago, come next September,' Maggie added.

And again the shoemaker nodded, as if he knew that, too; and Maggie caught sight of him doing so: 'Mr Ahern,' she said, 'maybe you'll tell us where his wife was all these long, forty years?'

But he was trying too hard to pull out a nail that had gone in crooked, to answer her; he was a poor fool of a man, at the best.

'Where was she, Maggie?' said the Blind Man, quietly.

'Running mad in the wilds of Kerry – there's a damsel for you!' she answered, flinging up her head.

There never was such a story.

'Maybe I'm too hard on her; but it seems she was a barmaid in some house there, and me young mason from Cork – he wouldn't be more than twenty then, I suppose – took up with her, and married her. Well, when the job was done, when the convent was built, and me mason thinking of bringing home his bride, lo and behold you, me lady escapes and there's no tidings of her!'

'Hoity-toity,' said John Ahern.

'Neither tale nor tidings of her. The poor man comes home to his empty shell of a house, and has to write off to America, begging and imploring his sister to come home and live with him, and save him from the lodging-house keepers. And so she did. And she earning good money and all at the gussetting, up she gets and comes home, and keeps house for her brother, and he a sour and a bitter man that would be getting worse and worse as the years went by. Well, if there's anywan will be rewarded by the God above for doing her duty, 'tis that girl Hettie Gorman, though 'tis an old woman she is now, by the same token.'

'She is that – you could tell it by the way she walks,' said the Blind Man.

'Well, sir,' Maggie took up her tale again, 'the years go by – well and good; but first I ought to tell you that Theig himself went down to Tralee, all the way, three times he went down, looking for her, and all in vain: even the priests couldn't help him; me fine lassie wouldn't be said by man or mortal, only taking her fling as long as she was young and handsome. He soon got sick of it, trying to bring the wanderer home; I can vouch for it myself he didn't sleep a night out of his little house in the corner for the last thirty-seven years.'

'Are you sure of that now?' said the shoemaker, foolishly. Maggie raised up her eyes and was about to say something very saucy when the Blind Man said: 'Go on, Maggie,' quietly and gravely; he was not a bit like John Ahern, he was now probably thinking of how very different from his expectation these long years of marriage had turned out for the mason. The thoughtful tone of his voice solaced Maggie, and she went on with more life and earnestness: 'At last after forty years, to make a long story short, the Missioners – the Redemptorists – and sure they're the hardest of all, come to Tralee. The tents are set up outside the chapel. The lights are blazing. The chapel is crowded to the doors, morning and evening and all day long; and everyone is talking about the mission, and back-biting the people who aren't taking advantage of it; and every morning the Missioners go round the lanes to the houses of the real bad ones – '

'Maybe they caught herself?'

'They did, as nice as tuppence; and they heard out her story, and they wouldn't promise her one bit of satisfaction till she'd go up to Cork and see whether her lawful husband was alive or dead; and in case he was alive, she was to ask his forgiveness and go and live with him if so he'd choose. And so she done. Over the mountains she came – who knows but she walked it? – anyway, and we all in here last night, saying our say, she steals up the lane outside, a poor rag of a woman, a poor sop off of the roads, not knowing what was before her, up the lane she steals and in by the house to the corner. She knocks at the door. Poor Hettie takes her in; himself was out. For a long time she can't speak with the fit of coughing that was on her, and the fright, too, maybe. Anyway, she outs with her story, and Hettie says to her: ""Tis business for himself; you must wait till he comes home!"

'Now here's a queer thing. Nor bite nor sup would she take, only asked and implored to be let alone, sitting before the fire, and the tails of her old skirt steaming, and the cough racking her, and when the fit would be over, nodding her head and shaking herself back and forward and not saying a word. The livelong night poor Hettie went about her business, sweeping the floor, or what not, and maybe killing the poor soul with the sight of the nice clean little house and all the comfort was waiting her all these years if only she thought well to come home to it.'

'That's right, Maggie,' said the Blind Man.

'What else could the misfortunate creature do only cry down her two eyes?' she then questioned us, with strong faith in her own insight.

'You're right, Maggie,' said the Blind Man, again.

''Twas near twelve o'clock when himself came up the lane. The two of them could hear his heavy boots pounding the paving stones. "That's himself," said Hettie. The poor thing took with a tremble. "Lave me out," she says, and up she jumps and makes for the door like a cat. But Hettie came between her and the door – them quiet women do be very brave, "As ye came so far, 'tis as good for ye to see himself," she says, and just then they heard Theig outside. Back the poor wanderer jumps again and curls up before the fire on the bit of a stool with her back to them all, and pulls the shawl over her head. And in walks the man-of-the-house! He came in heavy and silent, like he is always. Hettie says nothing. He says nothing. He looked at the poor thing, and thought 'twas how she was some poor traveller having a heat of the fire. At last he takes the candlestick and has his foot on the first step of the stairs and is going up to bed when Hettie says, very calm-like, "Theig," she says, "ye'd better talk to your lawful wedded wife." Erra, you'd think he was struck. He took one step into the room, and over with him to the poor trembling creature, and he drags the shawl back off her head, and holds the candle into her face, and then he jumps back and he ups with his fist and he says: "Get out!" "Get out!" he roars at her, and he hardly able to say that same with the smother of rage he was in.

'She didn't stir. He didn't know what to do then. "Get out of it," he roared at her again. She didn't stir, only clung against the wall. There wasn't a sound out of her. He had the middle of the floor all to himself. He turned to his faithful sister: "'Hettie," he says, "what brought her in?"

'"The Grace of God," she answers.'

'Look at that!' said the Blind Man, 'the Grace of God.'

'He wouldn't be pacified. He sprang at the door, and nearly tore it down off its hinges in his hurry to open it; and he says: "'Out with you, ye – , or there'll be human blood spilt on the threshold of this house this night!"

'The poor drudge got up, and pulled her shawl over her head, and gave one look at Hettie, meaning to ask her to intercede for her –

"You'll forgive her, Theig?" Hettie says, calm-like again.

"'Never, so help me!" said the wild man, and out he flings her, not caring whether she fell or stood, and he bangs the door behind her, and goes up to bed without a word out of him.'

'Well, that Hettie Gorman is a wise woman. She knew her place better than to open that door after he banging it like that. She just held her tongue and when she was ready, up she goes to her bed.'

'And then the Night Watchman – ' began the shoemaker.

'Go on, Mr Ahern,' said Maggie, folding her arms. He couldn't go on without spoiling it. He made a sign of submission, and Maggie went on: 'In the middle of the night, just before the dawn came in, poor Hettie woke up, for she thought she was after hearing a moaning. She tried to put it out of her head. She couldn't. And then it came again. She lit her candle. "What am I to do, in the Name of God?" she says. And the terrible moaning came up again. She got up then and went to her brother's door; she thought he'd be asleep. My dear, she found him sitting up in his bed, as white as a ghost, and he scared, and his eyes standing in his head. He could hardly talk to her.

"'Did ye hear it?" he said.

"'I did," she said.

"'Is it of this world?" he says, watching her face.

'What was he thinking but maybe the woman threw herself into the tide after the terrible things he said to her.

"'Forgive her, Theig," says Hettie, putting her hand on his poor old head.

"'Tis she's crying, you're sure?" he says.

"'Tis herself, and she's fasting, and falling with the weakness that's on her."

"'Tell her I forgive her, only to have her go away out of this."

'Down Hettie comes; but the poor thing, clung up against the door like an old cat in the morning, wouldn't take the forgiveness from any lips except his own – the priests wouldn't believe her. So up comes Hettie again: "'Put your head out that window, and say the one word, and leave the poor soul go away in peace."

'He did that. "I forgive you," he says, "all and everything, only go away in the Name of God, and don't trouble me ever again."

"'I'm thankful," she says, and away she went like a ghost.

'And mind you even that much couldn't happen unknownst. Who should be passing on his rounds but the Night Watchman, and he hears the words coming down in the night – "Only go away in the Name of

God, and don't trouble me any more" – and he sees the poor shadow of a woman gliding away, and he thinks and thinks, and blabs the whole story all over the place – God forgive him.'

This is one of the nights in the Cobbler's Den I remember most distinctly, for Maggie's tale took a long, long time to tell, and when it was over the Blind Man stood up and said: 'Glory be to God, it must be very late – I never heard the lane so silent,' and on that word we all listened and sure enough there wasn't a stir.

'I declare,' said the shoemaker, ''tis after twelve!' And so we all stood up, Maggie saying 'I'll be kilt' – and made, all of us, for the door. But Maggie pushed us back again as soon as we reached it – 'Whisht! Whisht!' she said. And sure enough we heard the sound of a sleepy old horse-and-car coming over the cobbles, and we saw the lantern shining as it moved along. Well, we stood silent in the dark old hall-way, and we saw an old scotch car, piled with Theig Gorman's furniture, go by, and there were all Hettie's geraniums, packed together into a table that was turned upside down. A gas-lamp was shining on them, and the flowers were nodding and shaking as the car jolted.

'That's all the fault of that Watchman, God forgive him,' said Maggie again. Theig Gorman went to live in the North Side, and we knew him no more.

V
The Revenge

When Maggie came in she said: 'The last of the Riordans is dead – God be merciful to her soul.'

''Tis a happy release,' said John Ahern.

'Well, 'tis; but in spite of everything, and the hard name and all, the Riordans are an old stock in these parts, and 'tis only natural that a person would be sorry after them.'

'Nora Riordan was never the same after Jer Madigan's funeral.'

'She wasn't, how could she?'

'That's twenty-five years ago,' said the Blind Man.

''Tis, and more,' said the shoemaker, and he took a mouthful of tacks, as if there was no more to be said.

''Tis twenty-five years next month, the twelfth,' was Maggie's way of confirming quietly the Blind Man's estimate.

''Tis more,' said the shoemaker, as well as he could, without look-ing up.

''Tis twenty-five years, neither no more nor no less,' said Maggie, again with that quietness which invites any amount of argument. The Blind Man put his stick out straight in front of him; it was his way of ruling: 'What does a few years matter to her now and she dead?' he said.

'Or a few pounds?' said John Ahern.

I knew that Nora Riordan was Mrs Kenneally's maiden name; in the Cobbler's Den old neighbours never lost their maiden names; in these lanes the very children will speak of their mothers as Nora Kelly or Julia Murphy, and at a certain stage of growth are often puzzled over their own names. But my memory did not go back twenty-five years, and so I did not remember Jer Madigan's funeral.

I beseeched them to let the telling of it to Maggie, knowing that we would never get to the end of it if it was John Ahern or the Blind Man that undertook it. For Maggie Maw could not be kept quiet; she would interrupt them at every second word, putting in little things they would have forgotten; the only chance, then, of hearing it out-right from start to finish, was to give it altogether to herself. After a moment's pause, she would begin as if the story lay ready before her mind; perhaps she used to be turning things over and over – she was not able to read. She began in a hard voice: 'The woman that's now lying a corpse – God be merciful to us all – in the Dead House of the Union – 'tis she was the hard woman and the able dealer. She could make money out of the stones, as the saying is. What good did it do her – ? The devil a ha'p'orth! No doubt she made it honest, but she made it hard. What she made out of the shop – I call that honest money – though 'twas made out of drink itself. But what she made by other means, *by other means*, well, that's what got her the hard name. Listen, till you hear it, child.'

Maggie would call anyone 'child' on occasion.

'There was one thing – she kept the best of whiskey – that can't be denied; and she kept a snug house, with a good fire in it, and a red blind on the window, that would be shining down the lane, shining red in the black pools of water at night-time when the gas would be lighting inside it. 'Twas a great help to her – the name the house had for the good stuff. There wasn't a better-known shop in the parish. It was only out of your own door and into Miss Nora's. If you had a visi-tor, or if it was a marriage, or a death, or a christening, or a boy coming home from the sea or what not – well, 'twas into Miss Nora's with everywan – our second home it was. But for all that, 'twasn't out of the house she made her money: 'twas this way: If you had an old father with a cough, or an old mother with a fatty heart, or a poor child wouldn't live to be a man – well, she'd come at the blind side of you and insure him or her – as the case may be – with a dead-man for a few pence in the week, or maybe a shilling, and then in a year or two or three there'd be my brave Miss Nora getting her twenty, or thirty, or maybe her forty pounds from the insurance company, neat and clean into her hands! When anybody in the place died, what we used to say was: "There's a score of pounds for Miss Nora!" And so it would turn out.

'That's how she made her money, the most of it, and not out of the house at all; and sure 'twas a mean and stingy way, and a way that couldn't try (thrive) with anyone. She insured Kate Madigan's old father, old Jer Madigan, as well as anyone else, expecting he'd die in a year or two; but sure he didn't die in ten years, not to mind two! There she was, paying and paying until she was sick and tired of it; to make it worse the poor old man turned daft in the end, went about laughing and smiling and showing his teeth at everyone, and talking about nothing else, up and down the lane, only how Nora Riordan was waiting for him to die and he not going to die at all! He got that small with the age that when he'd go into her house, his head wouldn't hardly reach up to the counter; and there he'd stand, not caring who'd be in the shop, looking up at her, and laughing, and he saying: "'I'm geh, geh, geh!'"

'That's so,' said the Blind Man, "I'm geh!" that's what he used to say.'

'Child,' Maggie began again, 'that was his way of saying "I'm dead, dead, dead!" making game of her, you know, he'd be; and after saying that, he'd come out, laughing like a poor idiot, and go up and down the lane again, telling everyone the great joke he was after playing on Miss Nora. My dear, she was belled all over the parish.

'Well, it went on like that, year after year; but faith'n she never gave in; she kept on paying her shilling a week, and at last in the middle of one of the hardest winters we ever had in these parts, after a terrible wild and stormy night, poor Kate Madigan found her old father stiff and cold in his bed. And, signs on it, she hadn't a penny in the house! Not a penny to wake him or bury him. What could she do but go down to Miss Nora's and explain her case? And so she did. And what did Miss Nora say? "He's dead – is he? Well, he wasn't in much of a hurry anyway!" That's what she said; and not one brown copper would she give poor Kate. She wouldn't even offer her the loan of it. Kate was a poor harum-scarum of a woman, and that hard answer made her frantic; indeed it made all of us frantic. I remember well myself the talk and the arguing, as it spread around the lane, and I remember hearing Kate herself calling down the curse of God on the Riordans, all that ever came and went of them and all that would ever come. I don't say that was right, but I remember it; there she was, standing all alone in the middle of the lane, her hair wild and streaming, and her shawl in a wisp, and the rain falling on her, and the night coming down, and she never caring a brass pin, and all of us pitying her, and peeping out of the doors, and waiting to know how 'twould all end. I needn't tell you, Miss Nora never came near the door at all. She was too respectable, my dear. But at last poor Kate stopped up, sudden and sharp, in the middle of a fit of screaming, and out loud she says: "I know what I'll do," and away in home she went. And we all said "She's distracted, poor thing – God guide her this night."'

'That's so,' said the Blind Man, 'distracted she was.'

'The day for the funeral came. There we were, snapping up our poor piece of a dinner to have it over us, and peeping out the window at the same time for fear we might be late. The coffin, a poor shell of a thing that would hardly hold together during the journey, the coffin went up to her top room all right; we all saw it; but beyond the coffin not another sign of a funeral did anyone see up the lane or down the lane. There wasn't a hearse nor a car nor a carriage nor a bit of linen nor a black band nor anything else whatsomever. Well, at last, and we taking our drink of tea, we saw all the men moving towards the house; and there sure enough was the coffin up on their shoulders, ready to start. Wherever they came from, a multitude of people had gathered round. There they were, a black mass of them around the coffin on every side. Down comes poor Kate Madigan herself, as harum-scarum looking as ever, her hair flying in the wind – and a bad wintry day it was. She stands in the middle of them, and up she stretches her hand, and her arm bare to the elbow – "Round the block, men!" she says, like a general giving his commands. And so they began to move, herself after the coffin, and her shawl back over her head. No hearse, no anything, only the coffin up on their shoulders and the crowds moving behind it. Well, they went up the Alley, around Coppinger's Lane, down Galwey's Lane, out under the archway, and along through Hatton's Court, and that brought them straight in front of Miss Nora's house. When they came near it, Kate Madigan catches the two ends of her shawl in her hands and stretches it from her on both sides, and up she lifts her voice, and begins keening poor Jer that was up in front of her in the coffin. She was that loud and wild in her screaming that dead and all as he was, you wouldn't know how he could keep himself from hearing her. "You left me to pull and to drag!" she says, "You left me to pull and to drag in a world of deceivers!" Everyone knew the meaning she had in them words. And those that didn't were very soon told it, I can tell you. On they passed; and Miss Nora all the time was inside, as stiff as a statue, and her face like marble, and she not daring to come and take a peep out through the window. On they passed, and they came at last back to where they started from, and maybe they thought to stop. Well, if they did, up again goes Kate Madigan's arm, and her fingers working with hate – "Round again, men," she says, and they obeyed her without a word.

'The crowds of the world were after them. I saw them myself this time and they coming out under the archway, and 'twas how they burst through it, burst through it like water out of a spout, and the coffin swinging to the right and to the left, and faith'n 'twas little peace the poor patient inside it was getting, between the jolting and the noise and the cries and poor Kate's keening. Again they went by Miss Nora's, and the house kept as silent as before. But if it did, there was poor Kate screaming like a witch, worse than the last time; she was after losing all control of herself by this; and when they reached the end she cries out again "Round wanst more!" Well, she won! The third time, there was Father Long standing in the archway, and he blocked their passage, and he spoke quietly to poor Kate, for he saw she was in no fit state to be reasoned with, and he told her to take the coffin into the house again for the night, and that next day there'd be a hearse sent up and everything else was fitting. She consented. And so 'twas done. And only the next day did we learn that the second time the cries came outside her window, Miss Nora fell down in a dead mag – stiff to the world, and had to be lifted up to bed. Well, as John-ny here says, she was never the same afterwards. And there she's dead now above in the Hospital after all the money she made, and the grand family she reared and buried.'

''Tis no good to be too covetous,' said John Ahern.

''Tisn't,' said the Blind Man, 'pinching and screwing up for the future, and sure when the future comes there's the Will of God there before us, the same as ever. If It means us to be mad, we'll be mad; if It means us to be poor, we'll be poor; if It – '

'If It means us to be blind, we'll be blind,' said the foolish shoe-maker. The Blind Man was staggered, but he was good enough for him.

'And if It means us to be a cobbler, a cobbler we'll be!' he answered, and he stood up the same as if he wasn't after saying anything at all. But Maggie Maw had to stick half of her shawl into her mouth and run.

VI
Maggie's Way

When it failed John Ahern to get poor Bridgie Heffernan away from the quay wall, to get her away from it and so avoid seeing the dreadful sight she would see if she remained, it was I who was sent to try to do what he had failed to do.

'She's clung again' them, and she neither saw me nor heard me when I spoke to her,' John Ahern had explained.

'You only asked her the one time?' the Blind Man questioned.

'The one time, and that itself was a great trial out of me, you don't know the look she have on her.'

I found Bridgie still clung against the bars of the slip, the slip from which her little boy, the only child she had left, had made his way into one of the empty fishermen's boats that always lie anchored there, and so had come by his death. With a bit of packing-case, he had paddled her out to where his uncle's boat – the *Lurline* – lay moored in mid-stream, and then in getting from one boat into the other he had fallen between the two and was drowned. That is how his companions explained it, and no doubt they were right. Well, there now was the mother, her bony work-worn hands clutching the iron bars, staring with mad eyes at the dragging operations that went on in the middle of the river. In the boat were three men: a large-bodied policeman filled all the stern, doing nothing it seemed except weighting the boat; the drowned boy's uncle, Jack Heffernan, in his thick fisherman's woollens, handled the rope to which the stroke-haul was fixed, while his son Jim, grasping a long pole, stood ready to catch the body when it would have come near the surface. It was to prevent her from seeing the recovery of the dead body of her only child that we were trying to get Bridgie Heffernan away from the slip.

The work went on in silence now, in slowness, too, but when six hours earlier they began it, there was noise enough, hurry, too, people on either riverside shouting directions and advice. One could not imagine how the body could have escaped the hooks so long, considering that it was quite certain where the boy had been drowned. Yet escape the hooks it did, and unpleasant imaginations had begun to disturb the minds of those people who had been looking on a long time. What must it have been like for the mother! She had become so silent and wild-looking that she stood now in the centre of a little cleared space, people watching her from behind or peeping at her sideways out of the corners of their eyes. When I saw that cleared space and noticed the wild white look she had about the eyes, I knew that I, too, should fail, and my heart sank. Little by little, however, I pushed through the crowds and at last got near her: 'Bridgie,' I said, 'there's John Ahern after wetting a cup of tea for you.'

What I will not forget is the way she turned her head to see who had spoken, and then she opened and shut her mouth a few times, moistening her lips with her tongue, as one might do after a long sleep. And her brows worked a little, as if she were trying to recollect what had been said to her: 'Bridgie,' I said again, 'John Ahern is after wetting a cup of tea for you – ' but before I had got half way through the words she had turned away, and her eyes were fixed again on the men in the boat. I lingered by her for some time, and remember noticing how you would not remark the sun shining on the water if it wasn't for the boat and the men in it. On them alone it seemed to shine, on the boat, the men, and on the white bright drops of water that were falling from the rope as Jack Heffernan hauled it in or dragged it along. But when you raised your eyes, there was the statue of the Blessed Virgin on the Dominican Church shining like gold, and beyond it and above it was Shandon Steeple shining, too; and all the windows in the houses on that closely-built hillside were flashing back the sun like signals or burning like flares. It was a golden, sunny evening.

When I looked again at Bridgie she seemed not to be seeing anything at all; listening she seemed to be, listening intently. Then I felt she wouldn't notice if I slipped away.

In John Ahern's there was a little crowd awaiting me. They wanted to question me. I forestalled them: 'Is Maggie after coming?' I said.

'No – there's no trace of her anywhere; – well – you didn't succeed?'

'Leave me alone for God's sake,' I said, 'and let us all sit down or scatter away out of this until Maggie comes.'

'Did you speak to her at all?' said John Ahern.

He had his new coat still on him, and he looked very awkward, standing up, instead of sitting down, not knowing what to do with himself.

'You know very well I asked her.' I was getting cross with them.

'Maggie Maw is never where she's wanted; that woman would break your heart sometimes,' he said.

Someone else took up the talk: 'Another evening she'd be in and out like an old hen.'

'Did ye try the market?'

'What's the use of saying that? I declare to God I'm sick and tired of answering that self-same question.'

'You're right,' said the Blind Man to me, ''twould be better for us to sit down and not to be losing our tempers; it might be better for you, John, to take off your coat and go on with your work.'

'I will not go on with my work,' he answered; he had often given the little lad who now lay in the river a penny for taking a finished job to the owner. 'I will not go on with my work – what a thing I'd do!'

'Well,' the Blind Man said again, 'you might as well; there's no one but Maggie will get that poor creature to leave her post, by all I hear.'

John Ahern would have answered back, but just then poor Bridgie Heffernan herself, the poor woman we had been talking about, appeared in the doorway: 'Excuse me, neighbours,' she said, and turned to look behind her, as if she didn't know what else to do or say; and there behind her, to our astonishment, was Maggie herself, her two hands steering the poor distracted creature along, just as you'd have to guide a blind man up a narrow gangway.

'You'll excuse us, John,' said Maggie then, 'you'll excuse us for making so free.'

We thought that a rather queer thing for her to say; but anyway she had done what we had failed in, she had got the woman away from the quayside. And so we trusted that her way was right. We pushed back and made room; and over to the table she piloted the distracted woman – and a quiet soul that poor Bridgie Heffernan always was – sat her down at it, poured her out a cup of tea, poured out one, too, for herself, and without another word they began to drink it. We kept our eyes away from them, and John Ahern took off his coat and hung it up, slipped on his apron, and sat down to his bench; the Blind Man took out his pipe and emptied it on the hob. And the meal went on, almost in dead silence, for a little while; suddenly, however, Bridgie looked around at us, a half-eaten piece of bread in her hand, and nodded, with a curious look in her eyes, once or twice at John Ahern. He nodded back. Then she said, breaking out suddenly into rapid speech: 'If you want e'er a little boy to run a message for you, or tidy up the place, a little boy you'd like to have on the same floor with you, or maybe 'tis an apprentice itself you'd be wanting, and sure he's nearly old enough for that same, maybe you won't forget my little Paddy, sir?'

'I won't forget him, ma'am,' answered John Ahern, bravely enough, for all his astonishment. She nodded again at him, as if more than thankful, and then turned to the Blind Man (he was sitting perfectly still, a bit of a penknife stuck in the bowl of his pipe), and said, again with the same hurried speech: 'And you, sir, God knows 'tis often I gave you my heart's pity and you going along through the crowds without one with you or a word out of you, and if he'd be any company to you, or any help at all, there's that little boy of mine – a willing little child, and you'd like to hear him speaking, although he has no more sense for a boy of his age – '

We saw Maggie suddenly stand up; we didn't know why: she had nodded at someone who had thrust a head in at the doorway. She took the broken piece of bread from Bridgie's hand, just as you'd do to an infant who had got tired of a crust; she then settled the shawl around her, took her arm and said: 'We'll be going home now, if you don't mind, Bridgie.'

We knew then that the signal through the doorway meant that the body had been recovered. Poor Bridgie was staring at Maggie, quite dazed it seemed. Trying to gather her wits, she said: 'Home?'

'That's your place, ma'am,' Maggie returned. And then maybe the poor bothered woman saw the tears running silently down from Maggie's eyes, for at that moment she came to herself and you'd think her heart would break.

'Look at that!' said the shoemaker, when they were gone.

'Maggie's a great little 'oman!' said the Blind Man, 'how did she do it?'

'No, but to get her to eat – that's what's puzzling me.'

''Tis queer,' said the Blind Man.

''Tis queer, and damn queer, too,' said the shoemaker, 'none of us could do it.'

''Tisn't that at all I mean.'

'Well, what do you mean, so-a?'

''Tis this: now there's us, we have a Maggie in this lane, and in the next lane or the next lane to it, maybe they have a Maggie Maw of their own – who knows? We don't know about their Maggie Maw, and they don't know about ours. Isn't that queer enough for you.'

''Tis,' said John Ahern, he was staring though his glasses up at the Blind Man, trying to follow what he was saying.

'The name of that policeman you were telling me about, John, and Jack Heffernan's name and Jim's name, too – they'll all be in the paper, and right, too; but will you find Maggie's name in it?'

'You will not,' we answered in one voice.

'You will not,' he went on, 'and I say she's after doing something none of them could do.'

'That's so.'

'Those grand ladies that do be going about, poking their noses into our little places, they're very knowledgeable right enough; could any of them do what Maggie is after doing this evening, and she neither able to read or write?'

'They could not,' said John Ahern.

'They could not,' said I.

'Faith'n, they couldn't,' said the Blind Man.

COWARDS?

I

Rossadoon is a promontory on the Kerry coast. It ends in two blunt
points that are not unlike the unshapely fingers of a giant's hand in a
Scandinavian story, only that one of them, that on the northern side,
is bigger in every way than the other, built up of huger cliffs, and so
higher and freer of the winds and the clouds. Yet it was that northern
point that the hardy people of old chose, when Christianity was still
young in the land, to give to God, building their little stone church
of four simple walls upon it, and burying their dead between that little
church and the steep edge of the cliff. Of that early church only frag-
ments of broken walls remain; hundreds of years must have passed since
Mass was last sung there above the sea; but the crowded gravestones,
many of them too neat, too new, tell us that the people of Rossadoon
lay their dead of today with those that died over a thousand years ago.
Too neat, too new, indeed, those shapely stones; and those on which
one meets with such an inscription as: 'Sacred to the memory of John
O'Riordan, of New Inn … Erected by his son, Michael J. O'Riordan,
of Portland, Maine, USA', those are seldom in keeping with the place.
Yet there, on North Point, among the crowded graves, will soon be
erected a monument far bigger, far richer than any of those that American dollars have paid for. It will be set up above the grave of Tomas
O'Miodhachain, and the inscription, in the purest of Gaelic phrasing,
will tell how he died in Mountjoy Prison for the sake of that land for
which so many others like him have died in every age.

And so Tomas O'Miodhachain is gone home for ever to North
Point, in Rossadoon – lying within ten fields of where he was born.

Colonel Hastings, too, has gone home, as if for ever, it seems, to his
old grey weather-beaten house in South Point. And it was on the self-
same day that those two men of Rossadoon went home – the rebel and
the colonel. But, as for that bright-faced boy – the colonel's only son,

Edward Pendrift Hastings, who, in a certain way, saw them home – he had gone home before either of them, not, however, to South Point with his father, nor to North Point with the rebel: in a soldier's grave he rests, not far from Arras.

II

It was on a day of bright grey mists, those mists that seem to hide not one but many suns, that the poor wasted body of the rebel was brought by train, like any other dead thing, to Cappaban. There its guard of young Republican Volunteers from Dublin delivered it into the keeping of the local company of Republican Volunteers from Rossadoon. The funeral procession was soon faced to the west, faced against that straggling, winding, up-and-down hillside road of rock and shale, which, growing ever narrower and narrower for seven miles, passes at last, as a mere track in the heather, between broken walls into the graveyard on the Point. At the start there seemed to be three funerals rather than one: in the middle of the road the gathered Volunteer companies of the whole countryside marched evenly and compactly, far too numerous and too fierce-minded to take any check from the squads of silent, heavily-armed police that were gathered at every corner of the road – marched with pipe music and draped drums and draped flags, the coffin in the midst of them, wrapped in the bright Republican colours, looking like an enamelled jewel-case against the hillsides, dim and grey in the mists. But on either side of the steady, disciplined marching of the Volunteers there streamed along an irregular crowd of the people of the countryside: men, women and children, old and young, with here and there an old farmer from the hills on horseback, his brain alight and fiery with memories of other fights, other heroic deaths, other memorable funerals. Later on, those horsemen, and indeed the whole throng, would of themselves form too into processional order and take their place behind the drilled men about the coffin, but at the start the three bodies moved along the road in a silence that was full of hidden, fiery thoughts, as the mists were full of hidden suns.

The countrymen from Cappaban and Rossbuidhe and Rossadoon itself, although they gave every heed to it, could not march like the pale-faced men who had brought the body with them from Dublin; but ever since Tomas O'Miodhachain himself had left them two and a half years before, their drilling had been neglected; and many a one of them, now swinging awkwardly along, had a thought that the lifeless clay in their midst was conscious of this lack of training in their bearing, was somehow rebuking them. Yes, the Dublin men marched better; but it was not that alone that set them apart, not that alone but this: they had realised, unlike the men in far-away Kerry, what death by starvation in a cell in Mountjoy really means, had weighed it against the other deaths that are incident to rebels – death in a hot fight, death in the dawn, facing a firing squad, death on the scaffold – and come to feel that more than any one of them it tested the spirit within, the spirit itself, unaided and alone. As they marched now in unbroken silence, without the least glancing to right or left, their lips seemed uniformly thin and set, their brows uniformly pale and bent and hard, for each of them was marching on in the silence of loneliness. And somehow as the march went steadily on, climbing the hill with no abatement of speed or steadiness, this realisation of what death in prison really means, had meant to their own neighbour's boy, began to rule in the spirit of the whole throng, as well as in that of the men of Dublin, to unify them, to silence them, to stiffen them. Even from a distance one seemed to notice it, to yield to it, as to something severe and terrible and threatening; and then were it not for the relief and the release that was in the music of the pipes one would scream out.

III

Colonel Hastings, sitting high in his trap, did not notice it, did not cry out, did not even catch the wild music that was shrilling from sea to sea. He had been away from home for the past fortnight, had been to the War Office in London, was now making for home in a chilling silence. He would have driven straight on and into the procession, his road cutting across its road, if his man had not touched his arm: 'That's the funeral – the crowd passing – '

'What funeral?' The colonel was staring and frowning at the black mass streaming so earnestly forward.

'The Sinn Féiner's funeral,' the man answered, timidly. 'Tom Mehigan's funeral, the boy that died in Dublin, in prison. They wouldn't like us to break into them … '

Then, perhaps, the colonel did notice that strange stiffness, that severity in the marching.

'Why should I?' he whispered, in so strange a voice, so choked a voice, that his man glanced up at him from under his brows.

And so they sat there, the colonel two cushions higher than his man, while the funeral flowed by below them on the road. The discoloured leaves of the trees dropped their mist-drops noisily about them.

Were he half the age he was, the colonel might have stepped into the ranks of the pale-faced men and marched with them. Like theirs, his brows, too, were bent, his lips thin and set, his eyes as hard as steel. And the voice that had whispered so strangely went well with this look of inhumanity, so new to him. It was this star-like gleam, this aloofness from the common warm stir of life, that made him akin to the young men from Dublin. His man, daring to touch his sleeve, had expected from him an outburst of fury, at the least a snap of vexation. His mind was full of the last meeting between the rebel and the colonel. It was at the one recruiting meeting that was ever held in Rossadoon. The colonel made his speech, had announced that he was sending his only son into the army, had asked the young lads of the place to step forward like men and join him. Not one had stepped forward. How the colonel's eyes blazed up, how he trembled with passion, how he flung his head in the air!

'I tell you what you are, you're cowards, cowards!' And then, his man remembered now, Tom Mehigan, in one spring, had leaped on to the fence beside the colonel: ''Tis the cowards that go!'

''Tis the cowards that stay!'

''Tis the cowards that go!'

''Tis the cowards that stay – by their dams!'

Too excited to catch up the phrase or its meaning, Tomas O'Miodhachain had then gripped the colonel's shoulder with his left hand, had flung his right towards the son who stood pale-faced by in silence: ''Tis he's the coward to go!'

''Tis you're the coward to stay – you and your men,' and the colonel wrenched himself free and raised his whip.

'Strike me!'

Then many men had leaped in between them, the police inspector led the colonel to his trap (this self-same trap), his men formed themselves into a thick body around it, and the Loyalist party moved off, the whole meeting remaining behind them intact, holding the ground as won, and chanting in a single voice: 'Wrap the green flag round me, boys,

To die were far more sweet,

With Erin's noble emblem, boys,

To be my winding sheet.'

It was wise for Tomas to leave Rossadoon after that; he went to Dublin.

All this was present to the old man when he touched the colonel's sleeve; but as soon as he heard his master's voice, 'He's after hearing some terrible thing in London,' he thought, and he glanced timidly from under his brows at the frozen face.

It was to get some account of his son's death in France that the colonel had gone to London. It was thought he would even go to France. Here he was come back far sooner than expected, cold and silent and aloof.

IV

Until they stopped up to let the crowds pass, the colonel had not spoken one word, had glanced neither to the right hand nor to the left hand. He did not even raise his eyes when, after long driving, his own place, still three miles away, rose up, like an old grey castle, against the rim of the grey sea. He had only stared straight ahead; and yet for all that would have driven into the midst of the crowds on the road if his man had not checked him. That old man, Maurice Dineen was his name, gave his master the true pity of the old retainer. Indeed he had to struggle with himself to keep his silence. He could have, and how willingly would have, broken out into a wild lament for the dead boy, in which there would be thoughts and words and phrases that no Hastings that ever lived could make himself for his relief. He had known the boy, had loved him, and loved him now the more for his hard fate, of which he had thoughts that must never be expressed.

Beyond count of time now, a tiny drop of rebelly Irish blood would suddenly leap to the surface in every generation of the Hastings. As in many another of the Garrison houses, their memoirs are parti-coloured. There's the story of one of them who fought for King James at the Boyne, of another who died fighting with the Wild Geese against the English at Fontenoy, of another who held lands in trust for the Papists when to do so was a high crime, of another who voted against the Union. And fortune has taken care that whatever there is of romance in these memoirs hangs around those wilder bloods that would not keep the safe path. When the young heir went to Trinity, what must he do but begin to learn Irish and lisp sedition! The old people at home shook their heads and smiled; 'A true Hastings!' they said. Then came the war; and the young lad was brought home and sent into the army. If he showed no inclination for it, he made no protest. Every other Garrison house in the country was doing the same. After all, that was the tradition. And, once in the army, he went through the mill of training with such high spirits and brightness that the old colonel, in his de-

light, used to read his letters to his visitors, slapping the pages with
the back of his fingers and saying: 'A true Hastings'. But when the
Rising came and the sixteen leaders, some of whom the lad had met
with in the literary circles of Dublin, were executed, group after group,
the colonel no longer read to his visitors the letters that were still
coming to him from France, for they had become critical and snappish
– and occasionally framed little lyrics and sonnets on Ireland – A true
Hastings!

V

The procession had all but passed. Groups of women in black shawls
and black cloaks were fussily making forward, five or six abreast, to be
in time for the last prayers and the shots above the dead. They were
too hurried for speaking. But a rough man's voice began to cry out, in-
coherently and indistinctly, so that it was hard to catch his words: 'I'm
as worthy to walk as any of ye! 'Tisn't Tom Mehigan would reject me
– the Lord have mercy on his soul. I'm as good an Irishman as any of
ye, and Tom wouldn't deny that!' There was then but a mumbling, and
then a cry more passionate than before: 'Don't mind me coat, lave ye!
Don't mind it. Better men than me, they wore it and had to wear it.
Don't mind it, lave ye.' There was again a silence, and the very end of
the procession, old men limping on sticks and little girls hurrying them
forward, went by, too earnest to notice the outcry of the drunken soldier. 'I'm as ready to die for me country as any of ye. But no, I'm rejected! The little boys, they wouldn't have me, I'd disgrace them! The old
soldier would disgrace them!' There was wild indignation and surprise
in the words.

   The colonel's horse was now slowly, and with nervous forelegs,
stepping down the steep road. The colonel saw the open road below
him clear for a moment, but suddenly a huge, untidy figure in khaki,
with a red, flushed, dribbling face, came headlong into the space; staring after the crowds ascending the road from him, his two arms wide
in the air, he looked like a blind man on an unfamiliar road, groping
and sprawling. He was returning on his phrases, 'Don't mind me coat,
lave ye; better men than me had to wear it.' But the crowds were now
too far from him; he turned and lurched to the corner where the roads
met, and was about to fling himself there on the soft grass when he
caught sight of the colonel. He drew himself up, steadied himself, and
a strange and troubled look struggled in his eyes, and his poor dribbling lips worked a little. He saluted, and then, as if that was not enough,

he quickly snatched the cap from his head and held it in his two hands against his breast, as the people do when a religious procession is passing by. The colonel, grey and cold, still staring with fixed eyes, went on as if he had neither seen nor heard; but out burst the drunken voice again, warm and broken with sympathy: 'Don't mind them, sir; he was no coward; so he wasn't. He was no more a coward than that boy they are burying on the hill. He was a gentleman, he was, and good to the men, and if 'twas fighting for the ould land he was, by Christ, they wouldn't have to shoot him for cowardice!'

The colonel sprang bolt upright in his trap, blind and deaf and maddened. He clutched the whip and lashed his animal. He tried to speak to it. It was rearing in the shafts, its head tossing. 'Home, home!' he cried to it at last, hoarsely, hardly audible. The horse leaped forward and flew like the wind.

And so the colonel lies buried in the old grey house on the South Point, almost as deeply, it would seem, as Tomas O'Miodhachain lies buried in his grave on the North Point, or his own dishonoured son in his unmarked sleeping place in France. God be his comforting.

COLONEL MAC GILLICUDDY GOES HOME

I

Colonel Mac Gillicuddy having been now laid to rest with his Gaelic ancestors in Muckross Abbey, my life, I trust, will soon again begin to flow into its old channels.

The memory of the Colonel was becoming, perhaps, the faintest of all my memories – I had not seen him for years and years – when I chanced on this casual little paragraph in my morning paper: 'The lecture that Colonel Mac Gillicuddy was to give in Wexford Town Hall on "Cromwell in Wexford" has been prohibited by the authorities.' Then the Colonel is home from India, I thought. He had been wounded at the battle of the Somme, and these wounds, I knew, had unfitted him for further active service; I also knew that he had since then been put in charge of some commissariat department in India, and that he had had to make frequent journeys into the very heart of that vast land, as well as into Mesopotamia; but beyond this I knew nothing.

Anyway, he was now in Ireland and anxious to lecture in town halls – what had happened to him? To lecture, moreover, on 'Cromwell in Wexford', and in Wexford itself – whatever had happened to him?

Other colonels, it is true, had endeavoured to influence opinion in Ireland by lecturing on Irish themes: I myself had heard a colonel lecture on 'The Wild Geese' in quite a sympathetic way, and not without some show of learning; but then this was before the Rising in Dublin at Easter, 1916, and the colonel who had done so was by nature a flashy sort of person. Colonel Mac Gillicuddy was different: a silent, brooding sort of man, somewhat of a student, he would not be twenty-fours hours in Ireland, his native land, without perceiving that all such methods of influencing Irishmen had become useless, the temper of the people having changed so much.

I found a faint smile beginning to play about my lips. I thought of Mac Gillicuddy himself – a quiet, brooding man with pursed lips and a top-heavy brow – why, his very appearance on the platform would kill the life of any lecture hall in the world, though it were lit with a hundred arc-lamps and festooned with red and white flowers. And then his theme, 'Cromwell in Wexford'! What other picture could that bring before the mind than the slaughter in cold blood by the Cromwellian soldiery of the 300 noble women of the town as they gathered for sanctuary about the stone cross in the market-place – surely an extraordinary story on the lips of a British officer! Then the place he had chosen – Wexford itself! And then the time – November, 1919, when the nerves of all Ireland were strained almost to the breaking point! Even as this thought flashed on my mind, I looked through the paper, and there, spread all over it, were stories of arrests, of midnight raids for arms, of prisoners hunger-striking in prison, of shootings, of jailings, of further proclamations of martial law. And I had only to look through the window to see soldiers marching by, armed to the teeth. Of the Colonel's desire to lecture on 'Cromwell in Wexford' at such a time, in such a place, I could make nothing, except that something had happened to him.

II

I saw no other mention of that lecture in the papers; a fortnight afterwards, however, I received a short note from him, a fact surprising enough in itself, for during his two years of service in France and since in India – eventful years – he had not written me even one letter. His note made no apology for all this, neither did he make any inquiry of how these years had passed for me; he simply mentioned, casually it seemed, that he intended staying three weeks longer in Drogheda, *studying on the spot the details of Cromwell's massacre in that town!* How long he had been there already, why he had chosen to delve into those terrible things, and why he should trouble me with them – all this had not crossed his mind, it seemed. His postscript was queerer still: 'Have you seen Tate's book on *Kitchener in Africa?*'

That I noted. I had not heard of such a book, but since Mac himself had served under Kitchener in his African wars, it was likely to be authoritative or he wouldn't have referred me to it. 'Tate's *Kitchener in Africa,*' I wrote in my notebook; and even as I did so a sudden thought jerked, *jerked* the pen from the paper: why Mac himself must have witnessed some terrible slayings in his time, perhaps even taken a hand in them!

I stood up straight. I no longer smiled: his deadly earnest face, which now was all my vision, forbade it. I had to put away my work and go out into the streets. With a nervous, unrestful stride, that I found impossible to control, I went from hilltop to hilltop, without purpose. Fagged, yet quieted somewhat in spirit, I reached my lodging again about eight o'clock at night. A postcard stood against the foot of my lamp. I saw that it was in Mac's writing. I turned the other side and read these words, 'Syed Ameer Khaldoun's book on India also'.

India! I could hardly touch the food they put on the table before me. And yet there was nothing like a definite thought in my mind – nothing, only the sense of a far-off background that I was afraid to examine, a background of outrage and blood and horizon-flames tonguing the distant skies; and against this distant background I would see, all the time, Mac Gillicuddy's brooding face, his top-heavy brow, his pursed lips, his gloomy eyes!

III

I had just settled down of an evening three weeks later on to resume the reading of Tate's ill-advised book on Kitchener in the Sudan when the Colonel was announced. I couldn't take my eyes from his face. He had changed, he had aged, withered; but these changes I might have looked for: he was verging on the middle age, and his life had been a hard one. It was not these changes in him that held me in wonder: it was a certain expression that would come across his face, chilling the air; and I could feel that he had somehow come on new standards and that he was now judging the world by them: at such times I would halt midway in a sentence, hoping he would not guess the conclusion I had intended! And often, until his whole face looked distorted, his right eyebrow would climb up his forehead, slowly, slowly; and the eye itself, so exposed, would then glare mercilessly into one's very brain! His very appearance disturbed me deeply. He did not speak of India or Egypt; his mind was too full, at the moment, of Drogheda and Wexford. Every detail of Cromwell's (or as he had taken to pronouncing the name, Crom'ell's) massacres in these places he had amassed, sifted, examined and arranged; and I could see that by dint of brooding on them, the terrible scenes, the locale of which he had been so familiarising himself with, had become alive for him, were burning as fiercely before his inner eye as if, like a poet, he had created them out of some central theme of human vileness. Noting how he would linger, involuntarily I was sure, on certain incidents – the killing of infants in the crypts of St Peter's Church in Drogheda, or the dragging with ropes of an old priest over the cobblestones – noting his rigid air of concentration at these moments, I could feel that the energy of his mind was exactly that of a poet's in the throes of creation: he was, I was certain, in the midst of passionate confusion, blood was flowing beneath his eyes, steaming, and the odour of it was in his nostrils.

I was really glad when, at two in the morning, he rose to go. I felt I should accompany him, for his ardour of mind was such that he might easily go astray or walk into the river, yet this I could not bring myself to do: he had exhausted my powers. When I shut the door on him I spread myself, dressed as I was, on my bed, forcing myself to think on anything, on everything, except on those wild scenes he had been speaking of like a living witness … I kept my eyes in the clutch of my left hand … After a long spell of this artificially-nurtured coma, as it were, I sprang up suddenly, caught up Tate's book on Kitchener and hurled it into the fire, for an insidious, morbid craving to dip again into its horrors had begun to form itself in my quietening spirit.

IV

The next morning he called to tell me that he was starting at once for Kerry. Cromwell, I gladly recollected, had never visited Kerry, and I remember I said, ''Tis the very place for you – a charming land, wild, romantic, yet gentle, somehow, with mild winds from the sea. Besides, it is the home of the Mac Gillicuddys.'

'Yes; I have been told they were a branch of the O'Sullivans.'

'That is so.'

I was glad to find him in so contained a mood. I expected he would satisfy himself with south Kerry, with Kenmare, or Waterville, or Killarney itself, with its magnificent Macgillicuddy Reeks, the mountain land of his ancestors; but a few days later I had a few lines from him from Ballyferriter, which is in the north. Ballyferriter, he informed me, means the Town of the Ferriters, an old Norman family; and then he added: 'In Killarney I visited Cnoc-na-gCaorach (the Hill of the Sheep) where Pierce Ferriter, the warrior poet, the prince who was head of the clan, was hanged, a priest on one side, a bishop on the other, in the time of Cromwell.' I could not help muttering, 'Still harping on his Cromwell'; but I read on: 'From my bedroom window here I can see the whole of Smerwick Harbour; as I write the moon is shining on Dunanore.'

Smerwick! Dunanore! – And not another word, only the two names – two names that I had almost forgotten. It was not for nothing he had gone to Ballyferriter! I could picture his gloomy eyes looking out on the still waters of that haunted bay. I should have gone with him.

The very next morning I had a letter from him which was, to say the least of it, incoherent. It puzzled me. There were lines in it, dashed down I could see, about Sir Walter Raleigh, about Lord Grey – terrible judgments; then there were homely phrases: 'Among the Irish-speaking people of this place I find the word for sixpence is *raol*, which surely is the Spanish word *real*.' Then following right on that: 'I hear screams in the dead night,' and then, 'Why does one become sometimes and quite suddenly possessed of a wild gaiety in such spots?' Every sentence in the letter, all but two, was quite intelligible, but as a whole it was without sequence: it was no more to be understood than the broken phrases a soldier, after a day of battle, flings from him in his restless sleep. It happened that I had just been reading Mügge's *Life of Nietzsche*, and I recollected how he tells that the incoherency of the philosopher's letters was the first hint his friends had of his approaching madness. I grew suddenly afraid. I picked up a time-table, and in less than an hour I was journeying towards Dingle, which is the nearest station to Ballyferriter.

V

I found him weakly struggling with his excitement. While eating the plain fare, the home-made bread, that had been put before me, I noticed that his face was becoming more and more haggard: the invisible fingers of a fixed idea were dragging at his cheeks. He could not help rising from the table to survey for the twentieth time the quiet bay outside, and he would scan its distances as anxiously as if he were fearful that an enemy squadron might at any moment round its rocky headlands. He was soon hurrying me along beside its gentle waters. For December it was a day of wondrous mildness, and never were any waters so limpid and beautiful in colour. They fell on the golden sands in just one long wave, that caught the mellow tints of the sky as it rose and broke lazily in foam. To our right, a black stump of a ruined stronghold stood a little way back from the waters. The Colonel pointed it out to me, and told me how it had belonged to the Fitzgeralds, when they were overlords of all this land, and how one of them, when nearing his end, had asked to be raised up so that his last vision might be the waters of his beloved bay. The Colonel spoke in a wistful tone, and I began to hope that this quiet country of St Brendan and many another life-forsaking hermit – so far from the turmoil of the world – might again win him to peacefulness. But the next moment, standing where San Josepho's Spaniards, three hundred years ago, had made their fight, he was, with an edge on his voice, pointing out to me the traces of the fort they had thrown up, and was showing me where Raleigh butchered the whole 800 of them to death, they having first surrendered to him their arms. Feeling that edge on his voice, I drew him unsuspectingly from the spot, and kept him pacing by the lisping and breaking waters almost till midnight, hoping that by first tiring out his body the great peace of the wide moonlight night might the more surely win upon his spirit.

I had just got into bed with a certain flattering thought that my ruse had not quite failed, when I heard him tapping hurriedly at my door. Before I was half dressed he was in the room.

'Look! Look!' He had flung up my window, his hand was stretched into the night: when I drew to his side I could see it trembling. Beyond it, was all the sweep of the bay, dreamy-looking in the moon, and quiet slopes of shadow were laid upon the hills. But, of course, my eyes were fixed on that spit of land where Raleigh had done his slaughtering, for towards that the trembling moon-white hand, as I instinctively knew, was fiercely stretched.

'Ah, my God! my God!' he was breathing, and I could feel his limbs trembling. 'Horrible! horrible! horrible!'

'What? what?' I said.

'The cries, the cries,' he whispered. I could, by the sound of his voice, tell that there was no natural moisture left in his mouth; it was scarcely speech that came from him. He was hanging on to me, and his trembling shook me. Could it be possible that he was beholding in vision the murdering of 800 defenceless men? Saw it as an artist would – in vivid groupings of destroyer and destroyed?

I peeped at him. His teeth were chattering, and his hands clutched my shoulders heavily, as if his legs were giving way; he was shrinking back from what he was glaring at. Yet the only sounds to be heard from outside were some sea-fowl quarrelling above a school of sprats (as I took it) in the mouth of the bay – sharp cries or melancholy, long-drawn and wailing. Was it these cries that were playing havoc with him? I felt my own ears greedily gathering them in, I felt myself yielding to them, I found them taking on some strange hurry and wildness. Bah! I shook myself. But he was trying to speak, and I thought it was the word 'Cries' I again heard.

'Rather inadequate,' I flung out peevishly, thinking, perhaps, to break the spell that was on him; the cries of the sea-birds just then were very far away, and indeed, not unpleasant in the still night. How could anyone mix them up with the wild screaming of a massacre? But I had tugged at some tightened nerve in him. He leaped from me, back into the room, and the heaviness of weakness was gone from him. He was now all nerve and sinew. He was glaring at me: 'Inadequate! inadequate! That's just it.' He spoke as if the problem of his life had been solved.

'Inadequate! Laughable! Laughable, when you think of the horror of it! It is that that makes one reckless in such businesses. Wild, inhuman' (how he was glaring at me!) ' – delighted to give the edge of the sword on a grey pate, or a soft breast, or a child! – "I will make them squeal," you say, you can't help saying it when the passion of slaughter is upon you, but you … *you can't make them squeal – loud enough!* and then, and then … my God! my God! Shut it! shut it! The curtains. Those also – oh! my God! my God!'

He had flung himself on the bed, burying his face in the pillow. I knew he felt himself swooning off, dizzy; and seeing that he was beyond making any effort to get a grip of himself, I said no word to him, only gripped his limp hand firmly, firmly – there is no other medicine for such a crisis – until, little by little, the terror passed from him.

VI

I was careful not to let him again out of my sight. As the death-still night went on – oh, what a land of holy silence it is! – he won back almost to his own self and tried to force me to my bed, protesting that it was not kind of me to treat him like an invalid. I shook my head, and there I sat until the inevitable reaction had come upon him, and he was sunken into an unrestful sleep.

The night was chilly, and there was no fire in the grate, and, not caring to rouse the household, my only plan was to slip quietly into the room he had left and rifle it of the blankets and wrap myself in them; which done, there I kept vigil over him, like a shepherd in an eastern land. Sometimes the loud scream of a sea-bird would cut through the night, and I would glance at him to see if he stirred to it. But, no. Then the silence would deepen and my thoughts would follow the strong-winged bird over the wide waters. I began to recollect all that I had ever learned of the massacre Raleigh had made in this lonely land; and the slaughters that have been made by others in this country before and since, connecting one with another; and how it came about I do not know, but suddenly, with firm assurance, it came to me that Mac Gillicuddy was picturing all those terrible scenes in the light of his experiences in Africa and India and Mesopotamia! Certain phrases in his letters, certain words I had heard him use, certain inquiries he had been making of me, began to swarm back on me, one summoning another, and at last I almost shouted out: I have it, I have it! – the fixed idea that is harrying him into madness!

With confidence I bent my eyes on the bed. He was whining, squealing like a young puppy in its first illness; but I didn't mind: I could cure him! Now he was still, quite still, seeming as if he were listening to things far away – that sense of strain, I noticed, never once went from him, asleep or awake.

Then little spasms of terror would cross his white features, which he would try to shake off. Yet still I did not lose confidence that now, understanding his disease, I could make a cure.

Of course we left Ballyferriter the next day. To catch the first train from Dingle we had to leave in the dark of the morning, and dark it was, the moon having sunken. A curious thing happened: in a wild, lonely place near Lord Ventry's woodlands, groups of silent-moving figures began to pass us on the road. The whole country, as everybody knows, was disturbed at the time by groups of armed men raiding in the nights. I grew timid.

'Who are these?' I whispered to the old driver.

'Whisht!' he snarled at me.

'But who are they?' I persisted.

''Tis little sense ye have, for an Irishman,' he said. I then said:

'Are they Sinn Féiners?'

'How would I know?' he growled at me.

The Colonel had caught the words, 'Sinn Féiner', it seemed. He gripped the driver.

'Halt awhile, driver,' he said. 'I want to see these men; I won't be long.' He was just leaping from the car, when the driver, with some magic word he had, set the horse prancing. I caught the Colonel's arm.

'Are you mad?' I said to him.

'Mad!' and he flung his head up; the horse was still rebelliously dancing along the road.

'Yes, mad,' the driver shot at him; 'them fellows would destroy you, and the likes of them clothes on your back!' The Colonel was still in khaki.

The figures had vanished. We were recklessly rushing along through places where there was not the faintest glimpse of light of any kind upon the road.

VII

When I had him seated in the train I began to think of the remedy I would try. Since he was haunted by the vision of the reverse of the British Empire I would speak of its obverse. After all, one could make out a case for it. Had it not spread Christianity, I would say, into those wild lands, throwing some certain share of its wealth and its choicest children into the work? Then, its glorious pioneers – their gallant forces, their fame – might one quote of them: 'Only the actions of the just, Smell sweet and blossom in the dust!'

Then I would attempt to show what a blessing those vast hinterlands are to a mother-country, how they are as a very sporting jungle for the younger sons who, remaining at home, must gamble away the estates. Lastly, I would speak of the stream of wealth that has been for centuries flowing into England itself from those seemingly inexhaustible sources. Of that one could speak with confidence … So I would speak to him; but I would not begin yet awhile, for he was sunken into some deep reverie: he had not yet quite shaken off his wild visions of the night.

We stopped at a little place called Emlough, if I remember right, and resuming our journey I made an attempt to speak; but he raised his hand, motioning me to silence. Soon afterwards a crowd of English soldiers, very tired-looking, armed to the teeth, got into our carriage, and I thought I saw the Colonel shudder. To start with a colonel a discussion on the two sides, the glory and the shame of the British Empire in a carriage full of soldiers might lead to the most unimaginable results as things were just then, so I was forced to hold my peace. And these soldiers kept us company until we reached home! I could see that their presence had made Mac Gillicuddy very excited. And there were other incidents as well to play upon him. In Tralee we saw groups of armed policemen lining the main street; presently we saw military motor lorries bringing some Sinn Féin prisoners to trial – young lads, they stood daringly upright in the hooded wagons, with bare steel all round them. We noticed how the people moved quickly through the streets in a sort of gloomy silence, peering into the hooded wagons as they passed in quick succession.

It was dark night when we reached the city. The next day I would make my first attempt to win Mac Gillicuddy from that fixed idea that was ruining his mind.

VIII

We were weary. I threw myself into a deep chair. The Colonel seated himself at the table, opened the evening paper he had bought at the door as we entered, and became engrossed in it, it seemed. Presently he rose. 'Pardon,' he said carelessly, and went out, the paper still in his hand.

He spoke so calmly, as if by having at last made up his mind on some definite plan, he had crushed his excitement into quiescence, that I thought of questioning him as soon as he returned. But there was no sign of his returning! I went seeking him at once, with a growing agitation in my mind. He was nowhere in the house. Without a moment's delay I was rushing through the streets, sharply peering at all that I met or overtook. And the streets were crowded and uneasy. As in Tralee and Dingle they were swarming with squads of soldiers with their helmets and packs on them; and batches of heavily-coated policemen, with white, strained faces, went silently and swiftly about whatever business they had on hand. Military motors and military lorries were recklessly tearing though the dimly-lit darkness. And the people seemed hurrying too, and silent.

For fully three hours I dived hither and thither through wide and narrow streets – through squares lit by arc-lamps and through filthy passages where there were no lamps of any kind. In an alleyway a poor beggarman was singing; his hair was long and matted, he had a thick, unkempt beard, he wasn't four feet in height, an old overcoat that he was wearing soaked water from the muddy ground. Yet he was singing heartily, and the name, Ireland, was in every line:

"'Tis Ireland, 'tis beautiful Ireland,
Ireland, the gem of the sea,
Oh, my heart is at home in old Ireland,
And I wish that old Ireland was free.'

He had a pair of nigger's bones in his right hand, he flourished them to the rhythm. I don't think I should have noticed him, but in three different places I came on him that night. I began to think in the end that maybe he was not a beggarman at all.

Exhausted, I again reached my lodgings in the market square; how wide, free and airy it was after the narrow streets! The moon held half of it in a white still light, the other half was black with shadow, in which a few odd lamp-lit windows glimmered very warm and mellow, contrasting with the wan moonlight.

'My friend has not returned?'

'No, sir; there is no trace of him. Johnny, here, saw him going out.'

'Well, send in whatever you have; I'm fainting.'

'Yes, sir; and there's the paper.'

I had little mind for it, but as it lay there on the table, I saw in scare headlines: 'Massacre at Amritsar!

2,000 Indians Shot Down by the English

500 Killed Outright.'

There was little other information except the name, General Dyer. I must confess I did not cast one thought on those murdered Indians, nor on their murderers; my one thought was Mac Gillicuddy. This was the news he had been so intent upon; it was this dreadful story, come so pat upon its hour, that had sent him out – and he had gone so calmly out! Though the paper trembled in my hand, my weariness had fallen from me. I was sweaty and cold, yet anxious to be up and doing; the shock those three lines of print had given me had called out those reserves of spirit that in such moments so dominate the mere body.

'I must find him,' I said. I swallowed some cups of tea, one after another, and rose up to make again for the streets.

At that moment I heard steps on the stairs, and in flung Mac Gillicuddy himself, quickly and nervously! An appalling wistfulness was in his features, his eyes were wide and pale, his lips weak. He threw himself into a deep chair and buried his head in his hands. And these hands, too, seemed so pale, long-fingered, sweaty!

'What has happened?' I said.

Without removing his hands from his face he shook his head. He wouldn't speak.

Meanwhile, outside, the whole city seemed to have gone into riot; that it was in train for it I had noticed in my rushing through it. The tramp, tramp of soldiers went by, the rattling of their horses and wagons. Far away a rebelly song was being sung firmly and defiantly. Suddenly we head cries and screams, and hundreds of voices: 'Release the man, release him!' 'Shame on ye, ye – ' 'Shame!' 'Shame!' 'Shame!'

I listened to it all, still staring at the broken figure sunken into the chair. Again I heard the cries, 'Release him, release him!' and 'Let him go, ye – ' And then all the cries, shouts, running, singing, seemed to gather up into one long, loud, triumphant roar. I leaped to the window, I saw a great crowd below, a group of policemen in the centre, buffeted by the people, and a wild, squirming little figure in their grasp – my little ballad-singer, I thought. They were all in the moonlight;

but a different crowd were surging into the square from a far-off angle, singing; and it was their coming that had caused the cheering. The little prisoner squirmed more than ever, and at last the policemen had to let him go. They then formed up into a dense mass, and began to fight their way back towards the opening they had come from. All was confusion; stones began to fly through the air, glass was broken. Little knots of people stood still, clutching one another, and others began to whirl around the knots, like currents in a rock-strewn river. Presently, other shouts, yells and screams, screams of terror, arose in another corner of the square; very shrill, they were, very high-pitched; and at once the whole crowd broke into a wild stampede: an armoured car had entered from a side street at a tearing rate and was encircling the square; the place emptied itself in a flick of time, lay again open to the moonlight and to the broad shadows. Still the car tore around it, circling it three times. At last it stood still. At its first coming Mac Gillicuddy had dragged himself wearily to my side; together we had watched its antics; now we were staring speechless at it, as it stood there, throbbing in the moonlight in a pool of shadow; it seemed to look around to see where next it should make a spring. We saw two young heads rise above it. They laughed. They spoke. If Mac Gillicuddy caught the words, I did not; but he raced from the room as if struck by a whip. I leaped after him. I flew down the stairs. He banged through the glass doors. I opened them. I saw him making headlong for the car. The two heads turned towards him. Then down they went. He leaped at the car, crying out – I know not what. A succession of revolver shots rang out, seemed to fly everywhere. Then the car blew a cloud of smoke and moved. He was all limbs, right in front of it. I could see nothing for a moment – only a lifting cloud. Then in, beneath, that little cloud I saw a figure crawling slowly on all fours, like a beast, stupidly, heavily – a most ridiculous posture. It only went a little way, when down it flopped, kissing the ground. And all the time the car circled the square. It swerved to escape the bundle that now lay in its path, and then shot swiftly out of sight by the side street it had entered from. There, in the middle of the moonlight, lay Mac Gillicuddy, dead, with his secrets.

It seems he had gone to the Sinn Féin headquarters and laid certain plans before them for the wrecking of the British Empire, offering his services in the carrying out of them. They would not listen to him. It was then he returned to me, a man who had suddenly given way to despair.

He sleeps in Muckross Abbey. Hundreds of other Mac Gillicuddys – soldiers also – sleep there, too. Considering the story of his life, the manner of his swift death, it is curious to try to imagine how those old Gaelic warriors received him, their kinsman. With aloofness? or with kindly welcome?

I, who knew him so well, I can picture him only as a poor abashed and tongue-tied figure, shrinking away from their hard gazing, their fierce brows. May he rest in peace.

His name was Reen, but they called him the Colonial: their way of pronouncing the word, however, could not easily be set down here. They had never used it, scarcely ever heard it until the newspapers during the Great War had dinned it into their ears. In New Zealand he had lived his many years. There he had landed in his young manhood, toiled upwards, found himself a wife, built his household, in course of years married off his three sons and his two daughters, all to the wrong people, it seemed; there at last he had buried his wife, upon which he had thrown in his hand, sold off everything, and made straight back to the rocks and the fields of his boyhood. Without warning one summer afternoon he drove into his sister's house in West Cork, a man still hardy, if grey-haired, erect enough, bright-eyed, and with the firm voice and free ways of one who had not won through without sweat and bitterness.

I

It was the quiet end of the farmer's year, a day in early October. The Renahans since morning had been building what they called the home rick. In the close beyond the cow sheds was its place from time out of mind. More than two months earlier, in August, before the corn was fit for cutting, they had built their main rick, also in its traditional place – where the pathway that wound up the side of the *cummer* towards the hill-top was widest.

It was a gully for the north-west wind, this close of theirs, and they had been glad to put a crown on the day's work and get themselves within to the warmth and merriment, the fire and the card-playing. They were a large family on whom the scatter for America had not yet fallen. Even without the others who had been assisting in the work – Phil Cronin, the labouring boy; Pat Lehane, a neighbour of theirs; Kitty Mahony, a neighbour's daughter; and one of the Lynch boys –

the Renahans themselves were numerous enough to fill the flag-paved, lamp-lit kitchen with bright and noisy life. They were all in their characteristically careless working clothes, patched and repatched and unpatched, stained with mire or sulphate of copper, many-coloured, loose-fitting; and one could not but notice all this because of this Colonial relative of theirs sitting on the settle between Kitty Mahony and the blaze of the fire. How different he was from the others! This ingathering he had foreseen, perhaps had foreseen Kitty Mahony's visit, and had made himself ready for it – had shaved himself, had put on his newest clothes – he had many suits of them – chosen his heaviest watch chain, his best linen; his boots he had polished; and his thinnish hair, after drenching it with odorous oils, he had carefully brushed and creased. The others, all of them, had contented themselves with bending their long backs and washing their hands in the current of water that ran from between two rocks swiftly across the close. It was their way mostly to keep their tattered everyday caps on their heads, indoors or out; and their hair was anyhow. Kitty Mahony was the only one who had taken any care with herself before coming across the fields from her father's house; she, however, always looked clean and tidy. Everybody knew that she was to marry the eldest son of the house, Mat Renahan.

Phil Cronin and Pat Renahan, the second son, were trying to recapture a way of dancing the 'Blackbird' they had seen at Dunmanway *feis* the Sunday before, three days ago. Again and again they had tried it. They would break down, begin to argue, resume the clatter, and break down once more. The musician – the youngest of all the boys, Tim – as soon as the rhythm of their feet went into confusion, would at once take the fife from his lips, lean down over his knees, and without a word, again begin his teasing of the sheep dog which, with stiffened limbs, lay stretched between his feet on the flags.

The old Colonial gave his head a critical shake: 'No,' he said, 'that's not it; that's not a bit like it,' and he turned and put his lips almost against Kitty Mahony's shapely ear: 'They're clumsy, see? They are clumsy, you know.' 'Isn't their own way just as good?' she answered him, carelessly, without turning her head. In the dance she was taking but little interest. She was eager for her lover to return from Dunmanway: she had had no thought that he would not be in his own house before her that evening. Her eyes were firm on the open doorway, on the chilly luminous space of sky that lay beyond the firelit figures moving and dancing on the flags. Yet even these few words the old man was glad to hear: 'Yes, but they're clumsy all the time. They couldn't put any finish on it even if they had the steps, not what you'd call finish.'

But the dancers had resumed.

Every now and then the father, John Renahan, without a word would plod slowly, bulkily, heavy-footed across the room, disappearing into the dairy for something or other. Massive, silent, heavy-featured, he thought but little of disturbing the laughing group in the middle of the flags. He would hulk through them in a straight line like a surly bull making through a herd of milkers. Without breaking the rhythm they would draw aside, lifting up their chests. They were so used to his ways that they took no anger from them. Once again he entered from the close and passed through them without a word, without a sign. As he did so, the girl's thoughts took on sudden and passionate life. All those about her, the dancers, the others, were nothing to her either. They were there in that kitchen and he she would have there, was elsewhere. 'I wish he'd come, oh, I wish he'd come' – her passion spoke within her so earnestly that she feared she had said the words aloud. She looked from one to another, turning her eyes only, and when she caught the annoying voice again in her ear she was almost relieved: 'There's a great change in everything, in everything. They're awkward.'

She nodded twice, and he was encouraged. He raised his voice this time, speaking to the whole room: 'You may give it up. You can't master it. You're that awkward.'

The dancers slackened off, and Pat Lehane, an onlooker leaning against the wall, took the pipe from his mouth: 'Of course we're awkward, and as you'd say, damn awkward too. And 'tisn't for want of instruction we're awkward. Our little priest, down from the Altar itself he's at us; and I'm afraid 'tis little improvement he's making in us. And the master, he says our equal for awkwardness isn't in Munster. And the returned Yanks, and they doing nothing at all themselves only strealing round, they're the worst of all. The awkward squad, that's what we are. The awkward squad that can't learn nothing.'

He was big, bony, high-coloured, with large flashing eyes, like an excited horse's, and a drooping moustache of strong hairs with dew drops pendulous at the tips of them; when speaking he threw up his head as if to give the voice free passage from the strong gristly throat. In gurgles and splashes it gushed from him; and the moods of his impetuous heart were felt in the uneven flow of it. 'The awkward squad that can't learn nothing,' and he threw his hand carelessly in the air as if there never could be question of amendment.

They were puzzled how to take him, but Tim, the musician, pointed his fife straight out at the dancers: 'The awkward squad,' he said, and throwing back his head, went into uncontrollable laughter. It was a way out. It took hold of them all; and the dancers began to look around for corners of seats to sink upon. The whole floor space in the centre of the room then lay vacant, the light falling on it.

Phil Cronin had already risen to get down the pack of cards when, whatever madness had seized on him, the old Colonial rose and stepped deliberately into the gaping space. 'Play it up, sonny,' he said to the boy, with such a motion of the hand as he might use to call a porter in a railway station.

The boy gave him a swift glance, tightened his fife with one firm twist, blew in the hole of it, and started the tune, his eyes looking straight out from under his brows at the waiting figure. Very erect he stood, silent, in the glow of the fire, his arms stiffly downwards, his head raised, and an inward expression on his features: he was listening, listening – delaying to let the music take full possession of him. As silently they all stared at him. Then he sprang out. With a lightness, even daintiness, with a restraint that puzzled them, he was tapping out the rhythm as he had learned it more than sixty years ago before decay had come upon the local traditions. But the onlookers were not impressed. They were soon aware how limited his steps were; and to them who had often seen prize dancers from Cork city or Limerick, where the dancing is even better, his style seemed old-fashioned and slow. And of course after a few minutes there was but little life left in the aged limbs. They sagged at the knees. Noticing this they took to encouraging him, whispering wondering remarks on his skill and timing. The old fool danced and danced, would dance until he dropped, it seemed, although by now his performance was little better than a sort of dull floundering.

Pat Lehane then took to letting yells of delight out of him as if he could not help it: 'Whew! Whew!' he cried: and soon the others were joining in. In the midst of the bedlam John Renahan, the father, entered in his silent way, made across the room, brushing almost against the floundering figure whom, perhaps, the touch of a finger would now overturn. Silence fell upon them all. The fife still sang out, but not so boldly. The dancer floundered more helplessly than before. The tapping had become a sort of scraping and sliding.

As the father reached the door of the dairy room he looked along those ranged against the wall and without raising his voice said: ''Tis a shame for ye.'

Their eyes followed his rounded back as he went from them; then they looked at one another shyly. But the dancer held on. Somebody began to clap gently. They all took it up, and Pat Lehane reached his hand to the tottering figure and led Reen back to the settle.

The creature was trembling violently – one noticed it as he wiped his streaming face. His chest was heaving.

II

They heard the son of the house turning his horse and cart into the yard. Soon afterwards he entered, a bag of bran dragging heavily from his right arm.

As he sat eating his supper, he was given in whispers a glowing account of the Colonial's skill as a step-dancer. The Colonial himself, now in the centre of a little circle who, at the other side of the room, were shuffling and dealing the cards, let on not to hear what was being told to the young man. Yet they knew he was taking in every word of it. For all that whenever he played a card he raised his lips towards Kitty's ear, telling her that he was winning because she was there beside him.

When she saw that her lover had finished his meal she stood up from beside the Colonial. She could not further restrain herself. Her eyes were hot and flashing, her colour heightened. But the Colonial also stood up. He said with some huskiness in his voice, with some difficulty in making it carry: 'Maybe Mat is tired after his journey?'

Mat had been through three or four years of guerrilla warfare, captaining his district. There were but few places in Munster he had not been in. He moreover had been in prison and following that in an internment camp. He had learnt to shift for himself. From the colour in Kitty's cheeks, her angry eyes, her eager, parted lips, he guessed that the old man had been pestering her. He too took fire; yet he held himself in. He looked at him silently, and his smile broadened like the cold sunshine of a March day across a tract of bare countryside. 'Do I look tired?' he said.

Old Reen was confused: 'But if I went along with you, along with you, some of the way?'

The lover had put a cigarette between his lips. He leant across the table, stretching out his head until he had the tip of the cigarette above the chimney of the lamp that hung on the whitened wall. Kitty was standing uneasily in the middle of the floor. They heard the Colonial's voice again: 'My hat is upstairs.'

The cigarette had reddened: taking it from his lips Mat said nonchalantly: 'Up with you then.'

Stumbling in his eagerness Reen made up the stairs for the hat. He glowed to think what a surprising lot of things about dancing he would say to the two of them, things they could never have heard of. When he had disappeared, the lover impulsively flung open the door, held it open for the girl, put his arm about her shoulders passionately, and turned to those within: 'Give us half a mile start on that champion dancer of yours, half a mile – that's all we ask.'

They were gone, their spirits leaping within them.

When the Colonial came down with his new black hat in his hand, the roomful were very intent on their cards. He made straight out, pulling the door to behind him. Then the card playing ceased and there was a blank silence.

The father broke it saying: 'I wish to God that old idiot would go back to where he came from. And I don't like what that pair is after doing either. I don't like it at all.'

His words took the merriment out of the gathering. Soon afterwards all except the sons and daughters of the family made out, but it was through the back door they went out. Their heavy boots were heard clamping up the rocky passage that led to the bohereen. That way they would not chance to come on a poor flustered creature groping in the darkness, making onward in sudden and reckless starts or standing still listening for any little stir that might let him know whether the lovers had gone east or west. Only in a dull way those neighbours felt that they should not care to come upon an old man so bothered in his thoughts. What a fool he was! – sixty-nine years of age, if a day, yet willing to let it slip from his memory that his life had been lived out, that his hair was grey, and that his arms would be empty for ever more. They gave no thought to the lovers. Yet, and for no reason it seemed, the spirits of the two of them as they made onwards began to leap with so astonishing an energy within them that their limbs for trembling could hardly keep the ground. Swifter and swifter they made on, whispering, wondering, why they could no longer maintain their laughter.

The Awakening

I

Ivor O'Donovan knew it was Ted Driscoll had called him: raising himself above the edge of the bunk he was just in time to see him manoeuvring that bear-like body of his through the narrow little hatchway, to see the splintery shutter slap to behind him. At the same moment he heard the Captain clearing his throat. The bunk opposite was his, and now Ivor saw him, all limbs, mounting awkwardly yet carefully over the edge of it. What between the sprawling limbs, the ungainly body and the hovering shadows above them, the place was narrowed to the size of a packing case. The timber work of the cabin had become so dark with the smoke of the stove that neither shadows nor limbs seemed to stir except when their movements were sudden and jerky. Ivor soon heard the Captain gathering his oil-cloths from the floor with one hand while with the other he dragged at the bunk where the cabin boy was sleeping; this Ivor knew, for as he sat up he caught the familiar words: 'Come on, come on; rouse up; they'll be waiting.'

The Captain he then saw disappear through the toy-like hatchway.

Ivor O'Donovan himself with a stifled groan descended lifelessly from the bunk to the floor. He drew on his sea boots – they had been his father's – drew his oil-cloths about him and in turn thrust his hand into the warm pile of old coats and sacking in which the sleeping boy was buried. He shook him vigorously: 'Come on, come on; they'll be waiting,' he said, and then hurried aloft into the drizzling darkness and took his place with the others.

The tightness that he felt on his brain from the moment Ted Driscoll had roused him seemed natural, not unexpected; nevertheless he groaned to recollect the cause of it. Now, however, as he settled down to his night's work, planted in the darkness there at the gunwale, braced against it, facing the Captain, the dripping fish-laden incoming net between them, he noticed that the tightness had somehow slackened, was still loosening its grip of him, so much so that he had some fear that it would again suddenly pounce on him with its first heat and violence.

Ted Driscoll and Tom Mescall were forward at the windlass; beyond them the boy, bending down, was coiling the rope they passed to him.

It was very dark. Everything was huge and shapeless. Anchored as she was, tethered besides, clumsy with the weight of dripping fish-spangled net coming in over the gunwale, the nobby was tossed and slapped about with a violence that surprised him; flakes of wet brightness were being flung everywhere from the one lamp bound firmly to the mast. Yet the night was almost windless, the sea apparently sluggish: there must be, he thought, a stiff swell beneath them. What most surprised him, however, was to find himself thinking about it. That evening coming down the harbour, he would not have noticed it. The whole way out, his back to the sea, he had stood upright, his feet set wide apart, his hands in his belt, glum, silent, gazing at the cabin boy who, sprawled upon the deck, was intent upon the baited line he had flung over the stern. But as far as Ivor was concerned that patch of deck might have been free to the sun: his own anger, his passion, was between him and the world. That afternoon he had waited for Chrissie Collins for two hours. At the very start he knew, he *knew*, so at least he told himself she would not come. For all that he had gone hot and cold, again and again, while waiting for her. He had broken from the spot impulsively: a moment later he had trailed back again, giving her one more quarter of an hour to make good in. Then when his rage was at the peak, hurrying down to the jetty, he had suddenly caught sight of her, all brightness, stepping briskly up the hillside, the schoolmaster walking beside her, as eager as herself. Her head was bent, her eyes were fixed on her dainty toe-caps, and she was listening complacently to the schoolmaster's blather. Only that he should have to tear through the village and it filled with the gathering crews, he'd have told her what he thought of her.

With his eyes downwards on the sprawling limbs of the boy, he had indulged, as if it were the only thing for a man to do, the heat of the passion that that one glimpse of her had aroused in him.

Now, ten hours later, braced against the timbers, swaying and balancing, freeing the net, freeing the rope, grabbing at the odd dog fish, the odd blob of seaweed, the tangle of seawrack, flinging them all, as they came, far out, clear of the rising meshes – he was puzzled to con-

trast his present indifference with his stifling anger of the afternoon.
Yet he was not pleased with himself. This calming down of his seemed
like a loss of manhood. His mind could not, it appeared, stay fixed on
the one thought. He found himself noticing what he had never noticed before – how the mackerel, entangled in the meshes, would catch
the light of the worried lamp and appear just like a flight of shining
steel bright daggers hurtling by him from gunwale to hold. Never to
have noticed so striking a thing before, how curious! But had the Captain ever noticed it? He glanced shyly at the aged face opposite him
and started, for the Captain, he saw, had had his eyes fixed on him, all
the time, perhaps! And Ivor recalled, reddening slightly, that also that
afternoon while lost in his own passionate thoughts he had caught him
observing him with the selfsame silent gravity. Why should he do it?
He was Captain. But the boat was his, Ivor's; and one day when he was
somewhat older, and when his mother was willing to trust him, he
would sail it. But this was unfair, he felt, for the Captain, this Larry
Keohane, had been ever and always his father's dearest friend and
shipmate, had sailed with him till he was drowned, had indeed been
with him that very night; and afterwards he it was who had undertaken the management of the boat for them; and in such a way that
not a penny of the fish money had ever gone astray on them. Later on,
now two years ago, he had taken Ivor on board as one of the crew, and
taught him whatever he knew of sailoring and deep sea fishing. There
was surely plenty of time yet for thinking of playing the Captain. Besides, the selling of the fish was trickier work than the catching of it.
His eyes fell on the claw-like hands of the Captain, they were twisted
with rheumatism, and a flood of kindly feeling for this grave and faithful friend suddenly swept over him with such power that he found his
own hands fumbling at the net without either skill or strength in them.
To glance again at the Captain's face he did not dare.

'Up, boys, up!' he impulsively cried to the windlass men as if to
encourage them. In the clinging darkness, although the drizzle was becoming lighter and lighter, he could make out only the shapeless bulk
of themselves and the windlass: two awkward lumps of manhood rising and falling alternately, their sou'westers and oil-cloths catching
some of the flakes of the wet brightness that were flying around everywhere. 'Twas curious work, this fishing. Like a family they were, con-
fined in a tiny space, as far almost from the other boats as they were
from the houses on the hills where the real families were now huddled
together in sleep. The real families – each of them was different from

the others. Tom Mescall's was the most good-for-nothing in the whole place. Others had quite nice houses, clean and well-kept. But most strange of all was it to have him, Ivor, thinking of such things, his head calm and cool (and he thereupon grabbed a huge dog-fish from the passing net and with a gesture deliberately sweeping sent it far out into the splashing darkness).

II

The work went on and on and Ivor could not help all kinds of thoughts from crossing his brain, nor help noticing the onward rush of them. The dragging of the net was done in silence, no one speaking until they each and all were sure that they had had a fairly good catch, and that all the nets were heavy. Ivor then was aware that some dull and lifeless conversation was passing to and fro between the men at the windlass. He was hailed suddenly by one of them, Ted Driscoll: 'Look where Leary is, east.'

Far off, east, Ivor saw a tiny light. As he watched it the other voice came through the darkness, half speaking, half calling: ''aith then he wouldn't be long swinging on to the Galley in there.'

'Is it Leary, do you think?' Ivor asked the Captain, and he was answered: ''Tis like the place he'd be.'

Ivor then sent his gaze ranging the sea noting the disposition of the boats. They were far off, nearly all of them. Some were miles beyond Galley Head. Others were away towards the west. Here and there a pair of lights seemed to ride close together, only seemed, however, while an odd one, like Leary's, played the hermit in unaccustomed waters. Far to the west the great light of the Fastnet every few moments threw a startling beam on the waters and, quenching suddenly, would leave a huge blackness suspended before their very eyes, blinding them. He noticed how, little by little, the timid lamps of the fishing fleet would in time manage again to glimmer through that darkness. He bent himself once more on the work, thinking over and over again what a curious way they had of making a living. On the land at the time of night every one of the houses was a nest of sleep – chilly walls and warm bedding. After all Chrissie Collins was a farmer's daughter, a small hillside farmer, a 'sky' farmer. Farm houses had ways of their own. Fishermen also had ways of their own. The next time he met her he would hold his head as high as hers.

The dragging went on and on. The unending clanking of the windlass, the wet mass of the net, the grip of his feet on the narrow way be-

tween gunwale and hold while the boat tossed and tugged, the sudden
flashes of the lamp, the long silences of them all, the far-off lonely-look-
ing lights of the other anchored nobbies and ketches, the bold startling blaze of the Fastnet, and above all the stream of shining daggers
sweeping by – for the first time in his life he reckoned up the features
of the fisherman's calling, and felt some sort of pleasant excitement in
doing so, as if he had heard some good news or come upon some unexpected treasure. He could not understand it.

When the last of the nets was in they tidied the decks, pitching
the sea-wrack into the sea. He heard the Captain say to Driscoll, whose
head was bent down on the confused mass of fish and net in the hold:
'Good, and a fair size too. I'm very glad.' 'I'm very glad,' repeated Ivor
in his mind, wonderingly, yet feeling that the words fitted in. He noticed Driscoll and Mescall, their arms hanging heavily after their
night's work, their sea boots lumping noisily along the deck, going aft
to the little cabin, making down the hatchway without a word. The
boy had gone down previously. The waft of the smell of boiling fish,
of boiling potatoes, that came from the smoke pipe told of his toil
below. To Ivor it was very welcome. He was hungry; and besides they
would presently all meet together round the little stove. 'I'm very
glad,' he whispered, not knowing why. And the smoke, he saw, was
like a lighted plume rising from the top of the iron pipe.

The Captain drew closer to him. He took the fragment of pipe
from his mouth and, smothering the glowing bowl in his fist, pointed
sou'west: ''Tis Casey that's going in.'

'Is it?' Ivor said, also picking out the one craft in all the far-scat-
tered fleet that had got under weigh, that – very slowly, for there was
scarcely a breath of wind – was making for the land.

'Maybe 'tisn't,' the Captain then said.

'I'm sure 'tis him all right,' Ivor said, though he was not sure at
all.

They stood side by side following with their eyes the distant slow-
moving light. There was scarcely a morning that some boat or other
did not hoist sail the moment their catch was made and hasten in.
There was always some special reason for it. And the other craft, every
one of them, would make guesses at the boat, as also at the cause of
her lifting anchor in such haste. The others were content to make the
pier any time before the buyers had received from other fishing ports
and from Dublin itself their morning telegrams fixing the day's prices.
Ivor thought how it was nearly always something to do with the real

household, with the real family, that brought a fisherman to break that way from the fishing grounds before the others. Sickness, or the necessity for some early journey, or the emigrating of a son or daughter. 'I remember your father, one time we were out, and far out too, south the Galley, ten mile it might be, how he called out, and we not ready at all: "That'll do, boys, we'll make in."'

The Captain's quiet husky voice stopped, and Ivor wondered if that was all he had to say; but the tale was taken up again: 'That was twenty-two years ago this month.'

Ivor was once more astray, he could not find reason in the words.

'Yes,' he said, quietly.

'That night he expected a son to be born to him; and he wasn't disappointed.'

Ivor knew that he himself was the child that on that night came into the world; but what kept him silent was the Captain's gravity. Such matter among them had always been a cause for laughter. Ivor was nevertheless glad that the Captain had spoken seriously; for all that, fearing to betray his own state of mind, he answered: 'That's not what's taking Casey in anyhow.'

The Captain did not seem to hear.

'All night long,' he said, 'I'm thinking of things that I saw happen out here on these waters for the last fifty-four years.'

Ivor raised his head in astonishment. Why should such recollections have set the Captain examining him the whole night long?

'Strange things,' the Captain resumed, 'strange voices, sad things too, very sad, things that should not happen.'

After all, the Captain was in the humour for spinning a yarn, that was all. But, instead of the yarn, the Captain, scanning the sky, merely said: ''Tis going south; the day will be fine, very fine.'

Ivor too felt a slight stir in the air, and from the hatchway Driscoll called them down.

'With God's help 'twill be a fine day,' the Captain said once more, throwing the words over his shoulder as they moved aft, one behind the other, sauntering along in their heavy sea boots.

III

The air in the cabin was reeking with the smell of fish and potatoes, and so thick with fire smoke and tobacco smoke that one could hardly make things out. There was hardly room for the five of them. The boxes they sat on were very low and the men's knees, on which they held the plates, seemed to fill the whole space. One felt the warmth against one's face like a cushion. Yet Ivor welcomed it all – the heat, the smell of the good food, the close companionship – not alone for the comfort it all wrapped him round with but for the memory it raised in him of those many other nights on which he had experienced it, his body as cold as ice and his fingers unable to move themselves. The others were already eating lustily and noisily.

'Not too bad, not too bad,' he cried out cheerily, planting himself between Driscoll and Mescall, just because they were head to head and nose to nose in earnest argument. They took no notice of him, continuing it still across his very face. Driscoll, who was the simplest of them, was showing how Mrs O'Connor, the shopkeeper who supplied them with all and sundry, had done him out of two-and-elevenpence, and Mescall, who, in spite of his harum-scarum wife and family, was the merrymaker, was explaining how she had tried the same trick with him and how he had laid a trap for her and caught her – a trap so clever that Driscoll had no idea how it worked or how by using it he could recover his two-and-elevenpence. The boy was heard plunging vessels in a bucket of water. All the time the Captain held his peace, and Ivor, noticing it, glanced at him, wondering if he were still recalling what he had seen happen on the fishing grounds during his long lifetime upon them.

Leisurely yet ravenously the meal went on, and when they thought of it, or at least so it seemed, first Mescall and then Driscoll, who had had no sleep till then, threw off their sea boots and disappeared into the darkness of the bunks. In the same haphazard way Ivor, the Captain, and the boy returned to the deck.

IV

At last they had her moving: her sails were flapping, coming suddenly between their eyes and the dazzling flood of light outwelling from sea and sky. When they filled, when she settled down, Ivor heard the Captain say in a voice that sounded unusual: 'I suppose I may as well go aft.'

Unable to account for the words Ivor answered in mere confusion of mind: ''Tis better, I suppose,' as if the matter was not quite clear.

Silently the Captain went aft to the tiller, and Ivor, as was his custom, threw himself down on the pile of rope in the bow: there was no more to be done. He felt the streaming sun, into which a benign warmth was beginning to steal, bathing his body from his hair down. After the work of the night, after the food, a pleasant lassitude, as thick as his thick clothing, clung to him. The cabin boy was already fast a-sleep on the deck, cuddled up like a dog, his face buried in his arms. Ivor felt sleepy too, yet before he yielded to it, he recalled the memory of the handful of them, cut off from all other company, working silently in the drizzling darkness, the tossing lamp momently flashing in their eyes and lighting up their dripping hands. He recollected too the rise and fall of the awkward bodies of the two men at the windlass, the clanking of the axle, and the uncompanioned boy beyond them working away in almost total darkness. Clearer than all he recalled the flight of glittering spear heads sweeping by between himself and the Captain. Then also the group in the smoky cabin, the hearty faces, the blue and white plates, the boy plunging the vessels in the water. How different from what was now before his eyes! The sea was wide, wide; the air brisk, the seagulls screaming, quarrelling, gathering the schools, dashing at the transparent crests of the waves or sweeping in great curves to the east, the west, everywhere, their high-pitched cries filling the air with a rapture that opened the heart and at the same time alarmed it. Yes, very different, yet his pictures of the night time – the groups silently working in the darkness, the gathering in the little cabin – these were dearer to him just now than the bright freshness of the morning. He recalled the unexpected words of the Captain – 'I'm very glad.'

At last the drowsiness that he would keep from him overpowered him.

He awoke to find the boy's hand timidly unclutching his shoulder: 'Himself wants you.'

Rising up he caught the Captain's eyes resting upon him with a calmness that surprised him, that disturbed him. He went aft.

'You're wanting me?'

'Sit down there, Ivor, there's a thing I have to say to you.'

Fearing some reference to Chrissie Collins, some questioning, some good advice, Ivor sat down without a word. The Captain blurted out: 'Ivor, boy, 'tis time for you to sail what belongs to you.'

As he spoke his hand lifted from the tiller – an instinctive giving up of office. Instantly however it fell upon it again. Ivor perceived the action with his eyes, not with his mind, for the words had sent a thrill of delight through his whole body. Everything he had been noticing that night of nights was in that overwhelming sensation – the darkness, the clanking windlass, the shining fish, the cabin, the seagulls, everything – but he caught hold of himself and said: 'But, Lar, why that? Why that?'

'Because 'tis time for you.'

'But why so? 'Tisn't how you're going from us; what's after happening?'

'Nothing. Nothing. Only all the night I'm thinking of it. 'Tis the right thing. Herself is at me to. If there's a touch of wind in the night, she don't sleep a wink.'

'Oh! If the boat goes we all go.'

'You can't talk to them like that. Anyway 'tis right. 'Tis your due. We got on well, Ivor. Them that's gone, they deserved as much. We done our best, all of us.'

'Lar, 'tis better wait till my mother hears of it.'

'If you wouldn't mind I'd give you Pat to be in my place. He'd be better for you than a stranger.'

Again that thrill of delight went through him. He thought at once if the Captain had not offered his son, a stranger would have to be brought into the boat, one of those unlucky creatures perhaps who had given the best of their lives sailoring the wide world over, creatures who were not trustworthy, who had bitter, reckless tongues, who destroyed the spirit of goodwill in any boat they ever got footing in. That danger the Captain had put aside. There was therefore a clear way before him, and a boat's crew after his own heart.

'I'm thankful, Lar, and herself will be thankful; but what will you be doing with yourself?'

A little smile grew upon the Captain's face, and both of them raised their eyes to scan the hillsides they were approaching. In the sun which now lay thick upon their brown-green flanks, nestling in the zig-zag ravines they saw the little groups of houses where the fishermen lived. Some of the cottages, snow-white, faced full in the eyes of the morning, sunning themselves. Others were turned aside, still asleep in the shadows, catching a bright ray only on chimney head or gable.

'Wouldn't I want to sit in the sun and smoke my pipe as well as another? That will do, Ivor. Ted's coming up. He's after smelling the land. In the evening I'll fix up with your mother.'

V

It was a Saturday morning. That night and the next they would all sleep in their own houses, not in the boats.

In the evening the Captain went to Ivor's house, and, as he said himself, fixed things up with his mother. Then he shook hands with them all, with Mrs O'Donovan, Ivor, his two sisters, and his young brother, who was only a boy. He then set off up the hill for his home.

Afterwards, standing up before the bit of glass nailed against the wall, Ivor stood shaving himself. His heart was blazing within him, his cheeks burning, for the Captain had been speaking his praises, and all his people had been staring at him.

It had been a day of uninterrupted sunshine, and now a bright heaven, slow to darken itself, although the sun had been a long time sunken, darkened to blackness every ridge, bush, tree clump, roof and gable that stood against it. On the roads and fields it still threw down a persistent glow; and Ivor went in and out the doorway praying for the dusk to thicken. In the midst of the Captain's praise of him he had felt a burning desire to see his boat once again with his own eyes, to be sure it was still there at the pier, where, with scores of others, it was fastened. He wanted to feel the tiller beneath his right hand – that above all. And yet he would not care to have any of his neighbours see him doing so. Nightfall was never so slow in coming. At last, however, with a yearning look at the still livid sky he set off down the path towards the roadway. He could gambol, he could sing, only that at the same time he had thoughts of the heavy responsibility that in future would rest upon him. He strove to calm himself, to walk with the appearance of one who had no other business than to breathe the cool air of the evening. He knew there would be groups of men still in the public-houses as well as along the sea wall; and these he wished to escape. Before entering the village he vaulted over the wall, descended the rocks, and made along by the edge of the waters. At a point beyond the farthest house he climbed on to the road again, and, more assured, made towards the deserted pier. At its extreme end, almost, his *Wildwood* was moored. The pier itself, the debris on it, the fish boxes, the ranks of barrels – as well as all the conglomeration of boats along its sheltered side – the whole had become one black mass sharply cut out against the livid waters of the harbour. On a standard at its very end a solitary oil lamp, as warm in colour as the waters were cold, was burning away in loneliness. Towards it, and as quietly, almost as stealthily as if on a guilty errand, he steered his way. He was glad when the piles of barrels so obstructed the view that no one could spy him from the road. Doubtless the news was already abroad; by now the men were surely all speaking about it; as for himself, it was very strange coming at the time it did, coming, without expectation, at the tail-end of the night when for the first time he knew what it was to be a true fisherman. He was glad Chrissie Collins had her schoolmaster. It left himself as free as air. And thinking the thought he breathed in the pleasant coolness of the night, yet could not, it seemed, gulp down enough of it. Glad of the darkness, of the loneliness, he suddenly threw out his two arms wide apart, stretching them from him, and drew the keen air slowly and deliciously through his nostrils. And breathing still in the selfsame manner went forward a few steps. Then suddenly he saw a figure outlined against the tide, seated on some fish boxes, gazing silently at the bobby for which he was making! He knew it was the Captain. His arms fell and he stood quite still. 'Oh!' he said, in a sudden stoppage of thought. He turned stealthily and retraced his steps, fearful of hearing his name cried out. But nothing was to be heard except his own careful footfall; and before he reached the road again he had recovered himself. It surely was a sad thing for Larry Keohane to have his life drawing to an end. Why was it that nothing can happen to fill one person with happiness without bringing sadness and pain to somebody else? Yet the Captain, he remembered, that evening in his mother's house had been quite cheerful, had told them how glad he was that they had made quite a good catch on his last night, and what a peaceful night it had been! And what a fine boat the *Wildwood* was; and how happy he was to be leaving her in hands that would not treat her foully; indeed he could well say that he was flinging all responsibility from his shoulders; and that was a thing he had been looking forward to for a long time. And saying that, he had gone from them cheerily and brightly. Yes, yes, but here surely was the real Captain, this seaman staring at his boat.

Ivor waited, sitting on the wall in the darkness, for a long time. At last he heard the slow steps of the old man approaching, saw him pass by – saw him very indistinctly for the darkness, yet knew that he had his hand covering his pipe in his mouth and his head on one side, a way he had when he was thinking to himself. He waited until the footsteps had died away up the hillside; then he rose to resume his own quest towards the nobby. He found he could not bring himself to do so. He did not want to do so.

With slow lingering steps, with stoppings and turnings, at last he too began to make towards his home. His head was flung up, almost flung back. More than once he told himself that he didn't ever remember the sky to have been so full of stars. Somehow he felt like raising his hand towards them.

The Emptied Sack

I

Urged to it by his son, John Connole made up his mind to do as the other potters had done; to throw aside the ancient methods, the antique gear he had inherited from his fathers, as they from theirs, and to install – it was his son's word – to install instead a modern scientific furnace in which the heat could be regulated to the hundredth part of a degree. Old Tadhg Kinnane, that dwarf-like creature, stooped and venomous, more than eighty years of age, whose body some intensity of brain rather than warmth of heart kept alive – what would *he* do then? With his heaped-up donkey-load of furze branches piled higher than his head he would no more be seen in the streets of Youghal, for furze was not the tinder used in the new-fashioned furnaces.

'And the poor creature,' Jack Tattan, one of the potters, began, half smiling, his hands under his clay-white apron, ''tis little use he's now for anything else.'

'He's eighty, he must be eighty-three,' Fred Lincoln said, his eyes twinkling against the sun; he had just come from within.

'Why should he be working at all? What is he working for? All he earned his whole life long, what did he do with it?'

''Twill be worse for him than the *Calliope*.'

'It will that.'

Forty years ago when the *Calliope* lay along the jetties all the windows of the hillside towns gazed wide-eyed at her bright shapeliness. Her gilded points and lines, her whiteness, her sparkle, her shining newness, had bespoken welcome for her from the townsfolk; her crew, from captain to cabin boy, were given the run of the port. Tadhg Kinnane was then in the prime of life, forty years of age, yet had for all that already buried his household – parents, wife, children, all except one daughter – had buried them in Ardmore of the Saints across the water. That daughter he had taught to keep house for him – if house it could be called. In due course she had grown into the custom of accompanying him to the town with his load of furze; still later, whenever he was busy working for the neighbouring farmers at the harvest or ploughing, she was become venturesome enough to undertake herself the delivery of the furze branches at the potteries. She would start off before the sun had risen, would pilot the ass and cart down the rough mountainy *poirsin*, along the white roads, and, at last, through the cobbled streets of the town; would look, it seemed, neither to right at the sailormen nor left at the 'prentice potters, but make straight on for one or other of the yards – there were many of them then – would sedately receive the payment, would make her household purchases, always at the traditional shops and in the traditional way, and arrive, oftentimes late at night, at the lonely cabin in the hills with a mouthful of gossip for the sun-burnt, sun-drowsed exhausted man stretched along the settle patiently awaiting her, his pipe in his mouth. He was not sharp enough in eye or brain to notice that those visits were having more and more attraction for the rich-blooded ripening girl. Her lips were girlish, soft, and full; she had a tender grace and innocence about her, her brows were light, well-shaped; her eyes timid and as dark as berries. She could not speak without blushing. Reared apart from womenfolk, she felt awkward when alone with them. She feared their questioning.

Forty years ago, then, after a long day's threshing in Pierce Fielding's barn, Tadhg Kinnane lay stretched in that patient attitude on the settle awaiting his daughter's return from the town. He saw the dust thicken, the bats make their own of the sky, the earth darken, grow heavy and cold after the going of the sun; and then, one by one, he watched the stars coming into the heavens silently, silently. From the settle it was that he saw the night fall. At last he arose slowly, and slowly went out, sitting on a block of wood by the door. The pale wide glare of the afterlight startled him, so frank it was, so untender. Yet the coolness, after the labour of the day, found welcome in his limbs; he stretched out his legs, rested his back and head against the wall, and sleep fell on him. When he awoke, suddenly, as if a whirring bird, with a cry, had struck him one stroke, a dark-blue silent night, gemmed with stars, was standing upon the earth. His hands were cold, and a soundless wind was feeling softly at his features. It was some moments before he realised that the fear he felt all about him, like a chilly, invisible garment, was due to his daughter's delay in the distant town. He groped his way into the hut, making for where the last spark of fire was still visible among the ashes; this, with the fire-wheel, he fanned up vigorously, indeed passionately. As suddenly he stopped and glared at the clock's face: it was ten minutes past one. It could not be so late, he thought; but from far away he heard a calf roaring, and the cry shook the heart in him, for it opened the spaces of the silent night, made it seem vast and lonely, vacant of any living soul to comfort one in trouble. No, it could not be so late, he reasoned with himself, yet again came that unrestrained cry of animal distress; and he felt he could not wait any longer. He plunged the candle into the fire, and set it lighting on the dresser. He reached for his coat, it hung on a hook in a roof timber, and as he flung it on he suddenly stretched an ear for other sounds that he fancied he had caught – the jolting of the ass cart as it made up the difficult, rocky passage towards the house. 'Ah!' he breathed, and the comfortable warmth of anger began to replace the chilly fear within him. Oh, he would speak to her, he would speak to her, and never again would she go alone into that cursed town of tradesmen and sailors. He buttoned his coat hurriedly, it would show her what he had been about to do; and, waiting, he stood on the threshold, alert, stiffened up, filling the opening, the night-blue sky before him, the glowing interior behind. Again, and more clearly, he heard the homely, drowsy, unhurried rattling, and he drank comfort from it. Then it ceased. But almost at once, again began. Once more stopped, for some time too. Once more began, stopped once more. 'God guide us, God guide us,' he breathed, and made hurriedly down towards the rambling, uncertain noises. He found the cart dragged obliquely across the passage, the ass cropping the long dew-cold herbage by the edge of the way. As for his daughter – she already was far on the sea in the arms of the wild young skipper of the *Calliope*.

Tim Tobin, then, had said the word that had renewed for them the story of Kinnane's far-off day of trouble. Bitter and all as old Tadhg was he had suffered his share, and had, as they said, shrunk into himself, closing not only his mouth but his heart. When one is come to that what is left except to bend upon the work of the day? And this he did. He would labour for the farmers round about, sometimes rising at dawn and travelling ten or fifteen miles to a harvesting or ploughing, and, come home, would be heard late in the night hacking and hewing in the furze thickets by the river bed or along the hills. He took on pottery after pottery, and kept them going, and neither the driving sea winds nor mountain floods nor rains ever hindered him or even delayed his coming to them at the right time. They it was that failed him, one after another giving up the ancient way. By this time, however, himself was getting old, was now more than eighty years; and for one so old the hacking out and the gathering and the piling of one load of furze branches was a full week's work.

'Do you know, I'm sorry for the old creature – in a way.'

'Um, um, you needn't then. He won't starve.'

'That's true. Still, what'll he do with himself?'

'Lie down and die; and indeed they're a long time waiting for him, his people in Ardmore.'

'Will he come today, I wonder?'

II

As if unaware of any change whatever, the old man dragged his little donkey, rather viciously, one thought, into the yard. Animal, tackling, furze branches, cart – and then the old man himself – face, whiskers, hair, hands, clothes – they all were of one texture and one hue – a rough, hodden grey upon which the dust of the long distance he had come was scarcely noticeable. As always, the animal made to swerve to the left where, it remembered, long tufts of bluish grass were to be cropped between the cobblestones; and, as ever, the old man snarled at it, 'Come on, you!' Then, 'Whu-ee! Whu-ee,' his hard old lips blew out, and he threw the reins carelessly on its back. He stopped suddenly, his head down, even more than usual, his brows bent, even more than usual, to that intensity of purpose by which he seemed to live. At last, fixing his thought, he hobbled forward quite briskly towards the open-air stairs which led up to John Connole's office. But again he paused, hesitating for a moment; and, as precipitately as he had gone from it, made back to the cart, from which, hurriedly, he began to fling the furze branches off about the yard. John Connole, who must have seen him, came on to the wooden platform at the head of the stairs: 'Take them up again, take them up, I say. And be off with you, be off with you, you old deceiver. You were told not to bring them.'

The old man stopped as he pulled one from the pile; he held it in his hand, awkwardly, like a defeated flag; such words he had heard before in other potters' yards. Timidly, quietly, he put the branch on the ground. 'Take them up, I tell ye. Didn't I tell you I was done with you? Be off with yourself.'

John Connole turned his back and went into his office. The old man raised his eyes towards where he had been speaking on the platform.

A little group were standing under a low wide archway: the autumn sun was playing about their feet, not on their heads or faces: 'There you are, Tadhg. There you are,' one of them called to him, not roughly. He could think of nothing else to say.

John Connole's son came across the yard. He was well-dressed, well-combed. He had some papers in his hand. He was puzzled for a moment to see the old man slowly replacing the branches on the cart: when he understood, he made a gesture with the papers towards the group in the archway: 'Give him a hand with them,' he said, and with the lightness of youth in his limbs bounded up the wooden stairs.

The men began quickly to fling the branches on to the cart, old Tadhg looking at them suspiciously. For them during the long, long years he had always been little more than a butt for their joking; they would begin again at any moment, he felt; but no; they helped him to swing the cart about on the rough cobblestones, to set it going, and all without one word of impatience. They then drew back, they had played their part. He peered at them, still suspicious, but, making sure they had no thought of gibing at him any more, he took a step towards them; 'Whisper,' he said, 'did ye ever hear this?' and he hissed out an Irish saying, which, translated, is 'Petting the dead and the dead laughing!' They could only keep their silence, staring at him. And he looked back at them, and smiled!

He grabbed the mouthpiece and led his swaying, carelessly built load through the gateway and out into the traffic of the main street.

III

It took him only a moment to make up his mind as to what he should do. He turned down a narrow sunless street of long-deserted warehouses. At the farthest end was a glare of light – the wide sky, the bright waters of the estuary. He made straight for the edge of the jetty, dragging the donkey after him with a callous vigour, its head screwed sideways up. He swung the cart about until its tailpiece was towards the waters. Then, muttering and growling he began, still with something of a false strength in his limbs, to pitch the branches into the sea.

If he had drawn his cart in at any other point of those all too spacious jetties, he might have finished without interruption, but now, suddenly, he heard, 'Look out!' shouted at him in an un-Irish accent. A sailorman with a noose of stout new rope across his guernsey, a-round his shoulders, was coming towards him laboriously: pressed forward at a sharp angle, his thin and worn shoes showed the play of the feet within them. It was not he who had shouted: it was another, whose duty it was to lift the rope over whatever quayside debris lay about. Again, this man shouted 'Look out! Look out!' and failing to raise the cable high enough above the cart, about half the load was swept off on top of old Kinnane: when the rope had passed by, himself, too, had been thrown and was sprawling in the midst of the branches. He had to turn on his face and hands to rise up. He did so as if there were need for haste, as if he had no time to think of what had befallen, or of the wet rope, the labouring sailorman, or the ship that like a dazzling vision was gliding to its moorings. He resumed without a thought, it seemed, and with the same surly vigour, his task of pitching and kicking the branches into the water. The last he flung in with all his strength. 'Take them with you, me fine salt water,' he snarled, and turned away. He at once began dragging his cart from the quayside. The men on the ship, some of them standing with mooring cables in their hands, thought doubtless that he had been fulfilling some daily task and now was setting off for home. He did not seem to have given one glance at the ship: her spars were bright against the rich blue of the sky; all about her were gleams, points of sun-fire, lines of light. One glance perhaps he had given her, no more, when, sitting in his cart, he started for his lonely nest in the hills.

IV
How many, many hundred times he had thus in the gathering twilight made homewards! The falling night, the cool airs, the silent winding road, showing dimly before him, the rocky heathery hills, now closing in on his path, now opening out again, all the time, however, rising higher and higher, growing darker and darker – it was easy for him in such surroundings to forget that this was the very last of all such journeys: that he would never see the potteries again. And so, now wide awake, shouting and pulling at the little animal, and now drowsing into sleep, his head bobbing and his hands hanging limp, resting on his knees – on and on he journeyed, mile after mile. His voice was sometimes heard: 'Go on, go on, can't ye', and no weakening seemed to have overtaken it. But, swinging around into that rising, stone-strewn, winding passage that led to his house, he suddenly felt afraid and cold and lonesome. Only a dismal and empty hut lay before him – as if it had not been empty and dismal for more than forty years! A cold and empty house! But as suddenly he saw out before him the ever-rising masts of a sailing ship, her spars, her cordage, shining in the sun! 'Go

on, can't ye!' he called out bravely, with a new ring in his voice, and from that until he threw the reins on its back, he gave the animal but little peace.

He removed the mouthpiece and left the ass to its haphazard grazing, the cart still tackled to it.

Meanwhile he had lit a candle, had closed the door, and soon was searching and poking in all the holes and corners of the room. Little cries broke from him. Sometimes he stopped, listening. He climbed up on chairs and fumbled at the roof timbers. At last he satisfied himself that no more remained to be done. In the midst of the place half a loaf of bread was hanging from a rafter by a string: it was his way of baulking the rats of it. From this he broke off some chunks and began hastily to chew them, still moving about as if unable to rest. He suddenly quenched the light, locked the door behind him, and made once more for the cart. He restored the mouthpiece, sat in brightly, and vigorously urged the animal back towards the town. It wanted an hour to dawn. 'Ah! ah!', 'Ah-h-h', he breathed out, showing his teeth – a cry that was full of triumph.

When he once more entered Youghal town, the pale morning was playing upon it; nevertheless, everything was still fast asleep, churches, shops, and houses deep in their dreams. Not a sound, not a movement – no door, no window stirring, no blind raised. The rattling of the wheels, even old Tadhg himself noticed how sharp and loud the sounds were. He was glad to turn once again into that deserted lane among the vacant warehouses. Again he made for the jetties. He tied his beast by the reins to some iron bars in a window frame. He hobbled forward, as with purpose, towards the dreaming ship. Silent she was, disdainful, yet his heart filled with warmth as he gazed up at her. Seagulls were flying about her topmasts, gliding and wheeling, crying out sharply their long melancholy notes. Her grey-painted side was high above his head: he had not foreseen the difficulty of waking so huge a mass into life. But soon he noticed that a young sailorman, smoking quietly, lazily, had been watching all the time. By way of greeting he raised hand and stick to him. He was afraid he might suddenly disappear into the depths of that huge contrivance. He drew nearer, hobbling, 'Whisper,' he said, cautiously beckoning the sailor to come closer – 'Whisper, what's the name of her?'

'The name?'

'Yes, her name, what's on her, the ship?'

'The *Hispaniola*. 'Tis all along her.'

'The *Calliope*?'

'No, the *Hispaniola*.'

'Whisper, whisper now: are they after changing it?'

'Change what?'

'The name of her. For why did they change it?' He was whispering up, his left hand at his mouth.

'They haven't changed it. *Hispaniola*, that's the lady's name.'

'Ah, ah, I'm telling ye now, whisper, 'tis the *Calliope* she is. Isn't it I should know that? 'Tisn't so easy to deceive me. The *Calliope* – and the Master – Captain Hinchion – that's the name. Look now, like a good boy – go in and tell him there's one here would like to make speech with him – and, whisper, 'twould be no harm to tell him that he won't be sorry at all if he's said by me. Go on now.'

'But he's not on board, your Captain Hinchion; he never was.' As he spoke in his somnolent voice the sailor raised his eyebrows, his two hands, the smoking pipe in the fingers of one of them, held loosely.

'He never was,' he repeated.

'Ah, he's not. He's not. You tell me that?' Perplexed, he stared piteously at the sailor.

'*Calliope*,' he whispered again, in a sort of staring vacancy.

'No, *Hispaniola*, Portland, Maine.'

The old man waved his hands with sudden joy.

'Portland, Maine – that's it. A hundred times they said it to me, 'tis where I'd find her.'

'Was she from there?'

'Portland, Maine, Portland, Maine.'

'Hold there a while now, will you?'

'No, no; stop! Come back.'

'I'll be back presently.'

'Ye will?'

'Certain.'

He vanished from Tadhg's eyes; but the old eyes never shifted; they were fearful the sailor might not return. When he did return he was accompanied by an oldish, blear-eyed, scrubby-bearded seaman, vicious-looking, scowling. His limbs were twisted with rheumatism. He fastened his gaze on Tadhg: 'The *Calliope*?' he muttered huskily, absently, his weary worn-out voice offending the freshness of the morning.

'Yes, yes.'

'Portland, Maine.'

'Yes, yes.'

'Captain Hinchion?'

'Hinchion – young. A bold lad. A bold lad.'

'Right you are. I seen her often. I seen her in Portland, Maine. In Caleta Buena. In Sydney … She went … '

He stretched his hand out over ship's side, he lowered it slowly, the fingers wide apart one from another. 'She foundered. Crew, Cap'n, cargo. Cap'n's wife. All of 'em. All.'

'They were drownded? All drownded, ye're saying?'

'You have it,' he nodded affably.

The old man glared at him, his jaw hanging foolishly. The seaman took no notice; he raised his head: calculating how long ago it was since the *Calliope* had foundered, he was, unseeingly, staring into the windows of the little town, blindly, although every one of them was a living torch against the sun.

'It's forty years ago.'

'Forty?' Tadhg repeated, in a dull and stupid voice.

'Forty, I said,' the seaman rapped out at him. He was a chronicler of the seas. Tadhg's head swung up in answer: 'The Captain's wife … she was my daughter. Maybe now, ye wouldn't believe that?'

Their eyes were fixed on him. There was something like a snarl of victory in his way of saying the words; and something like disdain in his abrupt turning away from them.

The young man laughed quietly. 'Queer old thing,' he said; but the other flung a string of filthy words after the retreating figure.

V

The spark of fire the truculence of the sailor had induced in old Tadhg lived but a moment; in a sort of stupor he got into his little cart and, almost without thinking, set out from the still-dreaming town towards his home. He had lost a whole night's sleep and, bright morning though it was, he had gone only a little way when his head dropped on his breast. It did not matter. Often and often before it had happened to him. All those who travelled that road were acquainted with him; had known him even in their childhood. To see him pass with his head fallen on his breast gave them scarce a thought. It was a little group of stranger tinkers that at last gathered about the cart, waking him up and telling him he had better be careful. Their wild faces, sun-dark, dirty, passionate, were about him in a ring. He stared at them stupidly. A middle-aged, bedraggled woman, with a child at her breast, folded into a shawl, was still shaking him, fearing he would drop off to sleep again. 'Good man,' she was saying, 'you'll come to mischief, you'll come to misfortune. For the love of God mind yourself. 'Tis many a good man met his death and he going the road like that.'

He gathered his wits. Anyone who had known him for the past forty years would, as answer to her words, have expected from him a snarl, nothing else: but no, his voice sounded weak, uncertain of itself: 'And, *a laogh*, 'twould be all one. 'Tis how, whisper, *a laogh*,' he drew the woman towards him away from the others. ''Tis how, they used to tell me they always come home in the end, and they broken, and every hand raised again' them, and they dark in themselves, and like a dirty slut upon their father's floor.' He raised his head and looked at her straight in the eyes: 'Let me tell you, let me inform you, 'tisn't like that she'd be with me, 'tisn't, 'tis not so, far from it, but in silk and satins, with bangles and ear rings, and – and – ' Words failed him, and he gave up, with an impatient gesture, the attempt to find them. 'Whisper, what a mistake they were making! 'Tis I could dress her out. 'Tis so. And, whisper, not a soul knew it, not a soul knew it – and I laughing at them! Laughing at them in my heart of hearts! All the years of my life, laughing at them in my heart of hearts!' And he shook his head with satisfaction to think how he had been laughing at the world all the years of his life!

The tinker woman nodded to show she understood, but indeed all she understood was that the old man was simple-minded and couldn't keep his thoughts to himself. Suddenly she saw all his strength go from him, saw him trembling and trying to control his tongue. 'But 'tis all one now,' he began to glaum his breast. 'My heart,' he said, 'is a cage without a bird, I'm an emptied sack! There is no spirit in me any more, nor strength nor life nor anything. But God's Will be done, the Will of God be done,' he gathered up the reins weariedly. He did not care how long the road was, nor how cold and lonely his cabin.

The tinkers drew away from him, moving quickly on. The woman began to speak: 'He's very old, that poor creature is. I didn't notice it at first. But I'd say he was a firm man in his day. A firm man. And he had the look of a miser. He was laughing, he said in his heart of hearts. Look at that now – his heart of hearts.'

But even as she spoke she was racing ahead eager to catch a glimpse of the town they had been making for since the break of day. Her bare feet as they swiftly padded along threw up clouds of dust from the sunny roadway.

The donkey cart meanwhile went on towards the distant hills, aimlessly, it seemed, straggling about the road. Every now and then the grey old head of the drooping figure in it would move from side to side, and 'Vo! Vo! Vo! Vo!' – the traditional Irish cry of sorrow – would break from the lips. Sometimes the cry was loud and unrestrained; sometimes smothered, only a groaning.

I

Dunerling East was its name, the model farm in all that countryside. Only after many years it had come to be so; and Michael Hodnett, the farmer who had made it so, lay fast asleep in his armchair on the right-hand side of the front door. As of its own weight his big strong-looking head had sunken itself deep into his deep chest. The sunshine of the October afternoon was depositing itself lavishly upon him, thickening upon him, it seemed, while slumber bound him there, so huge and lumpish, so inert, so old and fallen. Dunerling East just now was looking more model-like than ever before. The house itself had had all its sashes, its doors, its timber work painted afresh; its blinds and curtains had been renewed; its ivy growths trimmed; and the whole farm, even its farthest fields and screening thickets, spoke of the same well-being, the same skilful management. The sleeper might lawfully take his rest, his spirit had so indisputably established itself everywhere within the far-flung mearings. Even were he to pass away in his sleep, and stranger folk as reckless as might be, to come into possession of the land, many years must needs go by before Dunerling East became hail-fellow-well-met with the farms round about it, shaggy and scraggy as they were, waterlogged in the bottoms and bleached or perished on the uplands, unsheltered by larch or beech.

All this cleaning up had been done in preparation for the first coming together, after many years, of all or nearly all that were left of the family. The arrival of Stephen Hodnett, the third youngest son, from the States, had been the occasion. He had brought with him his young wife, and, as well, an elder sister of hers, a young widow for whose distraction indeed the voyage had been undertaken. Of all the sons of the house this son, Stephen, perhaps had done best: he was now manager of a large bakery store in New York. But the brother next to him in years, Finnbarr, had done well too. He was come, also accompanied by his wife, from Kerry, where he managed a very successful creamery. The son to whom the care of the farm had fallen, to whom indeed the farm now legally belonged, Nicholas by name, had maintained it in the condition to which his father, this old man asleep in the chair, had brought it; perhaps he had even bettered it, but, of course, the land had been got into good heart long before it fell to his turn to till it. Nicholas, though older than Stephen or Finnbarr, had never married: he would wait until his father's death. The only other son of the house was up in Dublin – Father Philip Hodnett, a curate in St Multose's parish. He was the one living member who was not present in Dunerling East. Within the house lurked somewhere the eldest living of all the old man's family, Ellen, the second child born to him. She looked old enough to be the mother of those mentioned, even of Nicholas, the eldest of them. She was sixty and looked more. Her cheeks were thin and haggard, colourless, her hair grey, and her eyes stared blankly at the life moving before them as if it were but an insipid and shadowy thing when compared with what moved restlessly, perhaps even disastrously, within the labyrinths of her own brain. On her the mothering of the whole family had fallen when Michael Hodnett buried his wife in Inchigeela.

From the feet of the sleeping figure the ground fell away downwards to a bracken-covered stream. Beyond the bracken it rose again; much more suddenly however, so suddenly indeed that the red earth showed in patches through the tangled greenery. Those reddish patches looked like corbels supporting the cornice-like ledge of the upward-sloping grazing grounds above. Just now, along that sun-drenched ledge, a procession of shapely deep-uddered cattle was moving from left to right, the beasts in single file or in pairs or groups, deliberately pacing. Thirty-one milkers were to pass like that, making for the unseen bridgeway across the stream in the hollow. Presently they would dip from sight and again be discovered in the tree-covered passage trailing up towards the milking sheds, the rich sunshine catching their deep-coloured flanks and slipping swiftly and suddenly from their horns and moving limbs. Anyone who had ever come to know how deeply the sight of that afternoon ritual used to thrill the old man, now so sunken in his sleep, could hardly forbear from waking him to witness it.

Behind the cattle sauntered Nicholas. His head was bent, and in his right hand a sliver from a sally tree switched the cattle along. Although a working day, he was dressed in his Sunday clothes. His gaiters were new, rich brown in colour, and had straps about them; his boots also were new and brown. All day since morning his visitors, his brothers Stephen and Finnbarr and their people, had been away motoring in the hills towards the west – around Keimaneigh and Gougane Barra – and he had found the idle day as long as a week. 'Stay where you are,' he had said to one of the labourers who were digging out potatoes in the fields behind the house; 'stay where you are, and I'll bring them in,' and he was glad of the chance to go through the fields one after another until he was come to where the impatient cattle were gathered, anxious and crying, about the fastened gate. Their time for milking was overdue, and they needed no urging towards the sheds. When they were safe across the bridge he left them to themselves: by that time the first of them were already head-bound in the stalls. Closing a gate behind them he made diagonally up the sloping field. At his approach his father suddenly raised his head.

''Tisn't Sunday?' he said, and then, recollecting himself: 'They haven't come back yet?'

'Any moment now,' Nicholas answered. He then turned his back on him and gazed across the countryside where a couple of roads could be picked out. The weather had been very fine for some weeks and little clouds of sunny dust wavered above them.

'Are the cows in?'

'I'm after bringing them across.'

'Is Finn after looking at them?'

'Yes, he'd get rid of the Kerry, he said.'

'Didn't I tell you! Didn't I tell you!'

He had filled up with passionate life. As he blurted out the words, he raised his heavy stick in his blob of a hand. Nicholas glanced away from him, and again searched the countryside with his eyes: 'They won't be long now: 'tis as good for us to be going in!'

He put his arm beneath his father's. He lifted him. The old man's right foot trailed uselessly along the ground. But his thoughts were on the cows: ''Tis often I do be thinking on the two beasts we had and we coming hither from Carrig-an-Afrinn. Scraggy animals, scraggy, splintery things.'

II

Mrs Muntleberry, the young American widow, and her sister, Stephen's wife, were both thoughtful, gentle women; it was plain in their quiet eyes, their quiet faces. After the meal, homely in its way, but good, they now sat bent forward earnestly staring at the old man who was keeping himself so alert and upright in their midst, ruling the roomful with word, gesture, glance. Of his power of work, of his downrightness, they had, of course, often heard from Stephen: in Stephen himself they had found something of the same character: until today, however, they had not realised how timid in him were the strong traits of his father's character. They had been motoring in a world of rock-strewn hillsides; they had swung into glens that struck them cold, so bleak they were, so stern-looking even in the softest tide of the year. Carrig-an-Afrinn they had not actually passed through: it would have meant threading slowly up many twisting narrow hillside bohereens in which their car could scarcely turn: perhaps also Stephen had not cared to have them actually come upon the bedraggled homestead – little else than a hut – from which the Hodnetts had risen. They had, however, gone as close to it as the main road allowed them, had seen, and felt almost in their bones, the niggardliness of life among those hillsides of tumultuously tumbled rocks. That wayfaring in bleak places had brought them to understand Stephen's father; even if he were no different this evening, had remained as he had been ever since their arrival – drowsing between sleep and waking, mumbling old songs, sometimes losing count of who they were – they would nevertheless because of this day's excursioning have more deeply understood the tough timber that was in him. But all the evening he had been quite different. The names of old places, of old families, had been in the air about him. He grew young to hear them, to bethink himself of them. They had aroused him. Stephen had forgotten many of them. He would say, ''Tis the Sweenys were north of Inchimore. 'Tis Keimcorravoola you're thinking of.' And of itself the place name or the family name was enough to spur the old man's brain to all manner of recollections. So it had been with him all the evening, alert as they had never seen him, a new man, and not a bit modest about his powers when young, whether at fighting or hurley or farming. His stick was in the air about their heads: and once without warning he had brought it down on the table, making them all leap to their feet and grab at the dancing tea things – down with all his force lest they should not clearly understand how final had been the stroke with which he had felled a Twomey man in a faction fight at Ballyvourney. And when in speaking of some other ancient wrestling bout he referred to his adversary's trunk, how he had clasped it and could not be shaken off, the two women looked at himself, alert yet lumpish before them, noted his body's girth and depth, and felt that 'trunk' was indeed the right word to use of such bodies.

Finn's wife, the Kerry woman, was enjoying it heartily. Her Kerry eyes, deep hazel in colour, were dancing to watch the old man's antics, grotesque and unashamed, were dancing also to note the quiet, stilly, well-schooled Americans opening the doors of their minds to comprehend adequately this rough-hewn chunk of peasant humankind. The expression coming and going on the faces of the three sons, she also enjoyed. She watched to see how they took every gross countryside word and phrase that would unconcernedly break from the old man's lips. Her own Finn she held for the cleverest of them because he had the gift of slipping in some contrary word that would excite his father to still more energetic gestures or more emphatic expletives.

In time old Hodnett had exhausted the tale of the great deeds of his prime: a gentler mood descended on him: 'Like you'd shut that door, or like you'd tear a page out of a book and throw it from you, I put an end to all that folly and wildness. Listen now, let ye listen now, this is what happened and I coming over here from Carrig-an-Afrinn.'

III

He told them clearly how on that day, which of all the days of his long life stood most clearly before his mind, he had made swiftly home from the fair at Macroom. Michael, his eldest son, a boy of about sixteen years at the time, had hastened down from the potato field on hearing the jolting of the returning cart. As usual with him he examined his father's face. He was at first relieved and then puzzled to discover from it that his father had scarcely taken any drink during that long day of absence from home, of boon companionship in the town. More than that, his father was going about in a sort of constraint, as if he had had something happen to him while away, or had come upon some tidings which now must be dwelt upon within himself. Yet he did not seem gloomy or rough, and he could be gloomy enough and rough enough when the fit was on him. Often and often after a long day in Macroom, he had turned in from the road, flung his reins on the horse's back, and without preface begun to heap maledictions on the head of the villain pig buyers from Cork with whom he had been trafficking. Today he was different: 'Is Johnny above?' he questioned his son as he loosed the horse from the shafts. The boy nodded.

'Up with you then. Up with you while there's light in it.'

The boy, climbing up to where he had left old Johnny, who was helping them to dig out the potatoes, was still wondering over the mood his father had returned in.

'What is he after getting?' the labourer asked him.

'Four ten.'

'He'd get more in Dunmanway last Friday.'

'He's satisfied. He says he is.'

Before long they saw himself coming through the gap. 'What way are they up along there?' he asked them, nodding his head towards the sloping ridges they had been digging.

'Small enough then,' his son answered.

The father stooped and picked up one of the potatoes. He began to rub it between his finger and thumb.

'They'll be different in Dunerling East,' his son said, complacently tossing his head.

As if that were the last thing he had expected to come from the boy's lips his father looked sharply at him.

Dunerling East was the farm he had been for several weeks negotiating the purchase of. It was ten miles away towards the east, ten miles farther from the hardness of the mountains, the cold rains, the winds, the mists. In those ten miles the barren hills that separate Cork from Kerry had space to stretch themselves out, to die away into gentle curves, to become soft and kind. So curiously his father had looked at him the boy wondered if something had not happened to upset the purchase. He was not surprised when his father, peering at him under his brows, spoke to him in a cold voice: 'The potatoes might be better. The grass too. And the cattle. Only the Hodnetts might be worse.'

Michael glanced at the labourer, then back at his father. He found him still skinning the potato with his hard thumb. But he could also see, young and all as he was, that his thought was not on the potato, big or little. The labourer had once more bent to his digging; and Michael, withdrawing his eyes slowly from his father's face, spat on his hands and gripped the spade: yet he could not resist saying: 'They're poor return for a man's labour.'

He scornfully touched the potatoes hither and thither with the tip of his spade, freeing them from the turfy earth, black and fibrous. They were indeed small.

The father seemed careless of their size. He stood there, a solid piece of humankind, huge, big-faced, with small round eyes, shrewd-looking, not unhumorous. He said: 'If I hadn't that fifty pound paid on it, I'd put Dunerling East out of my mind.'

He turned from them and made for the gap through which he had come. They questioned each other with their eyes and then stared after the earnest figure until the broken hillside swallowed it up.

It was a soft, still evening. Here and there a yellow leaf fell from the few scattered birch trees growing among the rocks which, on every side, surrounded the little patch of tilled earth. A robin was singing quietly, patiently – the robin's way. The air was moist; and because a break in the weather seemed near, they worked on, the two of them, until they could no longer see the potatoes. Then Johnny straightened his back, lit his bit of a pipe and shouldered his spade. Together both of them, taking long slow strides, made down towards the house. Suddenly the boy said: 'Look at himself!'

They saw him standing upright on one of the numerous ledges of rock which broke up through the surface of their stubble field. He had his back towards them. He was staring downwards, overlooking his own land, towards the straggling road, staring intently, although little except the general shape of the countryside could now be distinguished.

'Is it? Is it him at all, do you think?' old Johnny asked.

''Tis sure,' Michael answered. Then he cried out, sending the vowels travelling: 'Ho-o! Ho-o!'

His father turned and after a pause began to make towards them. Awkwardly they awaited him; they did not know what to say. He said: ''Tis at Carrig-an-Afrinn I was looking.'

Carrig-an-Afrinn was the name of the whole farm, a large district, mostly a hillside of rock and heather; they were standing in Carrig-an-afrinn: but they understood that what he had been looking at was Carrig-an-Afrinn itself – the Rock of the Mass, the isolated pile of rock by the roadside from which the ploughland had got its name.

They walked beside him then.

'I'm after hearing a thing this day I never knew before,' he said, and then stopping up and examining their faces he added: ''Tis what I heard: In any place where a Mass was ever celebrated an angel is set on guard for ever and ever.'

''Twould be a likely thing,' the old labourer said.

'I never heard tell of it,' Michael said.

'Myself never heard tell of it,' his father snapped out.

''Twould be a likely thing,' old Johnny said again, 'remembering the nature of the Mass.'

'Who was it told you?'

'One who was well able!'

The three of them turned and looked downwards towards the rough altar-like pile of rock where Mass used to be said secretly for the people in the penal days when it was felony to celebrate Mass in public. Only the pile of rock was visible, and that not distinctly, so thick the light had become.

'You know very well that Mass was said there hundreds and hundreds of times.'

The father spoke to his son almost as if he had been contradicting him. He received no reply. Then he added in a suddenly-deepened voice: 'Likely that place is thick with angels.'

The labourer uncovered his head without a word.

In stillness they stood there on the lonely hillside; and in the darkening rocks and fields there was no sound, except of small things stirring at their feet. After a few seconds, the farmer faced again for the house. Without thought, it seemed, he avoided the rocky patches. Indeed even at midnight he could have walked unperplexed through those rock-strewn fields. The others heard his voice coming to them in the dusk over his shoulder: ''Tis a strange thing that I never heard of that wonder until I'm just leaving the place for good and all. A strange thing; and it frightens me.'

When they found themselves free of the fields and in the *poirse*, or laneway, that led up to their yard, he said again with sudden passion: ''Tis a small thing would make me break the bargain.'

The boy flared up: 'A queer thing you'd do then.'

'Queer!'

'It may be years and years before we have the chance of buying a place like Dunerling East.'

He spoke the name as if that of itself were worth the purchase money.

'Carrig-an-Afrinn is not a bad farm at all.'

At this Michael burst out: 'Johnny, do you hear him? And he raging and swearing at them rocks as long as I can remember – raging and swearing at them as if they were living men and they against him! And he praying to God to take us out of it before his eyes were blinded with the years. And now he'd stay in it!'

Of that incident and of the night that followed it, the old man, forty-four years after, remembered every detail – every word spoken and every thought that disturbed his rest.

IV

Having given them to understand all that has been here set down, he went on: 'I tell ye, I didn't shut an eye that night, only thinking and thinking and I twisting and turning in my bed. When I looked back through the years and thought of what a poor place Carrig-an-Afrinn was – and there was scarcely a poorer – 'twas little less than a miracle to have me able to buy out a big place like this – a place that had been in the grip of the gentry for hundreds and hundreds of years. And up to that I always thought that I had no one to thank for it but myself – the strength of my own four bones, but after what I was told in Macroom that day, how did I know but that maybe it was in Carrig-an-Afrinn itself the luck was? and that good fortune would follow whoever lived in it like good Christians, and that maybe secret friends would help them, and they at the ploughing or waiting up in the nights for a calf to come, or a young foal or a litter of bonhams itself? Who knows? Who knows? And what puzzled me entirely was that I should be ignorant of all that until the very day, as you may say, I was settled on leaving it. It frightened me. While we were in Carrig-an-Afrinn no great sickness befell us or misfortune, except a horse to break his leg or a cow to miscarry or a thing like that; and I thought of all the strong farmers I was after seeing in my time, and they having to sell off their places and scatter away themselves into Cork or Dublin, or maybe to America itself. Sure this place itself, if ye saw it when we came hither, the dirty state 'twas in, the land gone back, exhausted, and the house and sheds broken, everything in wrack and ruin – 'tisn't with a light heart ye'd undertake it. But of course only for that I could not have bought it at all. So I said to myself, and I listening to the clock ticking at the foot of the bed, I'm undertaking that big place, and maybe 'twon't thrive with me. And if it fails me, where am I? That's what I said. If it fails me, where am I? I tell ye, I was broken with thinking on it. And all the time, and this is the queerest thing of all, I heard someone saying, "Carrig-an-Afrinn, Carrig-an-Afrinn. Carrig-an-Afrinn, Carrig-an-Afrinn." And not once nor twice nor three times, but all the night long, and I thinking and thinking. Of course, there was no one saying it at all, only maybe the beating of my own heart to be like a tune. But I was afraid. I thought maybe music might come rising up to me out of the *cummer*, and it thronged with angels, or a great light come striking in at the window. And sure enough at last I started up and I cried out, "There it is! There it is!" But 'twas no unnatural light at all, only the dawn of day breaking in on top of me.

'Tis how I was after dozing off for a little while unknown to myself, and I woke up suddenly in confusion and dread.

'That morning and I rising up, my limbs were like wisps of straw. I was terrified of the long day before me, and that's the worse way a man can be. But when I came out and stood in the broad sun, and 'twas a morning of white frost, I drew in the air to myself, and I took courage to see my poor animals grazing so peacefully on the hill, just like what you see in a picture. If the big farms broke the men that were born to softness and luxury, Dunerling East wouldn't break me, and I reared hard and tough! That's what I said, with great daring in my breast.

'Not long after that we moved our handful of stock east to this place. I laughed to picture the two scraggy beasts, and all the deep feeding of Dunerling East to themselves. And that same evening myself and Michael, Michael that's dead, God rest him, went over and hither and in and out through the length and breadth of this estate and round by the boundary ditch; and 'tis a thing I will not forget till my dying day what he said to me, my son Michael, that same evening, and we killed from the exertion. He stopped and looked up at me before he spoke: "'Look," he said, "why have you your hands like that?"

'My two hands, clenched, and stiff, *stiff*, like you'd have them in a fight, watching your opponent, watching to catch him off his guard, or for fear he'd spring on you. That's how I had my hands. And 'twas natural for me to have my hands like that, for what I was saying to myself was: I'll break it! I'll break it! And I was saying that because if I didn't break it I was sport for the world. Like a bully at a fair I was, going about my own land the first day I walked it!'

In recalling the labours of his prime he had become a new man. When they looked at him they saw not the stricken old creature whose days were now spent in the drowsy sun, but the indomitable peasant who had wrung enough from the rocks of Carrig-an-Afrinn to buy out Dunerling East from the broken gentry, and who then had reclaimed Dunerling East from its hundred years of neglect. When he could not find words to fit his thought his left eye would close tight, and one big tooth, that he still retained in his upper gum, would dig itself into his lower lip, until the struggling words came to him. And they noticed that his two hands had clenched themselves long before he needed them clenched to illustrate how it was he had tackled the reclamation of the sluggish marshlands of Dunerling East. The two Americans had drawn together, shoulder touching shoulder: they watched him across the table with wide eyes, their faces drawn. The creamery manager from Kerry dared no longer to put in his jocose word. He wished rather to be able to draw off the old man's mind from this renewal of the unrelenting warfare of his manhood. But no such word could he find: his father was abroad in a passion of fictitious energy: it would indeed be a potent word that could stay or hinder him. Every now and then the timbers of the heavy chair groaned beneath the movement of his awkward carcase. He was unconscious of it. It meant as little to him as his own exposing of the shifts, the meanness, the overreaching, the unintentional tyranny he had practised while he worked out his dream.

'My poor boy, Michael,' he went on, 'was the first to go. He was great for the work. For a boy that was slight and tender I never saw the equal of him. 'Twas how he had great spirit. A word was worse to him than a whip. When we'd be cutting the deep grass in the inches, half a dozen of us all in a line, and he'd fall behind, being young and soft, I'd say to him, "Ah, Michael," I'd say, "God be with the little fields of Carrig-an-Afrinn, you could cut them with a scissors"; that would bring him into line I tell ye. The poor boy. 'Twas pleurisy he got first; and we thought nothing of it: maybe we didn't take it in time. But what chance was there to be taking him into Macroom to the doctor, or from one holy well to another? The time he died too, it could not be a worse time. Herself was after bringing little Stephen into the world – and before she was rightly fit the harvest was upon us; and 'twas the first real good harvest we got out of Dunerling East. When I looked at it standing I said: "'Tis my doing and my boy's doing, and my boy is dead!" But herself was better than any man in a harvest field. Maybe she overworked herself. She wasn't the one to give in. The day she was laid in Inchigeela 'tis well if I didn't curse the day I came hither from Carrig-an-Afrinn. Father O'Herlihy was standing by. "The Lord giveth and the Lord taketh away," he said, and his hand on my shoulder, and 'twas all I could do to say "Amen" to that. There I was with a houseful of them about me and only herself, that poor thing inside, only herself to do a ha'p'orth for them. I don't blame her for being as she is – knitting, knitting, knitting, or looking into the fire and thinking – I don't blame her at all. What she went through after that, pulling and hauling and slashing and digging, 'twould kill half a parish. Up at four in the morning getting the pigs' food ready, or the mash for the calves; and milking the cows, and keeping the children from mischief. The only other girl I had, she was second after Nicholas there, I lost her just when she was rising to be of use to me. 'Twas a fever she got from drinking bad water. And the two boys I lost after that, one of them was the terror of the countryside. He turned against herself inside; he was wild and fiery. Mind you, he dared me to my face. He said what no son of mine ever said to me. I won't repeat it. I won't repeat it. The eyes were blazing in his head. The delicacy was showing in him. The brains of that kind is a terror. He went off with himself and left me in the lurch. And then he came back – one twelvemonth after – and 'tis like herself inside he was. Only bitter, and the health wasted. The same as any labouring boy he walked in to me. Not a shirt to his back, or what you could call a shirt. He shamed me, the way he was. And he dying on his feet. 'Twas a dead man was patrolling the fields for months before he took to the bed entirely. And I daren't say a word to him because he had a tongue would raise blisters on a withered skull. The other poor boy, his name was Laurence, was a handsome boy. Everybody used to say he's make a handsome priest. But sure at that time I couldn't dream of such a thing. It takes a power of money to make a priest. He died of pneumonia, and not a thing to happen to him only a bit of a pain in his side. Only for that I hadn't time to be thinking on it I'd be saying there was a curse on top of us; but no, because year after year the produce was getting better and better; and in spite of all the sickness and deaths and funerals – and funerals are the greatest robbers of all – the money began to rise up on me, and I could get in the help when I wanted it – 'tis often I had a score of men at the harvesting, besides what neighbours would come of themselves. Those there (he nodded at his three sons, all of them sitting with bowed heads, with pipes in their mouths, not daring to break across his speech) – those there, they only knew the end of the story. Ah boys, ah boys, the softness comes out of the hard, like the apple from the old twisted bough, and 'tis only the softness ye knew of. And then in the end of it all, the great change in the laws came about and I bought out the land and 'twas my own, as you may say. The day I signed for it, a sort of lowness came over me, and I remembered my poor dead boy saying, and he my first born, "Look how you're holding your hands!" Let ye listen to me now; I cried down my eyes to my own self that night because herself was in the clay. That poor soul inside, you might as well be talking to a cock of last year's hay, dull with the weather and the sun, you'd only get "yes" and "no" for an answer. And the rest – those here – were too young. What I did was to send over for old Johnny, old Johnny I would have helping me an odd time in Carrig-an-Afrinn, to come over to me, that I wanted him. God knows all I wanted him for was to keep me in talk against that terrible fit of darkness and loneliness would fall on me again. He came over and together we walked the land, every perch of it. He knew what sort it was when we came hither, and 'tis he was the man could tell the difference. What he said was, now, let ye listen, let ye listen to what he said, and he only a poor ignorant man: "After all, 'twas only a rush in your hand!" Now that was what a wrestler would say of another in the old times, "He was only a rush in my hands," meaning by that that he had no trouble in breaking him. That was great praise and yet it couldn't rouse me for I was after walking the land field after field; and one field I found was the same as another. That's a strange thing to say. Maybe 'tis how I was old and I coming hither. 'Twas in Carrig-an-Afrinn I grew up. There was never a man drove a handful of cattle of his own rearing to a fair that hadn't some favourite among them; and he sees the dealers come round them and strike them and push them, and knock them about, and he knows that they are all the same to him, that he sees no difference between one and the other, except one to be riper than another, or a thing like that. And 'twas so with me. I walked my fields and one was the same as another. There was no corner of them that I could make for when the darkness would fall on me. I knew 'twould be different in Carrig-an-Afrinn. And that's what I was thinking of when old Johnny said to me that after all Dunerling East was like a rush in my hands. I opened my heart to him. I told him I felt like the steward of the place, and not like the owner of it. He said 'twasn't right for me to be saying a thing like that, and 'tis down on my two knees I should be and I thanking God, but that the heart of man was only a sieve. The very next day and I still going about like that, counting up the great improvements I was after making since I came in, and arguing with myself, and yet dissatisfied with myself, I wandered up the hillside opposite, and whatever turn I gave or however the sun was shining, 'twas about four o'clock in the evening, I saw Doughill and Douse rising up in the west and snug away at the foot of Doughill I saw a little shoulder of a hill, and "Honour of God," I said, "if that isn't Carrig-an-Afrinn itself!" Let ye listen to me, I fell down on my knees in thanksgiving like a pagan would be praying to the sun! And from that day forward I had a spot of land to turn to when the black fit would fall on me. Mind you, 'twas a good time I found it, for while I was breaking the place and wrestling with it I didn't think of anything else, only to be going ahead and going ahead. But 'twas different when I could pay for the help, and I had time to look around, and the rent wasn't half what it used to be. Ah, the soft comes out of the hard, and the little lambs from the hailstones. If Dunerling East is a good property now 'twas many the hot sweat fell into the sods of its ridges. But sure them that could witness to that, they're all dead, except that poor thing inside, God help her; and 'tis she took the burden as well as the next.'

V

His voice fell and the glow of exaltation vanished from his features.

'They're all dead?' Mrs Muntleberry said, quietly.

'Dead!' the old man answered her, and having said it, his head kept on moving slightly up and down to some pulse in his brain.

'Then these,' she said again, and indicated the three sons with her eyes, 'these are a second crop.'

'A second crop,' he said, 'except that poor creature inside.'

They found it hard to break the silence that had fallen on them. Earlier in the evening both Stephen and Finnbarr had been, as one might say, themselves – Stephen, the bakery manager, a hustler, and Finn, the creamery manager, not unable to hustle also. But as the story went on, and, though they had heard it all in a fragmentary way before, they had scattered from the homestead without ever having made themselves one clear unified picture of what coming hither from Carrig-an-Afrinn had meant for their father. They had never seen him clearly as one who would not be beaten, no matter who by his side fell worsted in the struggle. Only the oldest of them, Nicholas, the farmer, could recall any of the dead, and he was a soft quiet creature, strong of body, but inactive of brain. The one mood, however, had come upon all three; they were not much different from what they had been before they had scattered, from what they had been when Ellen would still them by whispering the one word: 'Himself'.

It was Finn who first rose. He went and lightly beat the inverted bowl of his pipe against the bars of the fire grate. Then drawing with his strong lips through the empty stem, head in the air, he took a few steps towards the window and drew back one of the heavy curtains. The colour, the glow had gone from the day. Instead there were now everywhere filmy veils of mist. Beyond the sunken stream the hillside looked near and the screens of trees, ash and beech, seemed tall and unsubstantial: in the twilight softness the homely features of farming and cattle trafficking were hidden away. The scene was gracious and tender. They all stared through the window.

'It looks fine, so it does,' Finn said.

'It does; it looks fine,' his wife added, letting the words die away. The old man was listening.

''Tis what a traveller said, and he a man that had recourse to all the places in the world, 'tis what he said: that it had the appearance of a gentleman's place out and out.'

Mrs Muntleberry turned and let her eyes rest softly on his face: 'Still you liked Carrig-an-Afrinn too?'

He lifted his head; such words he had not expected: 'Ah, ma'am, ah, ma'am,' he said, making an effort to move his trunk so that he might face her directly, 'Carrig-an-Afrinn, Carrig-an-Afrinn, the very name of it, the very name of it!' And he stared at her with a fixity of expression that frightened her, stared at her in blank hopelessness of saying even the first word of all the words that rioted within him. He recovered. He swept his hand across his brow, toying with his hair. 'They tell me Pat Leary, who's there ever since we came hither – there's only the one year between us – they tell me he sits in the *cummer* an odd hour at the foot of the rock where the Chalice used to stand. His work is done. He'll catch hold of plough nor snaffle no more, same as myself. 'Tis a great comfort to him to sit there.'

She was sorry she had brought Carrig-an-Afrinn back to his thoughts.

'The heart is a sieve,' she said, watching him to see how he'd take old Johnny's word. But he was not so easily moved from mood to mood.

'You saw it today?' he questioned earnestly. 'You saw it today?'

'We went quite close to it. Did we see the Rock itself? Did we, Stephen?'

Stephen said as boldly as he could: 'Oh yes, we went quite close to it.'

'Ah, ma'am, Nicholas there, some day he's going to pack me into the motor car; and over with us to see it. It can't be long I have to stay.'

Before he had finished, almost indeed at the first word, Nicholas had risen and quietly taken down a shabby-looking old violin from the top of a heavy cupboard that stood in the corner. While they all looked at him he tuned it without a word, and to him tuning was no easy task. Then he stretched his two long legs out from the chair and began to play.

The instrument was almost toneless, and the player almost without skill. He played the old songs of the countryside, going straight from one to another, from a *caoine* to a reel, from a love song to a lively rattle about cattle-dealing or horse racing. Nerveless, toneless, yet the playing was quiet; and it was the music itself, and not the instrument or musician was in the fiddler's mind. After a while this the Americans noticed. Then the scratching, the imperfect intonation, the incongruous transition from melody to melody disturbed them but little. He played on and on; and they were all thankful to him. The room darkened, but the sky was still bright. At last he lowered the fiddle, a string needed to be tightened. The others at once broke into talk. Mrs Muntleberry was nearest to Nicholas. She had her eyes on the instrument. He noticed how at the word 'Carrig-an-Afrinn' which was again on the lips of the old man, her head had raised itself. He whispered to her, without taking his eyes off his task: 'He'll never see Carrig-an-Afrinn again.'

'No?' she whispered back, with a little gasp of surprise.

'Nor nobody else,' he went on; 'they're after blasting it away to make the road wider; 'tis how two lorries couldn't pass on it. I'm in dread of my life he'll find out. 'Twould be terrible.'

She turned her eyes on the old man's face. The music had restored him again to confidence. His eyes were glowing. He had re-established his mastery. 'Let ye listen, let ye listen to me,' he was saying.

THE STONES

I

Though John Redney's house was far back in the glen his straggling farm spread out into the river valley of which the glen itself was, as one might say, a side pocket, narrow and secret. In all its winding length there was no other house: it was even more lonely now than when long years before John Redney had played in it, a companionless child.

When the sudden downpour of rain towards the end of August swept his newly-gathered cruach of turf from the inches, leaving him without fuel for the coming year, he knew quite well that all down the valley, and on the heights as well, the farmers were shaking their heads over what had befallen him, were by adding this to that, proverb to proverb, memory to memory, strengthening one another's belief that such disasters did not overtake a man without cause. And the picture he made himself of them so grouped was a pain that almost overwhelmed the pain of his actual loss.

Only two days before, he had finished the ferrying over of the turf from the bogs on the other side of the river. He had thrown it out there loosely, not far from the bank, for, the very next day, he was going to cart it up the glen to the little rise where the Redneys had built their cruach as long as anyone remembered. That very evening he had sent his labouring boy over to Con Jer for the loan of his horse and man for the next day, for the one day only to help him in drawing the turf from the inches to that traditional ground. Con Jer had answered the boy that he came at a most unfortunate time, that he had never been so busy, that he couldn't think of letting him have even the horse not to mind one of his men as well. He said he was surprised that John Redney would not have thought of that himself. Innocently enough the boy repeated the words as Con Jer had spoken them. And so it was that the next day John Redney hastened down the glen, mounted a hillock at the mouth of it, and scowled at the swirling waters rolling his turf along the valley – good black turf, as firm a sod as he had ever cut, and a whole year's supply of it, and more.

The morning after, as he gazed at the drenched fields from which the sudden mountain floods were rapidly disappearing, he could not help recalling the very words the boy had brought back in his mouth from Con Jer, nor how they had set him on fire, maddened him until he had told him angrily that it might be a good thing for Con Jer to go up to Carrigavawring and have a look at his own effigy there. No, the exact words he had used were: 'Well, boy, Con Jer's effigy in stone, up there on Carrigavawring, if Con Jer went up and had a look at it – one look' – and there he had stopped. It had been in his mind to say that one glance at it would leave Con Jer with only very little thought indeed for crops or cattle or fences or anything else that concerned this world of living men. This, however, he had not said and perhaps it was better so. The boy had, he was certain, truly reported the words, only half aware of the threat in them; and repeated in that uncertain fashion, they had, it might be, raised more confusion in Con Jer's mind than if they had been made into a frightful story. What did he care! Let them now come together, the farmers of the valley, stick their noses into one another's faces, make out that his turf had not been swept from him without reason – it was all one to him. Con Jer would toss and turn on his pillow for many a night to come, wondering if what the boy reported was true and, if true, what would come of it.

More and more as he dully stared in front of him the river was reassuming its own true shape. Through the levels of the valley it curved from side to side with the light of the day, although it was a grey day, thick upon its surface, causing the pasture lands on either side to look dark and heavy. If the Nyhans had flung up a bit of a dam where the engineer had told them, there was an end to those sudden floodings; but no, the Nyhans hadn't it in them even to help themselves, when by doing so they would help another. The whole lot of them, the farmers on this side and the other, were against him.

II
It is a stony land. The name of it, Kilclaw, might mean the Stone Church or the Stony Wood. Nobody now knows which. The woods were felled some hundreds of years ago; but felling the trees had not been sufficient, for, that done, even the roughest kind of tillage was not yet possible until the little patches first marked out for it had been cleared of the largest of the stones embedded in them. The roots of them were found to be tougher than those of the wild ash, the moun-

tain fir, or the oak. Yet removed they were, dragged to the sides of the little fields, however they managed it, crop upon crop of them, year after year, decade after decade, century after century, until the stone mounds that now enclose the little patches of wheat or oats or potatoes take up as much, if not more, of the ground than the croppings within them. The boulders earliest removed were huge, huger than would now appear, for their bases once again are hidden deep in the ground. Half way up their flanks, sometimes all the way, they are clothed with brown and silvery mosses, or with innumerable layers of the tiniest fern. On top of and around and between them thousands and thousands of smaller stones have been piled or flung; and these, more exposed to the winds and rain and sunshine, have not clothed themselves at all, remain still unclad, may remain for ever unclad, unsoftened with verdure, bleached-looking, bare and stark. The people of the place fancy they see in them – those moss-clad boulders, those skull-like smaller stones that surmount them, effigies, images of their neighbours, never of themselves. A farmer using the *poirse* of a neighbour as a short cut for his turf or corn may suddenly behold in some place that he has already passed by some hundred of times, the rough effigy of one of the dwellers in the valley: if however, he be wise and of good heart he will keep his discovery to himself, for it bodes no one any good, this unexpected revelation of one's image in the stones.

John Redney never had been either wise or of good heart. His mind dwelt too much on things that were abroad in the air, in the darkness, drifting hither and thither. He was a poor lonely creature, living there in that unvisited glen, his the only house within it. His children were scattered far from him, were not writing to him, it was said, and his wife had become long since a poor sorry drudge to him. Having loosed that word effigy upon the wind, he went uselessly and restlessly strealing about his straggling fields more silent and gloomy than ever. He came to know that Con Jer had laughed at the threat, had said, 'And John Redney wants me to mount up to Carrigavawring and have a look at myself! I won't then, I have something else to do.' But Redney knew that if that laughter of Con Jer's was loud it was also hollow. He felt quite certain that Con Jer did not laugh in his heart when he laid his head on the pillow in the darkness.

III
At this time arrived one who had long since outgrown the beliefs of the hillsides – the ex-soldier, Jack Lambert, Miles Lambert's good-for-

nothing son. He had slaved and tramped his way in England, had been in America, Canada, and Australia – and nowhere had done any good. He had found himself in the Great War, first in France, then in Gallipoli. Again and again he had come back to his father's house and again wandered off from it whither he would. He had been at home this time only a week or so when the news was abroad that he had been seen in Redney's company traversing the most hidden and ill-reputed places at unearthly hours. Even on nights that were stormy and wild and without a glimpse of either moonlight or starlight, the two of them were heard going by. On quieter nights the sounds of the footsteps of the two of them had wakened people from their sleep, had caused them to lift their heads to listen. Johneen Kelleher had been out in his fields before the dawn drawing the stooks together, making them ready for the help that was to come to him as soon as the sun had dried the corn – and those two misguided men he had seen coming down from the stony hills where there were neither houses nor tilled fields nor traffic, and they looked as if they had been abroad the livelong night! Over his story a dozen heads drew into a circle; and one and then another remarked how much Lambert was changing; how he had taken on strange airs, had been found staring intently into this man's haggard, and elsewhere, in a place where he could have had no business, had suddenly raised his head above a mound of stones. Besides they had all noticed how, whenever he chanced to meet them now upon the road, he would look through them as if he knew the very thoughts they were thinking. Yet it was not he they blamed. He they knew was but the empty book into which old Redney was writing all the perversity he had ever indulged in that crabbed brain of his. Larry Condon broke up their discussion with a free gesture. What was Lambert but a common bummer, sponging on Redney, who, fool that he was, God knows he was queer since the day he was born, had been glad to find anyone at all to strike up a friendship with, to drink with, to gossip with; and none of them could deny that Lambert was a man of fine discourse when he had swallowed down a glass or two of good whiskey. They all knew as well as he did, that Lambert gave no credence to those beliefs of theirs. Since they had often defended their beliefs against him this they could not argue against, whereupon, silenced for the time, they broke the gathering and went through the darkness each to his lonely house. But by the next night some other tidings of the two secret men would have floated into some farmyard or other and another discussion would take place around the hearth.

The faces of the two of them, the look of intentness in them, began now to abide in the memory of all who crossed them. Whatever had come to possess them! the people asked one another. Were the two of them determined not to cease their searching until they had discovered the effigies of all the farmers of Kilclaw? Fear spread from house to house along the valley. There was not now a dweller in it who, if he spied the two of them coming towards him along the road, would not turn aside into some farmer's *poirse* to escape the peering of their eyes.

IV

They were an ill-matched pair: Lambert, the ex-soldier, brazen-eyed, straight-lipped, withered-skinned, impudent, and with a reckless way of striding along: old Redney, shy and tongue-tied, looking out from under his shaggy brows, his head down, his left hand clenched across the small of his back, his right hand tight and heavy upon the knob of his stick. With quick, uncertain steps, he made forwards as if his secret knowledge was no happy cargo. The neighbours would see him hobbling along with Lambert, always a little in the rear. They would see him stop up, his stick directed across a valley or along the flank of a mountain while Lambert's eyes searched the distance indicated; or Lambert they would find looking back over his shoulder waiting for the other as he clambered clumsily over those fences of loose stones. And the same anxiety arose again and again: 'Are they burying the whole countryside of us?'

'And what will they gain by it?'

'Nothing except the pacifying of their own wicked minds.'

''Tis a frightful thing for a man to know that he is already in the stone, that he is there to be seen for all time. If you woke up in the dead of the night, a wild night or a night of hard frost, you wouldn't like to picture it. You'd feel the frost in your shoulder bones.'

But those who gathered of a night time to Con Jer's were a quiet lot; Lambert and Redney might by dint of searching come on the images of the whole countryside and they would not lift an arm to prevent it. The younger men who met after the day in Dan Owen's were different. It was Pat Early, whose shoulder blow would fell a bullock, determined for that group what they should do.

The next day they loitered around the tumbledown cabin where their one smith kept his forge. Into its smoky background they retired, all of them except Pat Early himself, when they discovered that Lambert was coming along the road. From within they heard the approaching footsteps: they then heard Pat Early's voice: 'Lambert,' he said, with a rasping tone, 'Come over here.'

They heard the footsteps cease. Pat's voice they heard again: 'Come over here. I have a word to say to you.'

They could now see Lambert in the brightness of the doorway, his back almost towards them: 'Well?' he said.

'Did you hear Pat Nyhan is after dying on them?'

'I didn't: where would I hear it?'

Though he answered glibly enough, those within thought they saw him start when Pat flung the unexpected question at him.

'If you knew he was going to meet his end, sudden, and without preparation, you might have warned him: 'twould be a neighbourly act.'

They expected Lambert to deny, if only for safety's sake, any fore-knowledge of Pat Nyhan's death; but the words they heard were: 'Is this a place for neighbourly acts?'

His next word then they felt would be either of old Redney's cru-ach of turf that the August flood had swept down the valley or else of the Nyhans' failure to build the rampart which would for ever save the levels from the swollen river. Pat Early, however, gave him no time: he blazed out: 'Why don't you answer the question I put to you?'

'Question!'

'Did you know – did you know that something was in store for Pat Nyhan, some misfortune or other?'

'Two nights ago,' he answered after a slight pause and quite in a low voice, 'John Redney showed me him in the stone.'

They grew cold to hear him. And he had said the words in a way that showed that himself was no longer a mocker. Pat Early cried out quickly and with great strength and warmth, to their great relief: ''Tis a lie!'

Lambert, however, who had turned to go, was not disturbed either by the words or the force in them; he looked back and said in the same low voice: 'If he showed – the sight to me he can show it to you, that is if you care to see it, now the man's dead. Some people mightn't like to.'

The listeners gathered out noiselessly from the shelter of the forge, all of them; they feared that Pat Early was shaken, but again sturdily he answered: 'See what? A couple of stones! Do you think I believe old Redney has power over us?'

'But you'd face it?'

'I'd face a couple of stones anyhow.'

'We'd all do that,' John Morian added.

'By day or night?'

''Tis equal.'

'Very well; I'll tell himself.'

V

It was now the end of November. The night, it seemed, could not hold any more stars, nor the air any more cold. Con Jer's son, Tadhg, was one of the whispering group. Others were Pat Early, his brother-in-law, Michael Glynn, the smith's son, Larry Mehigan, and the teacher's son, Jim Carey, who had ventured without his father's knowledge. Morian was with them also. Larry Mehigan was delicate: the piercing cold had urged to rapid walking, and they had mounted Knockanuller at one spurt before they were suddenly aware of his gasping, of his effort to keep up with them: 'Are we going too fast?' Michael Glynn said.

'I'll be all right in a minute,' Larry answered; but immediately he had to turn aside doubled up in a fit of coughing.

''Twas the cold made us hurry: 'twas a queer thing for us to do.'

'But 'tisn't good to be stopping here; that's the devil of a wind for him.'

'There's shelter beyond.'

''Tis more than twenty years since I was up in these places.'

'Who'd come up here? What business would you have?'

'We'll be going on now.'

'How far up he came to find poor Pat Nyhan's image.'

They thought of him rigid in his bed.

''Tis a frightful night to be dead on.'

They did not laugh. Another time they would have done so at such awkward words, but dimly in the starlight they individually spied out shoulders of whitish rock and boulders that looked like massive ancient, long-weathered skulls. The little narrow path they were on was bordered by some of those immemorial pilings of stones, large and small. The mounds kept the wind from them, but the open spaces of the bogland would have been more welcome to them. 'Look, they're waiting for us.'

Sitting in the shelter of an upright slab they saw the two figures; Redney's rigid grasp of the knob of his stick they noticed especially.

'Are ye waiting long?' Pat Early said, casually, he hoped.

'Mind ye,' old Redney answered, ''tisn't by my wish ye're up here at all; far from it.'

Pat Early thought he wished to put them off. 'If you can show us what Lambert said, 'tis right you should.'

'I can show ye that all right, since ye wish it.'

They all began to move forward. In the dim light the round water-worn stones in the *poirse* began to roll under their feet. Pat Early said: 'I see we would have done right to have our spectacles with us to see it.'

Only after a few moments the old man understood the words. He then said, calmly and coldly: 'There'll be light enough where 'tis. The moon's there already.'

As he spoke he raised his stick towards the brow of the hill, which was gapped and rugged with boulders and rocks. There the sky was becoming more and more luminous and the stars were gone. The moon they understood to be away towards the right. When they pierced through among the boulders they saw it suddenly, rising in splendour. Slabs of blanched stone, pillar stones of shadow, gaps of darkness – sharp-edged, were all about them in confusion. They felt astray.

'There's Pat Nyhan. The Nyhans were up here always.'

Even if, with his stick, he had not pointed out the particular group of stones in that long-deserted mountain farm ground they would have known it for Pat Nyhan. It was set up in a listening attitude, Pat Nyhan's attitude; just so he used to listen, his left ear advanced, for he had been for years a little hard of hearing. They recollected too having heard that the Nyhans had come from this place. As they looked they could swear they saw the stones stir. One or two of the men fidgeted, looking around. Others stared at the stones in a dull sort of way. They were conscious of a desire to strike old Redney or the ex-soldier, yet conscious also that that was not in the bargain. The ex-soldier stood a little apart from them, neither looking nor speaking. Suddenly Larry Mehigan with that burred and resonant consumptive's voice of his said: 'Up here too the Redneys were always. I heard tell of them.'

Their eyes swept from the image and fastened on Redney. He turned his back on them as if he would set off for home. Indistinctly he grumbled at them over his shoulder: 'Ye're after seeing what ye came to see.'

He put out his left hand and Lambert came and folded it in his arm, protectingly. They then began to move off, the two of them. The others hesitated. As soon as he had said the words, Mehigan had been taken with a fit of coughing. The stone desert was ringing with the sound of it, and the dogs in distant farm yards had awakened and were answering back. But the dogs' barking Larry heard no more than he heard his own coughing: his excited brain was working all the time; he would blurt out, not giving the spasm time to exhaust itself: ''Tis true what I say. Up here they were always, the Redneys.'

'Somehow that's true, I heard it said; 'twas said,' Morian gave his opinion earnestly.

They came closer together. They were thankful to Larry. His words excused them from looking any more at the stone image, listening in the way that a tall deaf old man would listen.

Larry's cough had ceased, and they began to hasten after the two others. When they got within a short distance of them they saw old Redney stop up rather suddenly and raising his stick, point out something to Lambert. A word however he did not speak. The whole of them stopped up where they were. Individually fright fell on them. They did not want to know what the old man was pointing at. Lambert seemed vexed and impatient. They heard his whisper: 'Come on, come on.' But old Redney seemed not to be able to move nor to change his attitude. The moon poured its light on them all: old Redney with his stick stretched out, Lambert a little apart from him, waiting impatiently, and the other group still farther apart, puzzled and anxious. The cold was intense, and the sparkling earth was as silent as the starry heavens. The distant farm dogs had put their noses again upon the ground. It was their own stillness made the men aware of the benumbed stillness about them.

'Come on, come on,' they again heard whispered very hoarsely, and Lambert made a stride towards the petrified figure of his friend. As he neared it they saw the stick fall clattering to the frozen ground, and the next moment they saw Redney fling himself helplessly into Lambert's arms, a thin whimpering wail breaking from him into the silence.

'Look!' the boy Jim Carey cried; and right beyond the two clutching figures they saw old Redney in stone! The image was dark against the sky and immensely larger than the poor stricken thing in the ex-soldier's arms. It seemed to mock him, the head of it stretched out in unrelenting eagerness. One glance they gave it and without a word broke from the place.

Jack Lambert a few days afterwards was seen driving from the place, no one knew whither. Old Redney was missed. His poor bedraggled wife they would see driving the cows of a night time to the inches. She kept her thoughts to herself. Only after weeks and weeks the men of the valley learned her husband had taken to his bed, awaiting his doom. In tongue-tied silence still he awaits it, his eyes staring out straight before him.

A Looter of the Hills

I

I told the woman that her little girl was now recovered and that there was no need for a further visit. In quiet thankfulness she accompanied me down the rickety stairs, and suddenly, and entirely by way of impulse, said: 'Doctor, there's another poor patient here, and you ought to have a look at him. His name is Phil Donaghy.' With that she tapped on a door I had not noticed in a sort of recess at the bottom of the stairs. As if she had expected no reply she had put her fingers on the handle when the door opened: she said at once:

'Oh! I didn't know you were with him, Nora. I'm after asking the doctor here to have a look at him: 'twill do him no harm.'

Nora, a decent-looking soul, started and gaped at us, and I, knowing the pieties of such people, said at once: 'The room will do well enough. And himself, too.'

Of late I have been noticing that so surely as that close-wedged mass of tenement houses, crouching there in the shadow of St Michael's, rises to my memory or actually comes into view from some terrace on the hills, it is this Phil Donaghy, the patient I was then to become acquainted with, that emerges from it as an individual. That network of lanes and alleys, lying in the skirts of that bleak-looking ungainly church, is his background. They are scarcely six feet wide, these lanes, and the houses in them are so high in the old-fashioned way, that they feel even narrower still. The houses cling to one another in ramshackle groups like a lot of tipsy sailormen, some of them tossing their heads, some of them gone in the pins, others sodden and dull, while others again are gay with all manner of patchings, stains and weatherings. The footpaths by which one navigates the district are hardly a foot in width, paved with cobblestones, as also are most of the lanes themselves; and when you leave these pathways and turn into the hallways you find but little difference. One trusts oneself to a dark twisting passage along which one feels with the feet cautiously; flooring, soundless with rottenness, is beneath them, or flags, or, it may be, common earth. They are so long, these passages, they shoot forward so fiercely, turn sharply aside, shoot forward again, that one imagines oneself as burrowing under the old church itself, for piles and piles of crazy masonry seem to surround one on every side and to be over the head as well.

The room I was led into was large enough, very ill-lighted however. The window was hidden away behind driftings of lace curtains that had gone the colour of a negro. I gingerly put one of them aside and saw that the little yard into which the window looked was like a dripping well sunken into that mass of burrowed masonry. The sky I could not see, but an expiring gleam of light falling down the greenish mouldy walls hinted of it. That yard was indeed a dismal prospect. I turned from it and found my patient hunched over a lifeless bit of fire in the grate. When he raised his undetermined face to me, the eyes melancholy, the brows lifted, I could think only of an empty shop.

'Stand up, my man,' I said; and when he did so, resting limply on the back of a chair, I noticed the huge limbs, the huge awkward-looking trunk, and I knew for certain there was peasant blood in him.

'Out in the air,' I said, cheerily, 'out in the air is the place for you – and what else have you to do?'

His eyes sharpened, searching me with some effort at keenness. Not only that, but the kindly creature who had been tidying the place for him – she was his brother's wife, and lived on an upper floor – looked up quickly at me as if I had said some surprising thing! In a moment she was all words: 'That's what I tell him, Doctor. He should rouse himself!' And she caught him by the sleeve: 'You should rouse yourself, Phil. Isn't that what I'm always saying to you? A thousand times, Doctor, I said as much to him myself. And what harm but there's not a foot of the country that he doesn't know by heart. He used to be forever scouring it, ever and ever; but that was before his mother died on him.'

The lump of manhood turned its slow eyes upon her and said – I know not what.

She looked from his face to mine: 'Yes, Doctor, that's right. 'Tis long before 'twill be forgotten – how we buried her, the flowers – '

I knew then where I was. That very funeral, six months earlier I had come upon it as it threaded the lanes. Crowds of people followed it, with some sort of hidden excitement playing through them, and the coffin was entirely hidden in flowers and greenery – not the fast-bound wreaths, shapely and meagre, that florists supply to order, but a wild profusion of branches, flowers, and leaves, heaped and gaudy.

II

Only for that his mother had come from the heart of the country she could never possibly have lived to be over eighty years of age in such surroundings. Up to that age she had been a busy woman, attending to the housework, shopping, going to Mass, taking her place in all the doings of the laneway. Then she had a stroke, as the people say, losing control of her right side, more or less. From that out the dark room, with the bed in the corner, was her kingdom. No more housework, no more shopping, or Mass, or Retreats, or Missions, or anything. Then, as will happen, the recollections of her simple childhood came more and more to the surface. To her overgrown half-wit of a son she would say: 'There's no knowing the damage a goat will do. The goat we had, it went into Colonel Seeve's place one morning before a soul was up, and it tore down and destroyed all the lovely shrubs in the lawn! What did it care about handsome places! And it came home and laid down, and had a lovely sleep for itself! Look at that for you! And not a mortal knowing where it was after spending the day. But when 'twas found out – Oh, then there was murder!'

Or she might say to him – to him who was true child of the city's heart: 'Sheep's milk is so thick you couldn't drink it without putting water in it. Now there's lots of people don't know that sheep have any milk at all. The people of this lane now, Betty outside, or Johnny Mahony, they never saw sheep's milk at all. Sitting there they were, and they downfaced me when I said that people used to drink sheep's milk and goat's milk too.'

Or again, although his world had never been any other than the laneways and the wharves: 'Up in the dark of the morning we'd be, boiling the potatoes for them. And maybe then someone would say, "Do you hear that? That's the Linehans." 'Tis the way we'd be listening to know if the others were taking the road. And one after another we'd hear them coming from all quarters. You'd think some of them hadn't gone to bed at all at all. Away to the fair with them then: into Macroom; and 'twould be the dark of night when they'd come back. Over the mountains they'd go: there are places there would frighten you to look at them.'

At another time she would be still further back in her childhood: 'Gathering brosna in the wood we'd be; and we'd be all right so long as the daylight held; but the place would get cold and still, and we'd be listening to know if anything was stirring; and we'd say we had no right to stay so long, and we'd run home with ourselves. But all the same maybe we'd stay longer the next evening or the evening after.'

As if to aid her in this recovery of her childhood's far-off life in far-off places the film on her eyeballs thickened, more and more hiding away from her the dismal surroundings into which her many years had narrowed. When, unconsciously, she had ceased the struggle to keep tally of what was going on about her, when her eyes had gone utterly dark, her head lifted itself higher and higher, the features relaxed, her face brightened, took on the appearance of a sky in which the winds have died and the clouds vanished – frank, open and serene, lighted from within.

Beside her was another simple nature, this gom of a son of hers, who was lucky if he poked out two days' work in a week. Only when there was a rush of shipping at the jetties did the stevedore beckon him to take his place in the run of corn-baggers or timber-heavers. For the most part, he loitered in his mother's room drinking in her chatter of a world he had never known. Who could say what images he made himself from the rambling gossip! Anyway he began to explore the countryside round about, one day taking to the hills on either side of the city, or another threading the river valley to the west. It was not long until in that darkened room buried under, lost among, those piles of crumbling masonry there were to be heard two voices instead of one speaking of the green hillsides: 'Little lambs they were, jumping about their mothers. Lively. Awful game. Look! Look, can't ye!' And if the aged eyes could no longer see his clumsy antics, his six-foot friskings, they could most certainly make themselves pictures of lambs that were as white as snow and pastures that were green and deep. Or it might be a braver vision he had raised for her: 'At the top of the field he turns them round … '

'The headland, Phil boy, the headland.'

'Turns them round; and the tackling and chains goes rattling: "Whoa! Hack! Back you! Back, I tell you!" And one of them puts his head up in the air. And he opens his jaws. You'd think he'd take a bite out of the air or the clouds! And the other fellow puts his head down, down, into his chest, like a magistrate in the court. And he drags them round like that – "Whoa! Come out of it!" And all the seagulls and crows!'

'But 'tis hard work, ploughing is,' she'd answer, 'and after a day of it, if the ground was heavy, you'd be only fit to throw yourself in the bed, like a log of wood. Isn't it often I see them! Often and often!'

Because his nature was simple and passionate it was his way to act out his thought; and, listening in the dim passage outside the door of their room you might hear coming from within, the swish of a scythe or the whirr of a reaping machine or the gossip of a group of gleaners or the unrestrained argument of a group of cattle-dealers at a fair. For, little by little, he had ventured farther and farther from the dens of the city and grown knowledgeable of the life of the countryside. It was a common thing with him now to rise long before the dawn that he might enjoy the spectacle of a fair. Sometimes he was paid a couple of shillings for assisting in the driving of the cattle, at a headlong pace, into the city to catch a steamer or train. But indeed, whatever he thought of it himself, it was not for the sake of the odd shillings he hung about the earnest bargainers like that: it was rather to find food for his own hungry mind and heart that in turn might feed that other hungry mind and heart imprisoned in the slumland of the city. She as well as himself had benefit of all he saw and heard in his excursions.

One day he had lain stretched for hours on a grassy bank gazing lazily at the mowers in the meadow. That evening his mother grabbed him to her suddenly and buried her nostrils in his clothes: 'That's a good smell. So 'tis. So 'tis. A good smell. A good smell.'

After a day of cattle driving the smell of the beasts was to her a delight, as indeed was anything at all that renewed for her the impressions life had made on her virgin soul eighty years before. He began to loot the hillsides for her sake. Armfuls of wild flowers he brought her, whole branches of blossoming trees or masses of trailing woodbine. In autumn he came garlanded with boughs of crab apple, tangles of fruity briars or even half a sheaf of corn. She would bury her nose in them, play with them, plucking the fruit and thorning her fingers while she did so.

III

Late one night in the springtime her daughter-in-law heard stirrings in the old woman's room. She went to her: 'Mother,' she whispered through the darkness, 'what's the matter? Is it how ye can't sleep or what?'

'Nothing, child, nothing is the matter. What a goose you are? Don't be rising like that getting cold for yourself.'

The voice ceased suddenly, the stirrings had again begun. The young woman groped on the table and lit the candle. She found a live lamb in the grip of the old woman. The animal was struggling to escape from the claw-like ancient hands.

Things had gone too far; there was a scene. The half-wit had only little to say while they threatened him with the law.

'I'm no robber. I never stole anything. I was going to take it back. Nobody would miss it. I gave it milk. I covered it with my coat. I never stole nothing!'

After that the two of them, mother and son, had again to fall back on the wild flowers, the hawthorn and crab blossom, which fortunately were now plentiful along the hedges. Into the midst of the lane dwellers as they sat at nightfall at their doorways, the harmless giant would break, his basketing arms letting the wilful blossoms fall as he moved along with odours in his wake. They would raise their nostrils and smile, sometimes wistfully, or shake their heads, remembering old times and places.

IV

Of a morning in autumn Nora roused her husband impatiently. As her custom was she had, first thing, gone to the bedside of the old woman. She was now returned: 'Something is after happening,' she said to him.

'What's up with you? Is it Nanny?' Then he sat up quickly: 'You're shaking.'

'The two of them is missing!'

'Merciful Father!'

When he had dressed himself, was come with her to the empty room – litter of bird cages, of withered boughs, of branches dry and crackling as it was – she said to him: 'I knew they were up to something. They had their heads together. That's what they were planning. And sniggering. Laughing at us.'

'I'll break his neck for him! I keep a home for him, and that's the thanks I get. Nothing but annoyance and trouble.'

The room soon filled with the neighbours, councils were held: the police, it was decided, had better be sent for. They best could trace them. In the police station telephones were set ringing; telegrams dispatched; hospitals communicated with. All, however, without result. Alone, or accompanied by a young policeman, Tom went from place to place, everywhere noticing as soon as the matter had been explained, a thinnish sort of smile break over the faces of the officials. And he felt ashamed of himself.

'You have tried them all, you say?'

'Every one of them; and the Poorhouse too.'

'Well, there's the river.'

Tired out, embittered too, he came home and told his wife what the police sergeant had said.

'Don't say it – don't say it, Tom,' she said, her finger on his wrist, ''tis before my mind the livelong day! We were hard on them; we were hard on them!'

'No, no. We gave them their own way in everything, too much of it.'

Towards nightfall they heard an authoritative voice in the hall-way; tremblingly they opened. It was the same sergeant. He looked at them – as his habit was – for a long time steadily and in chill silence. They felt miserably guilty. He asked them many sidelong questions, as also was his way, before explaining to them the simple matter that a horse and cart had been stolen from a farmer's yard a mile outside the city. No one in the lane, however, had heard any sound of a cart; and anybody else might have taken it as well as this half-wit of theirs. The telephones, the wires, were, however, all at work again, so he inform-ed them; and before long they would surely have news. Yet no news arrived.

Late that night Tom and his wife and a neighbour sat in silence, dispirited, fearful of they knew not what. The neighbour had tired of urging them to make their minds at ease, to go to bed, to be ready for whatever would be sent to them; no more than that he could say to comfort them. Yet the silence irked them all; so that at last the wife rose up and began to set about some homely task. Tom too raised his head from his long brooding. 'Do you know, I think I can tell where they're gone to? Come, Dinny, come with me. We'll get the ambulance from the Corporation.'

The sleeping Corporation watchman did not wish to set out on a wild-goose chase. They had to threaten him; if the aged woman was found dead from exposure her death would be laid at his door, he would hear about it.

The motor ambulance drove through the silent streets, making a great clatter. Into the country with them, mile after mile. Towards the west they made, then northwards, cutting into the heart of the hills. Yet in spite of the excellent lamps they had they could make only slow progress, for none of them knew the country when they were a score of miles distant from it; all they knew was the direction. The steady whirr of the engine comforted them, and they began less and less to fear the unforeseen. They wondered at the great silence, the great blank spaces of the sky as the darkness drew away. The sun rose up on their right, and they saw wisps of mist hanging from juts of rocks or laid astray along the hedges. The increasing warmth of the sun was sweet to them, yet Tom widened his eyes as he caught the tumultuous singing of the birds. Their morning rapture promised that everything would be the same, but he was quietly saying to himself that nothing ever again would be the same, and his look was piteous.

At last they quenched their lamps: the landscape was flooded with brightness. They climbed along the side of a straggling belt of ruined woodland; they made the ridge; descending, they swung round on to a bridge that crossed a foaming torrent diminished after the summer yet still very loud. Before them lay a broad valley with wide meadows and sloping fields of corn, unexpectedly rich and soft-looking in the heart of those craggy hills. But their eyes had scarcely scanned its features when they noticed down below them in the middle of the dust-white road a solitary farm cart standing perfectly still, its shadow laid sharply upon the dust. So still the picture they made – horse, cart, shadow, and the solitary clumsy figure gazing towards them as if he had heard the noise of the car from afar off, it struck them the group must have been as stilly as that for hours. Without a word they slowed down as they approached. The poor fool looked at them as if he had expected them. He gave them no time to question him.

'She was all right, not a bit afraid, talking, talking, asking me everything. She never stopped, only asking me everything. I'm telling you she was as game as paint till she heard that river there and it giving tongue out of it.'

What could they say to him?

They brought her home and never again did the gift of consciousness descend upon her. After seventy years of absence she anyway once again had breathed her native air, had heard the voice of her native vale, its birds and its waters, enough perhaps to give her blind eyes to see its fields heavy with harvest, and its households as she had known them in her childhood.

Her son – the melancholy fit will pass. He will again take to wandering on the hills, gazing at the flowers thick-strewn in the hedges, or gaping at the young things playing about their dams, his mind all a confusion, yet not uncomforted.

THE PRIEST

I

Because Father Reen had been reading all day the rain had meant but little for him. Since breakfast time he had not been disturbed, his housekeeper even had not entered, and he had reached an age, he was sixty-two, when a day of unbroken quiet was the best of holidays. Yet any more of the quietness might have taken the edge off his pleasure. In the afternoon, just in good time it seemed, an uncertain sunbeam floated tremulously across the pages of his book; quite unexpectedly, it had stolen in through the still streaming window panes. Father Reen, his mouth suddenly opening, raised his head and stared with his blue eyes, large and clear, across the river valley towards the mountains. He noticed that, even as he looked, hedgerow, branch, and rocky height were emerging through the saturated air, were taking form, unsubstantial still, yet no longer broken in outline. His house was in a good place for the afternoon sunshine; it stood on a rise of ground above the river and looked to the south-west. The soil was sandy, the paths in the garden well kept and kind to the feet; before long, in the mild November sunshine, he was pacing to and fro the full length of his little place. Between this pleasant place in the sun, and the study he had just come from, he had grown into the custom of passing nearly all his free time – too much of it, as he often told himself, for it meant further and further withdrawal from the life of the village, the life of his parish; but then where in the parish was such life to be come upon as he could profitably make use of? He was conscious that in this parish of his, as in many another round about it, there was, speaking from either social or cultural point of view, neither an upper class nor even a middle class – there was only a peasant class that had only comparatively recently emerged from penury, a class that needed spurring, that needed leadership, and that was not finding it. He had long since reasoned out that the time had come for the building up of a middle class, an upper class too, on native lines, to take the place of those that had failed; but as often however as this thought came to him he smiled, for he certainly was not one of those who get things put to right. Now, however, breathing the fresh air, which was chilly enough to make quick walking necessary, he fortunately was free from the thought of all this. Beyond the feel of the fresh air in his nostrils he was free almost from sensation. Film after film of moisture he saw lifting, dissipating themselves in the effulgence of the sun, leaving the wide river valley, the hundred thousand rocky scars and ridges that encumbered it, sharply drawn, one against another, if as yet without colour, a succession of grey tones. But the swollen river made no response to the light above it, for its waters had become stained, were heavy after the scourings from the fords and inches. He could see it tumbling along.

Whenever in his pacing he faced the west his eye traversed not only the river but the village beyond it. He saw the evening smoke of its homely fires ascending, each spire of it alive with the sunshine streaming through it. He had been so long in the place, first as curate and then as parish priest, that he had got into the way of whispering to himself such pet phrases as: My valley, my river, my river, my hills. This afternoon, the ascending smoke spires taking his eye, My people! was the phrase that possessed his lips. It seemed touched with the memory of emotion rather than with any living warmth. He had scarcely uttered the words when he stopped up in his pacing, for in that single patch of open village street that was visible to him, he saw a horseman swinging steadily along, making, he was certain, towards the bridge, towards this hillside, towards this house of his.

II

In less than a half-hour Father Reen was riding alone across the bridge and through the village, faced towards the west, towards Kilmony, a ploughland ten miles away on the farthest edge of his far-flung parish, where, the messenger had informed him, an old man was nearing his end.

Anyhow there would be no more rain. The sky was clearing, the wind was swung round towards the north. Now the sun was hidden behind a barricade of cloud, cold grey in colour, and thick, that rested all along the horizon, shafts of rich light ascending from behind it to the height of heaven. The sun would not show itself again; and the moment it was gone one would feel how hard the night was turning to frost. Father Reen was conscious of this as he made on at a good pace. Yes, the air would become colder and colder, the landscape barer and barer, harder and harder in its features. The village, which he had come through, was wind-swept enough, was hard enough and niggard enough in all its ways, yet it did not lack for trees in various groupings, nor for clipped bushes, shapely hedges, flower pots. And he remembered how, as he passed through, he had heard an outburst of reckless laughter from the stragglers in the forge – their meeting place as long as he could remember. He knew he would come on no other group of gossips as loud voiced or as merry as they: nor on hedgerow trees or clipped hedges or any flowers. Already he was aware of the denuded character of the landscape about him, every feature of it sharp and bare; he foresaw all the long roads and byways, little cared for, stone-strewn, with their surfaces swept away, deep-channelled by the rain torrents from the hills; and, very insidiously, uneasiness intruded on his peace of mind, not induced so much by the discomfort of the roads ahead of him as by the thought of Kilmony itself, to which they led – a place where the people were still living in wretched cabins, on the poorest fare, without a notion of giving attention to, or spending a penny on, anything except the direst necessaries of life – a place where he hardly ever remembered an old person to die without the lust of property troubling the spirit almost to the beginning of the agony. Against the fear that this foreknowledge aroused in him he struggled; he shook his head at it, he set his teeth, he grasped the reins more firmly, consciously giving himself to the onward rhythm of the gallop.

Already, he felt, there was thin frost forming on the pools beneath his horse's hoofs. And what a bite in the north-west as it blew across the marches and the reedy lakes! Soon the stars would begin to come forth sparkling with frost. Everywhere now slabs of rock, pinnacles of rock, hillsides of rock; and not a tree anywhere, not a bush even; scarcely a sign of humanity, hardly a human being. On an upland farm he had seen a boy driving a few scraggy beasts diagonally up a sloping field to the stall. Now, across the inch, he saw an old man bent under a huge mass of bogland cow-fodder, making for a gap – and between man and boy there were miles, it seemed, of rock and heather, of such desolation as hindered the growth of any community spirit, which, of itself, would little by little, induce a finer way of living. My people! My people! he thought, so good, so sinless, even so religious, yet so hard, so niggardly, so worldly, even so cruel; and again he blamed himself for not starting, for not forwarding some plan or other – sports or storytelling, or dancing or singing or reading or play-acting – anything that would cut across and baffle that lust of acquisitiveness which every-where is the peasant's bane. My people! My people! My people! and then: If only I were young again! But this, he chided himself, was but self-deception. What was really wrong with him, he told himself, was that he had unconsciously withdrawn himself from them, with those hard ways of theirs. They were leaderless, at least in the social sense. They had no initiative – yet he had left them to themselves lest – yes, that was it – lest – he was like a doctor falling into age, afraid to use any except the safest remedies – lest complications might ensue – yes, that was the phrase. But it was true he was ageing. And the best day he ever was he had not been one of those blessed people who get things done. Anyway, his duty as a priest – that, O thanks be to God, he had never neglected, so far as he knew.

It was dark night when he turned up the hillside on the ridge of which lay Kilmony – a place where every household was intermarried with every other household. Pluckily his horse stepped up the broken ground, his forehoofs smiting the rocky shelvings, impatient for foot-ing. When the ascent became a little easier Father Reen raised his head and saw the crest of the hill swarthy and sharp against the grey cloud-less sky, darker than it, full of roughnesses, of breaks and points, a rest-less line running east and west with here and there a bright star fallen upon it. He knew he was at the right place. Beyond that ridge, he re-membered, were immense slowly-rising uplands abandoned to nature, miles on miles, where sheep were driven to pasture at the end of spring-time, and left to themselves the length of summer, where turf was dug out, but where no attempt at tillage had ever been made. On his right he now noticed a haphazard group of gables; some of them had once been whitened, and these helped still to separate the whole group from the beetling background. He heard a gate opened, and dimly he made out a tall figure in the middle of the road – it was indeed little more than a rough pathway – standing against the sky awaiting him.

III
'Am I at Miah Neehan's?' he asked.

'Yes, Father. You're better get off here, the yard isn't too clean in itself.'

He dismounted, and already he felt the wind cold on his sweaty limbs.

'I'm in time?' he questioned.

'Good time. In good time,' he was answered, and then he heard the voice raised: 'Isn't it a wonder one of ye wouldn't hold a lamp for Father Reen?'

There was but a dull glimmer of light in the interior of the dwelling: he saw it reflected in the dung pit which, in the old-fashioned way, occupied most of the yard. By peering he made out the causeway of large boulders running through the mire to the doorway. All was just as he had expected. It was one of those places, now happily rare, over which the spirit of the bad old times, as the people say, still seemed to brood, a place where necessity was served, and that only. Among the dark figures in the doorway he saw movement – the effect of a harshly spoken word of his guide – and he was glad, for the sweat was chilly on his limbs. He saw now a flannel-coated middle-aged man emerge, shielding the lamp from the wind with a corner of his wrapper. He made towards him, and by the time he reached the threshold the figures were all withdrawn again into the interior. There were both men and women, but the faces of the women were so deeply hidden within the hoods of their cloaks that all he could see of them was a pale gleam. They were seated by the walls, but the men were standing haphazardly about or leaning their shoulders wherever they could find support. Tall and spare, a mountainy breed, their heads were lost in the darkness that hung beneath the ancient thatch. The fire on the hearth was uncared for; and not a word was passing among those present. He saluted them, his hat in his hand, and waited until the lamp had been again hung on its accustomed nail.

'Where is he?' he said.

There was slight pause before the reply came: 'Inside, Father.'

Before he entered the lower room, the only other room in the house, he turned towards where the voice had spoken, saying: 'Are his affairs settled, are they in order?'

No answer coming, he turned towards the man who had held the lamp for him, looking at him questioningly, but he, throwing down his eyes, slunk away into the midst of the others. He raised his voice then: 'Are his affairs in order?'

Just then, the man who had welcomed him on the roadway – he had since been seeing after the horse – entered hurriedly, looking like one who had been anxious whether those within might not have been scanting their courtesies. A voice in the semi-darkness, a woman's voice, met him: 'Father Reen wants to know are his affairs settled?'

'Oh yes; that's all right. In good order. In good order. You needn't give yourself any uneasiness about that, Father.'

He spoke challengingly, the priest felt, to those about them in the room. Indeed he had scarcely finished when one of the tallest of the men flung himself from his place and strode across the room to the doorway where he took his station, his back to those within, his eyes staring out into the black night. 'Sit down, sit down, Jack. Be easy.' He who had answered the priest's question it was who spoke, with the carelessness of contempt, it seemed, rather than in any spirit of good fellowship. But the man in the doorway answered him, flinging round his head suddenly and angrily: 'I'm all right here – just here where I am.'

It appeared to Father Reen the two were fairly matched. 'Very well, very well. Please yourself. Come on in, Father.'

A woman's voice said: 'Tim, you'd want a second candle within.'

'You're right. One is a poor light on these occasions.' He soon had a lighted candle in his hand, showing the way.

'Come on in, Father. Everything is ready for you. Quite ready.'

IV

Father Reen was alone with the dying man. In the squalid room, the rickety contrivance of a bed, the ancient coverings, the stained walls, the tainted air, he again found all he had expected to find. Above all he found his thought realised in the head thrown weakly back upon the pillow, the eyes of which had fastened on him at the moment of entrance. He could feel how grimly the old man's will – he was ninety-one years of age – had been exerted, had been struggling against the craving of the worn-out body for rest, for the lapse of unconsciousness. He drew near to the bedside, seated himself at its edge, and noticed how the old eyes were searching the spaces of the room; he then heard the dry and wearied voice speaking with a distinctness that of itself alone would acquaint one with the triumph of the will over every other faculty in the old man's soul: 'Whisper, Father, is that door shut?'

The priest rose, made certain that the door between them and the crowd of descendants and relatives outside was fastened, then seating himself again said: ''Tis all right.'

'Whisper,' the old head was reaching up to his face, 'I'm destroyed, destroyed with them, with them in and out to me all day, all night too, in and out, in and out, watching me, and watching each other too.'

It was a long time before he was satisfied he had done all he could, and could do no more, for that struggling soul, which, he was sure, would enter the next world before the night was out. But the moment he had caught sight of the old face, the tight wisdom of it, the undefeated will in it, the clasp on the lips, the firm old chin, and then the hard-shut fist like a knob on the scraggy forearm that would lift and threaten and emphasise – he knew what was before him – that he would have to call up all the resources of his own brain and will, having asked help from on high, and wrestle, and wrestle, and wrestle to dislodge that poor old peasant's handful of thoughts from that which had been their centre and stay for seventy or eighty years – the land, the farm, as he called it – a waste of rock and shale, bog and moor, that should never at all have been brought under the spade. He had more than his farm to stay his thoughts upon: as earnest of his long and well-spent life he had his dirty bank-book under his pillow with eighty pounds marked in it to his credit. No sooner was Father Reen aware of this than he knew that it would be easier almost to wrench one of the rocks in the fields abroad from its bed than to wrench that long-accustomed support from the old man's little world of consciousness without shattering it to insanity. Yet this at last Father Reen felt he had succeeded in doing; he thought he found a new look coming into the old man's eyes, overspreading his brow, some expression of hard-won relief, some return of openness, of simplicity, that may not have been there since early manhood; in the voice he thought he found some new timbre, some sudden access of tenderness, of sweetness; and, more surely telling of the new scale of values suddenly come upon by that old battler in a rough world, a flood of aspirations broke impetuously from the trembling lips: 'Jesus Christ, O welcome, O welcome; keep near me, I'm not worthy, I'm not worthy, but welcome. O Blessed Mother, pray for me, now, now' – a flood onward and never-ending once it had started at all; and Father Reen noticed how the two fists, twin knobs, equally hard and small, were pressed fiercely down upon the brows, side by side, covering the eye sockets, hiding almost the whole of the rapt countenance, except the moving chin. Limbs and all, the old peasant had become one knot of concentration, and the thought of what he was leaving behind him was not any longer its secret.

V

When Father Reen re-entered the larger room, the living-room, he found the crowd in the self-same positions as when he had gone from them; and he felt that not a syllable had passed between them. Tim, that master mind of the group, the man who had led him to the old man's bedside – he was one of the old man's grandsons – had the middle of the earthen floor to himself. He blurted out, almost with a touch of levity in his voice: 'You had a job with him.'

A murmur of sudden and indignant surprise broke from those against the walls. Father Reen shot one glance at the speaker, he could not help it, the fall from the plane he had been moving in was so terrible – and the man, suddenly realising his fault, made some hopeless, mollifying gesture with a limp hand, speaking no word, however. His wife, as Father Reen perceived, came forward, saying: 'Would Father Reen take some little refreshment? We could make a cup of tea? 'Tis a long journey is before you.'

He motioned her away from him, making for the door: he wanted with all his heart to be in the saddle and away under the stars.

VI

It took some little time to get the horse ready. He then had to lead it down that steep decline beneath the crest of the hill. As he did so he noticed a glimmer of light above him on the right hand side. He had noticed no house there when ascending; he would not have noticed it now only that he caught a high-pitched babble of talk above him, and, looking round, had spied the dim gleam of a window. As he looked he saw a flash of light – the door had opened – and he heard an angry passionate outburst: 'I'll have the law of him! I'll have the law of him!'

The door was suddenly shut to. There remained the angry onward confusion of talk and the dull glimmer in the tiny window. It was a son's house or a grandson's house, surely; and there was many another house in the neighbourhood thinking the same thought this night. Law, yes, and years and years of it over those stony fields and that dirty bank-book. But this much, he told himself, he had known from the moment of entering that crowded living-room.

The remembrance quickened his blood. With almost a touch of savagery he urged his beast forward the moment he found his legs gripping its belly. The hard roads invited it. They, with the frozen pools all along them, were bright enough to see by; there was also the tangle of starshine hanging somehow in the middle air above the landscape. For one no longer young he rode wildly, but then the Reens from time immemorial had been eager horsemen. When he came down on to the level ground he broke into a hard gallop; and when, after an hour's going, he had won to the better-kept road beside the lakes he rode as if for a high wager. He was flying not from Kilmony so much as from that fund of reflections all he witnessed there had aroused in him. That terrible promiscuity of rock, the little stony fields that only centuries

of labour had salvaged from them, the unremitting toil they demand-
ed, the poor return, the niggard scheme of living; and then the ancient face on the pillow, the gathering of greedy descendants – he had
known it all before; for years the knowledge of how much of a piece
it all was had kept his mind uneasy. He knew he would presently be
asking himself: Where do my duties end? And this hard riding of his
was but an effort to baffle that inveterate questioning. He rode like a
man possessed. If the rhythm of the riding, the need for alertness, the
silence of the black, stark landscape, the far-stretching lakes, the mass
of starshine in the air, weakened at moments the urgency of the question, it overwhelmingly leaped upon him, that question did, whenever he passed a lonely farm-house clung against its slab of protecting
rock at the base of a cliff, or espied one aloft on some *leaca* or other,
betrayed to the night by the lamp still dimly burning. Each and every
one of them seemed to grab at his very heart pleading for some human
succour that their inmates could not name. And all the time the hoofs
of his animal were beating out from the frozen road in perfectly regular rhythm: My people! My people! My people!

THE EYES OF THE DEAD

I

If he had not put it off for three years John Spillane's home-coming would have been that of a famous man. Bonfires would have been lighted on the hill-tops of Rossamara, and the ships passing by, twenty miles out, would have wondered what they meant.

Three years ago, the *Western Star*, an Atlantic liner, one night tore her iron plates to pieces against the cliff-like face of an iceberg, and in less than an hour sank in the waters. Of the 789 human souls aboard her one only had been saved, John Spillane, able seaman, of Rossamara in the county of Cork. The name of the little fishing village, his own name, his picture, were in all the papers of the world, it seemed, not only because he alone had escaped, but by reason of the manner of that escape. He had clung to a drift of wreckage, must have lost consciousness for more than a whole day, floated then about on the ocean for a second day, for a second night, and had arrived at the threshold of another dreadful night when he was rescued. A fog was coming down on the waters. It frightened him more than the darkness. He raised a shout. He kept on shouting. When safe in the arms of his rescuers his breathy, almost inaudible voice was still forcing out some cry which they interpreted as Help! Help!

That was what had struck the imagination of men – the half-insane figure sending his cry over the waste of waters, the fog thickening, and the night falling. Although the whole world had read also of the groping rescue ship, of Spillane's bursts of hysterical laughter, of his inability to tell his story until he had slept eighteen hours on end, what remained in the memory was the lonely figure sending his cry over the sea.

And then, almost before his picture had disappeared from the papers, he had lost himself in the great cities of the States. To Rossamara no word had come from himself, nor for a long time from any acquaintance; but then, when about a year had gone by, his sister or mother as they went up the road to Mass of a Sunday might be stopped and informed in a whispering voice that John had been in Chicago, or, it might be, in New York, or Boston, or San Francisco, or indeed anywhere. And from the meagreness of the messages it was known, with only too much certainty, that he had not, in exchanging sea for land, bettered his lot. If once again his people had happened on such empty tidings of him, one knew it by their bowed and stilly attitude in the little church as the light whisper of the Mass rose and fell about them.

When three years had gone by he lifted the latch of his mother's house one October evening and stood awkwardly in the middle of the floor. It was nightfall and not a soul had seen him break down from the ridge and cross the roadway. He had come secretly from the ends of the earth.

And before he was an hour in their midst he rose up impatiently, timidly, and stole into his bed.

'I don't want any light,' he said, and as his mother left him there in the dark, she heard him yield his whole being to a sigh of thankfulness. Before that he had told them he felt tired, a natural thing, since he had tramped fifteen miles from the railway station in Skibbereen. But day followed day without his showing any desire to rise from the bedclothes and go abroad among the people. He had had enough of the sea, it seemed; enough too of the great cities of the States. He was a pity, the neighbours said; and the few of them who from time to time caught glimpses of him, reported him as not yet having lost the scared look that the ocean had left on him. His hair was grey or nearly grey, they said, and, swept back fiercely from his forehead, a fashion strange to the place, seemed to pull his eyes open, to keep them wide open, as he looked at you. His moustache also was grey, they said, and his cheeks were grey too, sunken and dark with shadows. Yet his mother and sister, the only others in the house, were glad to have him back with them; at any rate, they said, they knew where he was.

They found nothing wrong with him. Of speech neither he nor they ever had had the gift; and as day followed day, and week week, the same few phrases would carry them through the day and into the silence of night. In the beginning they had thought it natural to speak with him about the wreck; soon, however, they came to know that it was a subject for which he had no welcome. In the beginning also, they had thought to rouse him by bringing the neighbours to his bedside, but such visits instead of cheering him only left him sunken in silence, almost in despair. The priest came to see him once in a while, and advised the mother and sister, Mary her name was, to treat him as normally as they could, letting on that his useless presence was no affliction to them nor even a burden. In time John Spillane was accepted by all as one of those unseen ones, or seldom-seen ones, who are to be found in every village in the world – the bed-ridden, the struck-down, the aged – forgotten of all except the few faithful creatures who bring the cup to the bedside of a morning, and open the curtains to let in the sun.

II

In the nearest house, distant a quarter-mile from them, lived Tom Leane. In the old days before John Spillane went to sea, Tom had been his companion, and now of a night-time he would drop in if he had any story worth telling or if, on the day following, he chanced to be going back to Skibbereen, where he might buy the Spillanes such goods as they needed, or sell a pig for them, slipping it in among his own. He was a quiet creature, married, and struggling to bring up the little family that was thickening about him. In the Spillanes' he would, dragging at the pipe, sit on the settle, and quietly gossip with the old woman while Mary moved about him on the flags putting the household gear tidy for the night. But all three of them, as they kept up the simple talk, were never unaware of the silent listener in the lower room. Of that room the door was kept open; but no lamp was lighted within it; no lamp indeed was needed, for a shaft of light from the kitchen struck into it showing one or two of the religious pictures on the wall and giving sufficient light to move about in. Sometimes the conversation would drift away from the neighbourly doings, for even to Rossamara tidings from the great world abroad would sometimes come; in the middle of such gossip, however, a sudden thought would strike Tom Leane, and, raising his voice, he would blurt out: 'But sure, 'tis foolish for the like of me to be talking about these far-off places, and that man inside after travelling the world, over and thither.' The man inside, however, would give no sign whatever whether their gossip had been wise or foolish. They might hear the bed creak, as if he had turned with impatience at their mention of his very presence.

There had been a spell of stormy weather, it was now the middle of February, and for the last five days at twilight the gale seemed always to set in for a night of it. Although there was scarcely a house around that part of the south-west Irish coast that had not some one of its members, husband or brother or son, living on the sea, sailoring abroad or fishing the home waters or those of the Isle of Man – in no other house was the strain of a spell of disastrous weather so notice-able in the faces of its inmates. The old woman, withdrawn into her-self, would handle her beads all day long, her voice every now and then raising itself, in forgetfulness, to a sort of moan not unlike the wind's, upon which the younger woman would chide her with a 'Sh! Sh!' and bend vigorously upon her work to keep bitterness from her thoughts. At such a time she might enter her brother's room and find him raised on his elbow in the bed, listening to the howling winds, scared it seem-ed, his eyes fixed and wide open. He would drink the warm milk she had brought him, and hand the vessel back without a word. And in the selfsame attitude she would leave him.

The fifth night instead of growing in loudness and fierceness the wind died away somewhat. It became fitful, promising the end of the storm; and before long they could distinguish between the continuous groaning and pounding of the sea and the sudden shout the dying tempest would fling among the tree-tops and the rocks. They were thankful to note such signs of relief; the daughter became more active, and the mother put by her beads. In the midst of a sudden sally of the wind's the latch was raised, and Tom Leane gave them greeting. His face was rosy and glowing under his sou'wester; his eyes were sparkling from the sting of the salty gusts. To see him, so sane, so healthy, was to them like a blessing. 'How is it with ye?' he said, cheerily, closing the door to.

'Good, then, good, then,' they answered him, and the mother rose almost as if she would take him by the hand. The reply meant that nothing unforeseen had befallen them. He understood as much. He shook a silent head in the direction of the listener's room, a look of inquiry in his eyes, and this look Mary answered with a sort of hope-less upswing of her face. Things had not improved in the lower room.

The wind died away, more and more; and after some time stream-ed by with a shrill steady undersong; all through, however, the crash-ing of the sea on the jagged rocks beneath kept up an unceasing cla-mour. Tom had a whole budget of news for them. Finny's barn had been stripped of its roof; a window in the chapel had been blown in; and Largy's store of fodder had been shredded in the wind; it littered all the bushes to the east. There were rumours of a wreck somewhere; but it was too soon yet to know what damage the sea had done in its five days' madness. The news he had brought them did not matter; what mattered was his company, the knitting of their half-distraught household once again to humankind. Even when at last he stood up to go their spirits did not droop, so great had been the restoration.

'We're finished with it for a while anyhow,' Tom said, rising for home.

'We are, we are; and who knows, it mightn't be after doing the damage we think.'

He shut the door behind him. The two women had turned towards the fire when they thought they again heard his voice outside. They wondered at the sound; they listened for his footsteps. Still staring at the closed door, once more they heard his voice. This time they were sure. The door reopened, and he backed in, as one does from an unexpected slap of rain in the face. The light struck outwards, and they saw a white face advancing. Some anxiety, some uncertainty, in Tom's attitude as he backed away from that advancing face, invaded them so that they too became afraid. They saw the stranger also hesitating, looking down his own limbs. His clothes were dripping; they were clung in about him. He was bare-headed. When he raised his face again, his look was full of apology. His features were large and flat, and grey as a stone. Every now and then a spasm went through them, and they wondered what it meant. His clab of a mouth hung open; his unshaven chin trembled. Tom spoke to him: 'You're better come in; but 'tis many another house would suit you better than this.'

They heard a husky, scarce-audible voice reply: 'A dog-house would do, or a stable.' Bravely enough he made an effort to smile.

'Oh, 'tisn't that at all. But come in, come in.' He stepped in slowly and heavily, again glancing down his limbs. The water running from his clothes spread in a black pool on the flags. The young woman began to touch him with her finger tips as with some instinctive sympathy, yet could not think, it seemed, what was best to be done. The mother, however, vigorously set the fire-wheel at work, and Tom built up the fire with bog-timber and turf. The stranger meanwhile stood as if half-dazed. At last, as Mary with a candle in her hand stood pulling out dry clothes from a press, he blurted out in the same husky voice, Welsh in accent: 'I think I'm the only one!'

They understood the significance of the words, but it seemed wrong to do so.

'What is it you're saying?' Mary said, but one would not have recognised the voice for hers, it was so toneless. He raised a heavy sailor's hand in an awkward taproom gesture: 'The others, they're gone, all of them.'

The spasm again crossed his homely features, and his hand fell. He bowed his head. A coldness went through them. They stared at him. He might have thought them inhuman. But Mary suddenly pull-ed herself together, leaping at him almost: 'Sh! Sh!' she said, 'speak low, speak low, low,' and as she spoke, all earnestness, she towed him first in the direction of the fire, and then away from it, haphazardly it seemed. She turned from him and whispered to Tom: 'Look, take him up into the loft, and he can change his clothes. Take these with you, and the candle, the candle.' And she reached him the candle eagerly. Tom led the stranger up the stairs, it was more like a ladder, and the two of them disappeared into the loft. The old woman whispered: 'What was it he said?'

''Tis how his ship is sunk.'

'Did he say he was the only one?'

'He said that.'

'Did himself hear him?' She nodded towards her son's room.

'No, didn't you see me pulling him away from it? But he'll hear him now. Isn't it a wonder Tom wouldn't walk easy on the boards!'

No answer from the old woman. She had deliberately seated her-self in her accustomed place at the fire, and now moaned out: 'Aren't we in a cruel way, not knowing how he'd take a thing!'

'Am I better tell him there's a poor seaman after coming in on us?'

'Do you hear them above! Do you hear them!'

In the loft the men's feet were loud on the boards. The voice they were half expecting to hear they then heard break in on the clatter of the boots above: 'Mother! Mother!'

'Yes, child, yes.'

'Who's aloft? Who's going around like that, or is it dreaming I am?'

The sounds from above were certainly like what one hears in a ship. They thought of this, but they felt also something terrible in that voice they had been waiting for: they hardly knew it for the voice of the man they had been listening to for five months.

'Go in and tell him the truth,' the mother whispered. 'Who are we to know what's right to be done? Let God have the doing of it.' She threw her hands in the air.

Mary went in to her brother, and her limbs were weak and cold.

The old woman remained seated at the fire, swung round from it, her eyes towards her son's room, fixed, as the head itself was fixed, in the tension of anxiety.

After a few minutes Mary emerged with a strange alertness upon her: 'He's rising! He's getting up! 'Tis his place, he says. He's quite good.' She meant he seemed bright and well. The mother said: 'We'll take no notice of him, only just as if he was always with us.'

'Yes.'

They were glad then to hear the two men in the loft groping for the stair head. The kettle began to splutter in the boil, and Mary busied herself with the table and tea cups.

III

The sailor came down, all smiles in his ill-fitting, haphazard clothes. He looked so overjoyed one might think he would presently burst into song.

'The fire is good,' he said. 'It puts life in one. And the dry clothes too. My word, I'm thankful to you, good people; I'm thankful to you.' He shook hands with them all effusively.

'Sit down now; drink up the tea.'

'I can't figure it out; less than two hours ago, out there … ' As he spoke he raised his hand towards the little port-hole of a window, looking at them with his eyes staring. 'Don't be thinking of anything, but drink up the hot tea,' Mary said.

He nodded and set to eat with vigour. Yet suddenly he would stop, as if he were ashamed of it, turn half-round and look at them with beaming eyes, look from one to the other and back again; and they affably would nod back at him. 'Excuse me, people,' he would say, 'excuse me.' He had not the gift of speech, and his too-full heart could not declare itself. To make him feel at his ease, Tom Leane sat down away from him, and the women began to find something to do about the room. Then there were only little sounds in the room: the breaking of the eggs, the turning of the fire-wheel, the wind going by. The door of the lower room opened silently, so silently that none of them heard it, and before they were aware, the son of the house, with his clothes flung on loosely, was standing awkwardly in the middle of the floor, looking down on the back of the sailorman bent above the table.

'This is my son,' the mother thought of saying. 'He was after going to bed when you came in.'

The Welshman leaped to his feet, and impulsively, yet without many words, shook John Spillane by the hand, thanking him and all the household. As he seated himself again at the table John made his way silently towards the settle from which, across the room, he could see the sailor as he bent over his meal.

The stranger put his cup away from him, he could take no more; and Tom Leane and the womenfolk tried to keep him in talk, avoiding, as by some mutual understanding, the mention of what he had come through. The eyes of the son of the house were all the time fiercely buried in him. There came a moment's silence in the general chatter, a moment it seemed impossible to fill, and the sailorman swung his chair half-round from the table, a spoon held in his hand lightly: 'I can't figure it out. I can't nohow figure it out. Here I am, fed full like a prize beast; and warm – Oh, but I'm thankful – and all my mates,' with the spoon he was pointing towards the sea – 'white, and cold like dead fish! I can't figure it out.'

To their astonishment a voice travelled across the room from the settle.

'Is it how ye struck?'

'Struck! Three times we struck! We struck last night, about this time last night. And off we went in a puff! Fine, we said. We struck again. 'Twas just coming light. And off again. But when we struck the third time, 'twas like that!' He clapped his hands together; 'She went in matchwood! 'Twas dark. Why, it can't be two hours since!'

'She went to pieces?' the same voice questioned him.

'The *Nan Tidy* went to pieces, sir! No one knew what had happened or where he was. 'Twas too sudden. I found myself clung about a snag of rock. I hugged it. I hugged it.'

He stood up, hoisted as from within.

'Is it you that was on the look-out?'

'Me! We'd all been on the look-out for three days. My word, yes, three days. We were stupefied with it!'

They were looking at him as he spoke, and they saw the shiver again cross his features; the strength and warmth that the food and comfort had given him fell from him, and he became in an instant the half-drowned man who had stepped in to them that night with the clothes sagging about his limbs. ''Twas bad, clinging to that rock, with them all gone! 'Twas lonely! Do you know, I was so frightened I could not call out.'

John Spillane stood up, slowly, as if he too were being hoisted from within.

'Were they looking at you?'

'Who?'

'The rest of them. The eyes of them.'

'No,' the voice had dropped, 'no, I didn't think of that!' The two of them stared as if fascinated by each other.

'You didn't!' It seemed that John Spillane had lost the purpose of his questioning. His voice was thin and weak; but he was still staring with unmoving, puzzled eyes at the stranger's face. The abashed creature before him suddenly seemed to gain as much eagerness as he had lost: his words were hot with anxiety to express himself adequately: 'But now, isn't it curious, as I sat there, there at that table, I thought somehow they would walk in, that it would be right for them, somehow, to walk in, all of them!'

His words, his eager lowered voice, brought in the darkness outside, its vastness, its terror. They seemed in the midst of an unsubstantial world. They feared that the latch would lift, yet dared not glance at it, lest they should invite the lifting. But it was all one to the son of the house, he appeared to have gone away into some mood of his own; his eyes were glaring, not looking at anything or anyone close at hand. With an instinctive groping for comfort, they all, except him, began to stir, to find some little homely task to do: Mary handled the tea ware, and Tom his pipe, when a rumbling voice, very indistinct, stilled them all again. Words, phrases, began to reach them – that a man's eyes will close and he on the look-out, close in spite of himself, that it wasn't fair, it wasn't fair, it wasn't fair! And lost in his agony, he began to glide through them, explaining, excusing the terror that was in him: 'All round. Staring at me. Blaming me. A sea of them. Far, far! Without a word out of them, only their eyes in the darkness, pale like candles!'

Transfixed, they glared at him, at his round-shouldered sailor's back disappearing again into his den of refuge. They could not hear his voice any more, they were afraid to follow him.

THE RUINING OF DROMACURRIG

It was a deserted-looking place between the main road and the sea, and because I could find no one to tell me of it, the whole countryside was so desolate, I took the by road that I thought must lead to it. I had not gone far when I found myself staring at a large old mansion set in a ring of stubborn trees. It was gone grey in colour, woodwork and all, and the three or four stone steps that led to the hall door had long since become unsettled; dandelion and tall grasses were growing up vigorously between the stones of them. The garden round about was a wilderness. Only with difficulty one followed the path in it. It brought me into some cobblestoned passages, also grass-grown, which were flanked with what were once well-set-out stabling for, it was clear, a large number of animals. Neither garden nor house had prepared me for such a range of stables, and I looked about me in some wonderment, noticing more particularly than anything else how utterly the southern sunshine and the winds from the sea had cleansed the place from any sign or smell of the horses: the stalls were shutterless, doorless, and looking at them one had the same feeling as when a person turns out his pockets to show us how empty they are.

I wandered round and round and at last discovered a sort of pathway that should, I imagined, take me again to the main road. I came on an old bare-headed man sitting on a bank as if he were a portion of it, as if he had been always sitting there. The look in his eyes told me he had been watching me all the time I had been exploring that broken dwelling place. It was he who told me of the ruining of the property, and something like this was his way of telling it.

I

'Tis only too well I remember every twist and turn of that long day, and the night that followed it. The news came to me maybe later than to anyone else, it was after three o'clock; and when I made over towards the house I came on the master himself, Richard Donegan, and he standing his full height in the midst of a crowd of them. I noticed how big he was, and that was but natural, for the rest of them were only a rabble of stable boys and horse boys and jockeys, jockeys in the making and jockeys that would never ride again, poor creatures that their misfortunes had twisted and broken. Tough they were, hardy and tough, but undersized, as was best for them. Himself was taking no heed of them. His eyes were glaring across the fields, out on the sea, and a flood of speech was gushing from his lips. 'I haven't looked at a horse for six weeks,' he was saying, 'I haven't mounted a back for two months – maybe ye don't know what I'm meaning by that?'

Well, we were hard put to think what was right to say to him, we were only poor hands at comforting a man in distress. Our voices and our way of speech itself were again'us. Some of us were saying, 'Yes,' and others 'No,' and others again only saying, 'Don't, Master' – saying it over and over again like what you'd say to a child. Maybe after all it didn't matter what we said, because 'twas little of it he noticed, his own flood of thoughts was that hot and strong within him. There he was staring over the heads of us across the pasture lands, not knowing how many of us were there nor who was absent. But 'tis often I thought since that the very smell of our clothes, the smell of the horses from us, and the look in our eyes, and our bony chins, and our big woollen mufflers, and our buttons, and straps, and leggings and all, were good for him in the way he was. For 'twas true what he said, that he hadn't flung a leg over a horse since his wife was given over. Indeed maybe he couldn't have a better medicine to relieve the poor foolish heart within him than the crowd of us to be there about him with the smell of the stables all over us. But that was a thing he didn't understand then nor indeed any of the rest of us either. He began to moan about his poor wife, saying that we could never understand what she was to him, saying that he knew he was a hard man and a wild man, but that his heart would now be empty for evermore, and that no one could comfort him. And although we knew he had some drink in him, as was only natural, we began to imagine that maybe after all he was not at bottom the harum-scarum creature we thought he was. He'd shake his head above us and cry out that his wife was always the flower of the meadowland – I remember the things he said quite well – and the star of the gentle dawn, and his treasure and his hope; and that she filled the day for him with sunlight, and many other curious sayings like that. And then he'd take a change and say that he was making too bold on us, and that we should excuse him, and that he was after having a great sweep, that is, a great blow, and that he wasn't master of himself, that he didn't know what he was saying nor where he was standing nor how he had passed the night. And at last he was for bringing us all into the house with him.

But the men around me whispered to me that that was the very thing the women in the house didn't want; that they were hardly done yet with the laying out of the corpse of his wife; and that they had asked some of the horse boys to take the creature out with them, and keep him away with them as long as they could. Yet in with him he would have us go, all of us, and we had to struggle hard to get the notion out of his head. At last I said to him that the house was the women's; that 'tis little they'd thank us to go in until they had the place ready for us; but that maybe he'd come down the yard with us to my place and take a bit of food there.

I made a mistake there. He blazed out in my face for thinking that he was such a beast of a man as to let a crumb of sustenance, even one crumb, and a crumb was a small thing, pass his lips at such a time. 'You mistake me, Jerry,' he said. 'It must be to sticks and stones I'm talking. 'Tis little ye understand a man like me. 'Tis little ye understand the nature of me. Ye know little of grief or sorrow if 'tis talking of food ye are,' and then again he'd call his dead lady the flower of the meadow-land and the lamp that was quenched, and a lot more like that; and at last he turned on us as if he'd scatter us away from him in his indignation: 'Ye're telling me to eat up and drink up or my health will fail me. What health has that poor white face inside, and it so thin too, and the candles burning on the two sides of her and the flowers smelling?' And he told us, and maybe 'twas true and maybe it was not, that 'twas often he caught his own breasts and tore them down, mad because he couldn't share some of the great strength he had in him with the poor white-faced woman who had gone so woebegone and delicate. And then he'd say that the world was badly contrived to have the good and the beautiful going so soon to the grave and useless stumps like himself spared to encumber the ground. But at last I won him over. He said that God knew he hadn't the strength to resist me, that a child could lead him, the way he was, with his mind distracted and the comfort of his house snatched away from him. The slender one who brought him victory was dead, he said, and the column was broke, and the wreath scattered, and a great many other things that he remembered in the songs and ballads, they were gushing out of his mouth as if he hadn't to think of them at all, as if indeed he had a great store of them gathered up in his mind.

Well, I got my arm in his, and with my eye I told one of the older jockeys to keep close for fear he'd stumble on me, and with a look I told another to go back to the house and tell them where the master was gone. The rest of them followed us a little way behind and not a word out of them. He was moaning and groaning as we went along, repeating over and over again, surprising us with the names he was putting on the dead woman, surprising us all, because we knew he was no man for the books or the music. Indeed his business at that time was too big for him to have leisure for anything else. And it wasn't the business alone – though it was then at its best, with horses coming to us for training from the other end of Ireland, and from England too, because of those soft splendid fields we had and the sands below and the lonely roads that were as good to us as if the master owned every perch of them. The property is a sad sight now, a sad sight and a lonesome sight. But it wasn't the business alone, I'm saying, it was all the trouble he'd get into, he was that careless about what he'd say and what he'd promise – things he could never bring to pass – and 'twas only into court with him and out of court with him, from one case to another, and figures and names and accounts all mixed up in his brain. And besides that, we'd have accidents, and sicknesses, and losses, and victories, which were worse maybe than the losses, and lies told about us, and himself rushing up to Dublin and over to London to get the better of his enemies; and he coming home in a week or two in such a state that you wouldn't like to be looking at him – the big purple face of him so blue and shivery.

II

We got safely beyond the garden and were coming along a path through the fields when we all lifted our heads to the sounds of hoofs in the distance. It was a sunny afternoon in March, bright and clear, sharp enough too, and the roads were hard. The hoofs were far off when we heard them. All of us knew it was Robby Leddy bringing Starlight home – the hope of our stable – and a lovely thing she was – bringing her from the railway station; and we knew that he'd be making haste and that he'd be proud and high in his bearing, for he was after winning on her from a big field in County Waterford. In spite of the trouble and confusion on us all we couldn't help listening to the fall of the shoes and they so smart and ringing. Maybe the master himself was the worst of us all for that. He stopped up his rambling hullago-

ning, and when I glanced up at him I saw his big mouth and it hanging open, dead and helpless, like you'd see the clab of an idiot. He had
the look of a man who climbs up a desolate mountainside and then
sees down below him on the other side a shining scenery, something
he didn't think to see. His head was flung up and his ears, as I knew
well, were full of the music. Suddenly he stepped out from us, as if he
was a new man, and across the field with him making for a gate where,
he knew, the horse would have to pass. We all kept by him, of course,
and when we had covered about half the ground he clamped his hand
down heavily on my shoulder and began to say that Robby Leddy was
a good boy, and that it was kind father for him, and that 'twas the pity
of the world, so 'twas, that he had such an unfortunate day for bringing such grand news home with him. What use was good luck now to
any of us, he said, or prosperity, and what was one horse above another or one jockey above another? But all the same, and he even saying the words, I knew he was listening to the beating of the horse's
hoofs as well as any of us.

One of the boys, his name was Timsy Gallagher, he ran ahead of
us; he took away the stone and swung the gate back into the field for
us to go through. Our master was the first. When he turned east he stopped up dead. And we stopped up too. We saw him staring at a high
trap that had been left standing beneath the bushes, the reins flung
over one of the branches. ''Tis Denis's trap,' he said, frowning as black
as night; and then he barked out at us: 'The news wasn't long travelling to them, I tell ye!'

But 'tis right for you to know that Denis Cashman was the brother
of the woman who was after dying. He was the one man in the world
that the master didn't want to see just then. He was tall and straight
and hard; his mind as tough as his body. He had no talk in him, and
no forgiveness. Soon after his sister married the master, the master
made him a present of a hunter; but only a few weeks were gone by
when Denis wanted to give the hunter back, so that he'd feel himself
at liberty to tell the master what he thought of him and the queer people he was bringing to Dromacurrig – visitors, a sort of company his
sister was never used to. It took half the countryside to keep him from
sending back the horse; it broke a leg soon after, and Denis, they say,
grinned a smile when he lifted the gun to put it out of pain.

Well, we were clustered about the trap, and the master had his
hand on the shaft of it when Robby brought Starlight swinging round
the corner in a way that would raise the heart in you. He lifted himself

up in the saddle to see us all there, master as well as the rest, to meet him; the poor boy's mouth was laughing, and we saw his white teeth shining. 'He hasn't heard the news yet,' the master said, bitterly.

The boy didn't hear him; all the same, he saw that something was after going wrong, for none of us spoke a word of welcome or anything, nor raised a hand. I think the master would surely do so if the sight of Denis's trap had not put him out. 'Twas Denis he was thinking of, his sharp bony face, his close-cropped sandy hair, the thin weather-stained cheeks, the frost-bitten ears. He knew by the trap that he'd have to meet Denis in the house later on.

Horses are delicate, you know. You'd think that Starlight too knew that things were not all they should be. She was nervous, wheeling and snorting, arching her neck, tossing and champing. The boy was trying to hear what one of the jockeys was whispering up to him; and once or twice Starlight nearly flung him over her head. At last he understood. He twisted the horse about with a strong wrist, touched his cap, and said: 'I'm sorry for your trouble, sir.'

The master nodded three or four times in a dull sort of way. Whatever was the matter with Starlight, she flung out wild, backing, and twisting, and shaking herself, and all of a sudden she went up in the air, her forefeet battling above our heads. 'Stop it! Stop it! Stop it!' the master cried out all at once, as dark as thunder. 'Twas to the horse he said it. But again she went dancing on the road, scattering us. And again she went up in the air. The master snatched the whip from the trap and brought the lash down with all his force on the hind quarters of the animal; once, twice, three times he brought it down as viciously as he could. 'Stop it! Stop it! Stop it!' he yelled out every time he struck it, without any shame, and he springing about the road at the horse's heels. 'Twas getting rid of his anger he was. I then thought of crying out: 'Take it home, Rob,' and the horse was off like a flash.

We then saw Denis Cashman, bare-headed, cold-looking, coming towards us. Maybe he thought 'twas his own horse was in trouble until he saw Starlight rushing by. But the master didn't want to wait for him, I think he couldn't bear to wait for him. So he stepped off swiftly to meet him. He put out his hand to him: 'Forgive me. I'm excited. That animal excited me. It excited me. It maddened me. I cut it down. I lashed it. I'd kill it as soon as I'd look at it. What's one horse to me now above another? The flower of my meadowland is mown down – my meadowland is wasted. But you're after seeing her. My slender lily, my poor wife. 'Tis a sad spectacle.'

Denis Cashman was one without any nonsense in him. The wild mad look of the master confused him for a second or two. He glared at him and then said in a cold sort of way: ''Tis no time to be excited.'

To that the master answered: ''Tis not. That's true. 'Tis no time to be blazing out. But the animal maddened me. The way it showed off – there! there! There, in that spot; and that poor thing inside between the candles!'

And with that he covered his face with his arm. It made no diffe-rence. Denis Cashman answered – like stones falling in a well: 'What is done is done.'

And he kept a glinty eye sideways on the master, challenging him you'd think. The master turned to me and said: 'We'll go on now, Jerry.'

But mind you I had to catch him and put him in the right direc-tion he was so bothered by the coldness of the other.

We made back into the field and although we did not turn around, for indeed we dared not turn around, we knew that Denis Cashman's eyes never left us till we were gone from his sight.

III

Now, we hadn't the master long sitting in the middle of us when, in spite of his fine words, he was eating and drinking too. Coming on nightfall the women sent over to say that the neighbours were gathering in for the wake, and that maybe 'twas the master's place to receive them. The oldest of us went back with him to the house then. I needn't say the place was crowded – his people are more than a hundred years in the parish, and her people – God only knows how many hundreds of years the Cashmans are in it – and of course there was plenty for all of us to do. We had to see that no one was neglected and that it wouldn't be in the power of anyone to throw a bad word at Dromacurrig after-wards. I stayed there till 'twas half-past two; and of course I'd stay the night, only that my wife's father, he was over seventy at the time, could hold out no longer. When I saw that everything was right the two of us came away. My wife's father, he was a living saint. Even as we came across from the house, there he was with the beads hanging from his hand.

'Twas a calm night with the moon shining full in on us from the sea. The air was lovely and cool and fresh after the heat of the rooms and the steaming glasses and the babble of voices, some of the farmers and the fishermen rising a little tipsy and inclined to sing only for the people beside them holding them in talk of the times that were past and gone. And do you know the thought that came to me and we coming along in the silence – that my poor old father-in-law with his handsome face and his bald head bent down by reason of his devotion – that he put a crown on the night entirely. Never a word passed between us till we reached the foot of the steps, when he blessed himself with the cross. Where we lived was in the middle of the stables, indeed there was a row of them beneath us. 'Twas for safety myself and one or two others were living above the horses. And a flight of stone steps led up from the outside to the couple of rooms we had. 'Twas when we got to the top of the steps, where there was a great big flag, that the old man and myself turned to look out over the harbour admiring the wonder of the night and the peace that was over everything.

Then I lifted the latch and went in. I knew the rooms would be empty, herself and the boys and girls were all helping at the wake. No sooner were we in than the old man left himself down into an old arm-chair he always made his own of, and I went groping for some matches on the mantelpiece. The moon was shining across the floor. I thought I heard something stirring out in the yard at the back. I stepped over to the window and looked out. The white-washed walls of the sheds and the tarred roofs of the stables and the polished cobblestones of the passages, they were all lit up with the brightness of the moon. I looked and I heard the sounds again, and when I looked better 'twas what I saw – the master himself and he crouched down and he fumbling at the lock of Starlight's stable! I remembered then that just before we left the wake someone said the master had broken down entirely, and had had to go up to his room. Starlight's stable was the room he made for when the course was clear! He was vexed, it seemed; he was jabbering, and his voice would rise and fall in the dint of his anger. I was petrified watching him there. The patient old man, behind me in the arm-chair, kept still for some time, then he said: 'What are you doing?'

'Be quiet,' I said.

Of course he was puzzled then. He said: 'The candle, why aren't you lighting it?'

'Be quiet,' I said again. 'Sit there.'

He saw that I had some reason for being severe with him. He sat still, his two hands flat on his knees. But then he too heard the bits of speech coming up from the yard, and he could not contain himself: 'What's happening out there? Who's there at all?'

It failed the master to open the stable door. Maybe he hadn't the right key at all. He gave it up, he moved aside to the air hole: there were laths across it. He put his hand through the laths, far as 'twould go. And whether Starlight came over to the hand or didn't come, a great change came into the master's jabbering. 'Oh, Ooh! Ooh!' he was saying like you'd pet a child of yours. And he was after forgetting the anger he was in. He called the animal his flower of the meadowland, and his star of victory, and every single thing he was after saying already about his dead lady! And mind you, 'twas a very different voice he had; you'd think 'twas a different man was there. There was music in his throat this time, I tell you, full of satisfaction and comfort. 'Twas that that set me on fire altogether – the same words to be sounding so different! I got red and angry. I drew away from the window. I couldn't help myself saying: 'Terrible, terrible'. I had forgotten about the old man. As old as he was he stood up.

'What's terrible? Who's abroad? Who's outside?'

I didn't answer him. I could only stride down the length of the room and back again.

'Is that the master's voice?' he said this time, because the daft creature outside was getting reckless, maybe he was after forgetting where he was or maybe the horse had come to his hand. I couldn't help saying: ''Tis.'

'Who is he talking to?'

I made no answer, I stood still in the middle of the room with no idea what was the right thing for me to do. But the master was growing careless of everything now. Louder and louder he gave out what was in him, and over and over again, just as he was doing in the evening. The old man suddenly straightened himself up: 'Is he saying – Slender lily flower?'

'He is.'

'Is he saying – Star of victory?'

'He is,' I said, 'stop now.'

But he couldn't stop, and I wanting to think what was the right thing to do. He blazed out indignantly: 'Why, them's the words Timsy Gallagher told me he was saying about the lady is dead!'

That surprised me, and it frightened me, too, for I was thinking he could find no meaning in what the master was saying, that he would think it the foolish gabble of a tipsy man. Just then I heard Starlight whinny and clatter in the stall, and the noise somehow instructed me what to do. I caught a chair and I drew it along the floor heavily, so that he'd be warned someone was after coming in to my house. Sure enough he heard the noise. He started, and then I saw him bend down and scramble along the walls guilty-like, disgracefully. He got off through the wicket.

I turned to my old father-in-law: 'What's after happening, don't mention it to a soul.'

As if my words didn't matter he said: 'Is he a Christian man at all?'

'Christian or no Christian,' I said, 'don't mention it to a living soul. There was nobody heard him but ourselves.'

But there was, although to this day I couldn't say who. Because after his wife was buried, little by little it went about that the master had been fondling the horse and saying those things to it while his wife still lay above the earth. One morning he was no longer to be found.

Here the old storyteller stopped up; but I wanted to hear more.

'And was he dead?'

'No.'

'And did he come back?'

'No.'

'And why not?'

'Because, because those who met him in foreign parts many years after have this to say of him: that the marks of Denis Cashman's horse-whip are to be seen to this day on his neck and cheeks, and will be there for ever. So how could he come back? I needn't tell you the place went to wrack and ruin: 'tis little the lawyers could do to keep such a business on its feet and the owner of it abroad spending his substance in all the cities of France and Spain.'

I came to understand afterwards that the women in the house, or rather on the second floor of it, were the old man's sister-in-law and her daughter. They were poor struggling people who, although the old man had really no claim on them, looked after him as well as they could in their poverty. What was really the matter with him was old age and its debilities – that and trouble of mind. Trouble he had been having all his life, I understood – mostly with his wife, whether his fault or hers I did not learn, so much of it that at last she went off and left him, taking their two children with her: they were just of an age, it seems, to be of use to the household. Up to that time he had held on to some clerkship in a bacon-curing factory. After that he was rudderless, living from post to pillar. When he was stricken down by illness, the sister of the woman who had left him came to the rescue, as I have said, herself and her daughter. And they had kept him with them since. They knew as well as I that nothing could be done for him. He knew as much himself. Indeed it was himself suggested, insisted on, my being sent for, to save trouble, he said, when his time came: if he dropped down on the floor, for instance, well, they didn't want an inquest over him, did they?

I found him cuddling over a bit of fire, hunched up in a deep old chair, his head sunken into his shoulders, his two hands, ever trembling, resting on the top of his stick, a heavy stick with thorns along it. I put my hand lightly on his shoulder: 'What's up?' I said heartily. He slewed round a little and raised his eyes to me. God help us, they told of many things that were up with him. After a moment, and with a little shaking of the head – he was very old – he said the one word: 'Everything!'

I thought there was some cynicism in the accent. But it was true. Not an organ was sound. And so I pitied him. It must have been many years since he had had freedom from pain. I thought of hospital treatment for him. I mentioned it. But the old woman, wisely, as I now know, thought he wouldn't listen to such a thing. She said I didn't understand. And saying so she drew me aside. While we whispered he rose, and without a glance at us or a word crawled into the next room and closed the door behind him. I can recall the bent-down figure, the scraping feet, the uncertain stick poking in his right hand, the left, extended, balancing him – I see the stretched fingers of it, long and frail, white as chalk.

It was a ramshackle sort of room we were in. It is in one of a group of very old tenement houses which, squeezing together, rise mightily up from a narrow quayside to bend themselves, it almost seems, over the waters of the river – the Shannon itself. The group looks very picturesque at a distance, weather-beaten, tall and grey; close at hand, however, one is conscious only of a general decay, slatterliness and unpleasant smells. No other part of the old city is so poor.

As I watched in silence his slow going from us into the next room, I became aware that the old house swarmed with people. Up the stairs and down the stairs they banged or slided or shuffled; their feet scraped, and by the eager voices one knew they moved in groups. A snatch of whistling, a fling of a song, a name called, again and again and again – and the traffic seemed to be part of the place, for I noticed that neither the old man nor the old woman nor the daughter, who kept all the time in the background, had taken the least notice of it. Indeed in the room itself there was, in spite of the manifold and curious noises outside, a sort of silence, a stillness anyhow; and as I wondered at this, and indeed also at the never-ending traffic, I felt the eyes of the two women resting upon me. They were ashamed, I think, of the rather discourteous way the old man had treated me. Then suddenly from the next room, into which the old fellow had retired, I heard with some surprise a run of speech start up and continue without pause. I turned towards the woman. I saw that she also had leant an ear to the speech. Then she nodded, not to me though, but as if she would say, 'That's it,' and casting a glance at her daughter she began to move about.

'You mustn't mind him, Doctor,' she said. 'He's after his share of trouble.'

'Who's with him?' I said.

'No one,' I was answered. ''Tis excitement makes him talk like that.'

'How?' I said, 'like what?'

'When the talk begins he forgets his troubles. You know he was waiting for you all day. No. No. You have your calls to make. We understand that, Doctor. But he's impatient. And 'twas a strain on him. He's not such a care as you think.'

'But you'd imagine there were three or four people talking with him?' I said.

She smiled, a chilly sort of light wavering in her features.

'There are,' she said, and then added, the helpless little smile still within her eyes: 'There's old Kilrenan, and young Kilrenan, and Phil, and the Young Lady.'

She stopped suddenly, and suddenly nodded towards the room: 'There she is – the Young Lady.' She listened. We all listened. I could hear a curious sort of whispering, all sibilants, it seemed.

'She was drowned, you know.' The phrase was intended to explain everything.

I turned on her with some indignation in my glance.

'Oh,' she said, ''tis all in a book. Everything about them, the Kilrenans, and about the Bunratty country, and this place, too, but 'twas different then.'

'Is he reading it?' I said.

'Not at all.'

'Has he the book by heart?'

'No,' she replied, in an off-hand way – and then went on: 'This is the new book. But they're all in the old book, too.'

'Who?' I said.

She jerked her head again towards the room.

'The people talking.'

'I don't understand. The new book, the old book, what do you mean?'

'The old book is the book he wrote.'

I could not credit it. I saw the poor creature in my mind. She added immediately: 'Of course 'tis fifty years since he wrote it. I'll get it for you.'

The daughter remained silent in the background; and I found myself listening with new interest to the changing voices from the next room. I should never have associated them with the poor decrepit creature I had seen disappear into it. They were so various, so swift – with life.

From across the landing the old woman returned, bringing the book with her. It was bulky enough. Its cloth cover was a dull red; its edges were black with filth, were rounded at the corners: its pages the colour of snuff. The title page was loose. I read on it – *The Wraith of the Kilrenans* by Maurice Prendergast.

The date on it showed that it was published in 1885, and in London. I thought the name rather pretty, though I had never heard of anyone named Kilrenan in County Limerick or anywhere else, but writers, of course, often invent such names for their characters. I held it gingerly enough in my hands, it was so dirty.

'And where's the new book?' I said.

'Ah, where?' she answered, with a very patient lifting of her head, and she went on: 'He never asks for the ink now. 'Tis years since he asked for it. But he says he has it all in his head. And he'll write it all out some day. It amuses him, I suppose. Sometimes he's quite silent: we don't hear a word out of him. 'Tis only when he's excited he runs on like this. Other times he's like, like a thinking man, not a word out of him; but he comes out to us then looking very glad, very glad, you wouldn't believe it.'

'And what's the new story about?' I said.

'Oh, the same as that. 'Tis how 'tis, the end of everything is to be explained in the new one. But he'll never write it. I don't think he will.'

She made me take the book with me, although she impressed on me that no other copy of it was to be had.

I exposed it to the bright sunshine for some days, and in the sunshine in my garden I read it. 'Twas quite a nice story, a bit romantic. There were old castles in it, and banshees, and lights on the Shannon, and very dark nights. I am no great judge of literature. I don't have time to study it much; but I couldn't see anything wrong with it. At any rate when I got into it, I wanted to see how it ended; and that's a good sign, I take it. And then I knew so many of the places referred to in it that I couldn't help taking a special interest in it. I think I have read other stories like it – old stories: I hardly remember them. But I'm sure I have often come on poorer yarns. He could make his people talk in a well-bred sort of way, perhaps a little too well-bred.

When I handed the book back to Mrs Dereen I slipped her a pound note. After all I had never seen another author in the flesh.

'Isn't it queer,' I said, giving it back, 'one never hears any mention of that book or the name of the writer.'

She seemed surprised. She looked at me for quite a long time. She was thinking of something, I could see. We were coming down the rickety stairs, and again I noticed the crowds of people who seemed continuously going up and down them, mostly unemployed young men, one thought. They took no notice of us. There was a sort of eagerness in them all that I couldn't understand.

'Do people know about it?' I said.

She smiled. We were standing at the street door.

'Do you see that old green gate?' she said.

'Yes.'

'That's the Dog Club – St Mungret's. Well, there's not a dog in their lists that doesn't come out of that book.' She had it still in her hands, she was weighing it. She went on: 'Did you never hear of Kilrenan the Fifth?'

'I did; certainly I did.'

'And Kilrenan the Sixth?'

'Surely.'

'And Mickey Weeping?'

'Right. That's right.'

'They're all in the book.'

'That's so.' I recalled the names.

'But there's one dog now they call Monaster. That's wrong. It should be Moncaster.'

'That's so. Ralph Moncaster.'

'They're forgetting.' She was a little indignant.

As we spoke young men in twos and threes, idle young men, I'd say, were passing in and out; they were full of youth, full of life, their eyes were bright. We could hear the old stairs creaking and doors banging.

'And what does himself,' I said, 'think of all that – giving the names to the dogs?'

'Oh, we never mention it to him. I heard one time that he didn't like it at first. He said they didn't know any better. But that's a long time ago. But really they mean no harm. Anyway, the present generation scarcely know he's there at all – and sure that's just as well. And they don't know where the names came from.'

He had refused to see me on that visit, and I have not since been sent for. But today as I passed over the bridge in my car, a news item I had read at my breakfast made me slow down so that I might rest my eyes on that group of old tenement houses he lives in. The news was that Kilrenan the Seventh, after winning the Clontarf Cup in Dublin yesterday, had been sold for £400 to an Englishman from Cheshire: it was also stated that the dog had been purchased in Limerick six months before for thirty shillings. Kilrenan the Seventh, four hundred pounds for thirty shillings – great news, yes, but I had some difficulty in spying out the towering old houses at all, for their heads were more than half lost in one of those wandering mists that thicken so often above the waterways of the ancient city. The ramshackle huddle seemed very retiring indeed – stilly, shy, and very grey in tone. But surely, I thought, there must be great glory coming and going about that green gate today, for glory is glory even if thirty shillings is not four hundred pounds; yes, and what great trafficking must be leaping up and down the stairs of that old house where such a crowd of the dog boys hive themselves. If on my visits there in quite ordinary times I had found their eyes with such light in them, how they must sparkle today! And to recall them was again to hear their swift feet on the steps of the crazy stairs, their calling voices, the banging doors. Great excitement indeed. But then I suddenly recollected the little group I knew of – silent in the midst of it all. By this the stir of that noisy excitement must have edged its way into that inner room, I thought; must have jangled the wits of the old writer so much that, even without knowing why, he cannot but have flung himself headlong into swift converse with the shadows in his brain to escape it all and the world it comes out of. I was tempted, but I hadn't the heart to go and see. I earnestly hoped that my thought was wrong. God grant, I prayed, that he is having instead one of his silent days, that he is hunched into some old chair or other, his chin on his breast, and his face full of quiet joy as he moves his puppets about, making the pattern happier.

DEATH OF THE RUNNER

Callaghan O'Keeffe died the other day; the Runner must be fifty years dead at least; yet at Callaghan's waking it was the Runner's end that kept the young men bent forward, listening, while the ancients discussed it. Going home in the dawn, the young men among themselves still discussed it. Of the Runner they had been always hearing; he was in the tradition of that countryside; but during the wake they had come more fully upon his story. They hastened now in a manner unusual with a wake watch dispersing. It was towards the inches they made. They crossed them. They stood still when the river chattered at their feet, loudly it seemed in the stillness of that dewy morning. They were at the spot where in those far-off days the Runner came by his end. They were all under the stress of one mood. 'It was from the south he came; it was to the south they took him home.'

I

Water was what the Runner dreaded most, but young colts he also dreaded; yet neither from young colts nor from running water could he long remain away. He was to be seen at every horse fair in that countryside. The buyers used to say it wouldn't be a horse fair without the Runner in it. They looked for his lithe figure, his lean and anxious-looking face; only to learn that he had been there before themselves. Tongue-tied and furtive he kept on the outskirts of the bargaining groups, to the bargaining itself paying not the least attention; the shapely animal in the midst of them was for him all that was there. Its quivering made him quiver, its nervousness excited him. When the argument was loudest, and the colt's head was stretching after the forgetful backward reaching hand, he would touch the neck of the animal or the flank, touch it, and no more. When the owner turned about with a 'Whoa' he was gone. Sometimes he would screw himself up to take charge of one while the group adjourned to some public-house to wet the purchase that had just been made; but he could not be trusted; one and then another of the drinkers, a measure in the hand, would suddenly appear in the doorway wiping his mouth: 'That's right, Runner,' he'd say, and return to the warmth within; but it might also happen that he'd find his colt tied up to a post or a window rail with no one by to watch it; 'Bad luck to him for a Runner,' he'd say, and make other arrangements.

When darkness fell, into the darkness the Runner would vanish. Ten miles or even twenty might lie ahead of him. He had his favourite houses to stay in; and wherever he stayed a lake or a river was to be found somewhere in the adjacent hollows. He would remain a few days, a week perhaps, and then he was gone; and six months, twelve months, might go by without sight or news of him. Then quietly, sometimes very unexpectedly, he would return.

The man of the house or some servant or labourer abroad in the fields, would suddenly stop working. 'Listen!' he'd say, and listening, his comrade, or comrades, would hear some old tune or other being whistled in a high key, sounding as if it came from afar and had been in the air for hours. ''Tis the Runner', they'd say, and some of them would set off to find him. Leaning over a gate they'd find him, or sprawled along a dyke, or sitting at the foot of a tree, travel-stained and footsore, his socks in his hand.

'Welcome, Runner,' they'd say, and he'd follow them to the house. The people in the house at his coming would always feel a sort of excitement take them, against which they would assure themselves, saying: 'The poor creature,' or they might say, 'He seems good, the fit is not on him.' Yet who could know when the fit, his fit of running, might not again overwhelm him? But then again, what if it did? He did no harm to anyone: it was only his affliction. For all that it was true that some sort of excitability entered with him: after all it was in the man himself, in his eyes, in his very frame, his hands. Better than the dwelling-house, a barn or shed suited him, for from such he could vanish if his time was come. Vanish then he must; and strong indeed the bars and bolts that would imprison him.

He was terrible to see at such a time, the unnatural energy that would possess him. He would rouse from his bed, jumping up, gathering to himself his old jacket, his boots, his old hat – he slept in his trousers always – and then without giving himself time to put them on, away he rushed, the madness of fear behind him. Running at his swiftest he made from the house, clearing gates and dykes, until he came to some pasture land or inch bordering some spread of water;

and round and round that pasture land or inch he raced until his legs could do no more; then he stumbled, dropped down, rose, made on, dropped again, face in the grass, breathless, moaning. And sometimes in the middle of the chase he would be seen to dart swift glances behind him; and hard words and curses would break from him; and sometimes also, in his desperation, he would fling his coat from him backwards over his head to baffle whatever thing pursued him; and dodge and twist a while, and forward then again more swiftly than before. When he lay on the grass, exhausted, no one came to him; it was better not to come; he did not wish it. After some hours he would rise and make away over the hills, wordless, shaking.

But the fit might not come. Then he was a quiet, conversible man, as they said, working with the others at the hay or at spreading the dung, and giving, indeed, a good return for the bite he ate. They never questioned him. They knew his story.

II

In Killavane his shrill far-off whistling travelled through the air, the languid air of a golden summer afternoon. The workers hearkened to it – for the last time as it happened; but that they did not know. 'That's awkward!' they said. It was awkward, because in Killavane it had always been his custom to stay with the Landys. With them this time he could not stay, for two of them were down with typhoid.

The far-off whistling, rising, falling, persisted in the air. In all that fertile valley on that luscious evening it was the one thing that was not mellow and restful. 'Look, take him down to Callaghan O'Keeffe's. Callaghan is away, I know that, but herself will be at home, and she's not the woman to refuse him, or anyone else.' That way it was settled, John Ronan took him down to Callaghan O'Keeffe's.

That morning very early Callaghan himself had gone into Cork for a doctor. Sitting with him in his high trap he had brought him out to the Landys. He had taken him again back to the city. There he had to rest his horse. It was not often in those days one went into the city. The doctor, too, was a gracious fellow. They enjoyed each other's company, enjoyed it so much that it was late when Callaghan returned to his house.

When he had eaten, he strode into the flagged kitchen, where he found the Runner on the settle, his long legs stretched out, his head on his breast in his drowsiness. Callaghan was flushed and full of speech. He rejoiced to have the Runner there, or indeed anyone from outside, as one might say. The happy day was not to finish blankly with his coming in over his own threshold, as he had thought it would. He shook hands with the Runner; he told him how welcome he was; he looked on it as a privilege, so to have his house singled out; it showed a nice spirit. He forced drink on the Runner, and the Runner accepted it for quietness' sake, toying with it, for he was no drinker; neither indeed was Callaghan himself, but the day had been such an exceptional day, and the night might as well match it.

And while he drank and spoke, his legs apart, the glass at his lips, and the hanging lamp above his head, the women and the men went about the business of the house and yard, making all safe for the night and ready at hand for the morning. They caught snatches of Callaghan's headlong raillery. He was saying: 'Look, Runner, 'tis twenty-five years they say since you first came to this side of the parish; that you can't deny; you'd be foolish to deny it; I can prove it against you. Don't deny a tittle of it. What follows, I ask you, or any man?'

When he said that he glanced about at some stablemen. Their eyes went from him to the Runner; they found him with his two great eyes staring at the master's face, awe-struck, puzzled. 'Well, I'll tell you. 'Tis for your own good you should know. Everybody except yourself, maybe, understands what do be chasing you through the fields and by the water in the night time – that is, I'm saying, when the fit takes you. And why wouldn't they understand? 'Tisn't because they don't hold it up to you they don't know it. You'd be a foolish man to think so. 'Tis how they wouldn't hold it up to you. They respect you too much. And I respect you too much. You are an afflicted man, a poor hunted sort of a man, a haunted man, I might say. And nobody likes to speak of it.'

After all that, he had to go to the decanter again. Work about the place had ceased. Indeed the men, as their custom was, were seated in any and all sorts of places about the wall, one on the bottom step of the stair ladder, all of them heavy-limbed, drowsy, desiring their usual bit of gossip before retiring. But this night was different. The presence of the Runner made it different.

They began to whisper, and one of them spoke out: 'Is it in the Long Field we'll put them in the morning?'

He meant the milkers. But the master saw that the man was only putting the word in between himself and the Runner, to distract him. He turned on him with thick sarcasm: 'You can take them, Timothy, in the morning and drop them, one by one, into the river – see?' And he released from his finger tips one cow after the other into the water. There was dead silence. His eyes were still on the labourer, impudently out-staring him. When he was satisfied that he had put him in his place and that he would not again dare to interfere, he turned to the Runner once more, who, for all his bigness of joint and limb, was shrunken together. 'Look, Runner, it's for your own good I'm talking to you. Leave it to no one to say otherwise.'

He paused to sweep the kitchen again with a glance, a glance that had power in it to gather their attention to him.

''Tis twenty-five years since you came this way for the first time, a strapping man I heard them say. I don't remember it myself. I was a child in the cradle. Well, I ask you as a reasonable man' – he paused and his voice changed – 'that colt, that colt you were so fond of ... '

The words made the men start, swift glances were going everywhere: it was a matter that no one for years and years had drawn up to the Runner. As for the Runner himself, he had stood up, leaving his glass on the table, he had drawn away from the master until the whitened wall stopped him; he backed against it as though he would stubbornly force his way through.

The master, with insolence all over him, drew a heavy kitchen chair forward, and seating himself firmly on it deliberately arranged his riding breeches with both hands: no one would hinder him from having his say out.

'Tell me, Runner, if it's more than twenty years since you tumbled your father's colt in the tide, since you wrestled with him in the water, since you held his nostrils beneath it? – 'twas a queer use for your manhood. Don't be afraid of me. Forgive me that. 'Tis for your good I'm recalling it. I'm not blaming you. I'm not condemning you. You had reason. You were right and your father was wrong ... 'Tisn't every farmer would say that ... I say it ... She was a labourer's daughter ... Even so ... You had the right of choice. You bowed down to your father. Instead of marrying her, you took your revenge on himself. An innocent animal! Queer use for your manhood. But I'm not condemning you at all. These men here know me. They know I wouldn't do the like to any of God's afflicted creatures. But I ask you, where's that colt tonight? Is it dead or alive, I ask you? or is it the same colt at all that's in it? Would you know it if you saw it? Is it likely you'd know it after twenty-five years?'

By the expression of wild wonder on the Runner's face they saw that he had never thought of that. Neither had they. It was a strange thought. Callaghan O'Keeffe, too, marked the impression he had made. He stood up, master of the moment, his eyes flashing, his mouth firm with triumph. A day of fine things was being gloriously crowned. He drew back a pace and lifted the heavy chair with two fingers of his right hand, and dangled it in the air as if it had no weight.

'Runner,' he said, 'have some sense in you; battle against it; 'tis in your mind that coal-black colt is running his races and not in the fields of honest people. Black, did I say? Black, why by this time 'twould be as white as Napoleon's horse that the snow fell upon – only shaggy, shaggy, I'm telling you, and with no spirit in it to be revenging itself on man or mortal; spirit in a twenty-five-year old!'

He laughed out, lifted the chair, tossed it from him to clatter on the flags. There was a rush through the room, and the Runner was gone from them. The men crowded about the master, who would follow, and prevailed upon him to be seated, putting a glass in his hand. He blustered a while, but began to sip at it.

'You'll see 'twill cure him,' he said; and they humoured him saying, 'Of course it will', and 'Very likely'.

He spoke on, not heeding: ''Tis the shock, the shock will drive the madness from him. Oh, he was shocked surely, and double-shocked, if I may say so. You saw it? You saw it? He was double-shocked, surely. Many a lunatic in the asylum would be cured if only he could be shocked like that.'

'That's so,' they petted him. ''Tis said, 'tis said, indeed.'

The master laughed until the house reverberated.

'The colt he was so fond of, why what way could he be by this time, only a spavined wreck, broken-winded, blinded, foundered in legs, filthy. All bones and the belly hanging, like a paling that would be falling asunder under the wind.'

Still blustering, they got him to his bedroom. The last they heard from him was, 'I tell you the Runner is a cured man from this night out.'

III

They returned whispering to the kitchen. They questioned what ought to be done. In the end they settled that it would be best to go about their business as usual, some to their own houses by the roadside, others to their beds above the stables across the yard. To search for the Runner, to try to induce him to return, to go near him at all would be only to add to his excitement. Yet instead of scattering away to their beds, they loitered about the kitchen, taking what comfort they could from their pipes. They were disturbed. They liked their master; they respected him; they were sorry for what he had done. But that they made no mention of. Still they lingered. And they pretended not to be listening; yet listening they were, an ear to the bedroom up the stairs, an ear to the silent night outside. But the house was very quiet; the summer night even quieter. Coolness established itself in the large old place at last, and one of them, Pat Tuohy, went out to look among the sheds. He returned.

'He's all right. 'Tis in the hay he is, the eastern end. He's restless, but he's sleeping. I didn't go near him. The light would wake him, I was afraid.'

'We can do no more,' he was answered. 'If the fit is to come, it will come, and he'll put it off, with the help of God. But it mightn't come at all.'

They went out, quietly. The hay shed they avoided.

IV

The men above the stalls slept uneasily. They woke up more than once, whispered a few words, and turned to sleep again. There never was such a night for stillness. When the dawn was just about to rise, Tuohy once again aroused the man nearest to him.

'Listen,' he said.

They listened.

'What is it? What do you make of it?'

''Tis hoofs.'

'Hoofs?'

''Tis hoofs and nothing else.'

'They couldn't have broken out – the young things?'

'There's no fear of that. I saw to them.'

They listened again. The heavy, very irregular clopping of hoofs could be heard. They both settled that the sounds came from the inches, which lay around from the angle of the house close by. None of the horses, even if they did break out, could have got to the inches.

'I'll go and see,' Tuohy said, ''tis best.'

He went out noiselessly. There was a pale twilight everywhere, and the richest dew that had ever fallen: everything was drenched in it. Yet the earth under it was dry and firm, for the summer had been rainless. There was a lively coolness; it promised well-being: the man breathed it thankfully, as he avoided the litter in the cobbles. Whatever glance he gave upwards, he saw the master silently watching him from his bedroom window. He stopped to see him there, so tight-lipped. The master didn't stir, he might have been watching for hours, his look was trance-like. Only his eyes moved. He spoke just loud enough to have his voice carry, and his voice was cold: 'Are you hearing anything, or why are you up?'

'We thought we heard something. Tim did.'

'What did he say?'

'He said 'twas hoofs.'

He saw how the master started.

'It must be hoofs, too, I'm listening to. Where was it?'

'Maybe the inches.'

'Where's the horses?'

'The colts are locked in. The others are up on the ridge.'

'How could there be anything in the inches so? They couldn't break through.'

'They couldn't.'

'Do you hear it now.'

'No; not since I got up.'

'Go round and see.'

Tuohy passed close to the hay shed. Everything seemed to be as he had seen it the night before. He stretched an ear as he passed. There wasn't a sound. It was better not to go near it so. He went under the trees down a short passage, undid a gate, and came upon the inch field at the other side of a screen of firs. The inches were hard with the long drought. There was a summer mist lying upon the place. As far as his sight could pierce there was not a thing to be seen. He was thankful, and was about to turn when he thought of pacing the pathway by the river's side to the farther end. He went along it. The river flowed on, very gently, yet alive, saying its say quietly, as it had been doing the livelong night. He would go to the dyke so as to be able to reassure the master. Sally trees and alder trees grew in clumps, half in the water. He stepped out more quickly, thinking the master would be impatient.

Rounding a clump of alders he came very unexpectedly on an aged animal, an old shaggy horse, gone grey with age: he was reminded of a very old sheep dog. He was startled to see it rise up clumsily from its knees. It turned and made off, heavily clopping the ground. It had a long flowing tail. It was none of their horses. It was Singleton's horse, the tinker's horse. They must have arrived during the night and turned the old creature into the inches. It had happened before. He was glad to be able to bring such a story to the master. When he found him still at the window he cried up to him brightly: 'There were hoofs all right! Singleton's old warrior, no less. He had the whole place to himself.' He expected the master to blurt out what he'd say to Singleton; he said no more than: 'Singleton's?'

There was then a pause; after which the master said hesitantly: 'Is the Runner gone? I didn't hear him.'

Tuohy answered: 'In the hay shed he was. I suppose he went during the night. Will I look?'

'Do.'

He found the hay shed empty. He told the master.

'Maybe I went too far last night. Will he spread it about do you think?'

''Tisn't likely he'll mention it at all.'

'Maybe so. 'Tis time to ring the bell.'

Tuohy clanged the bell that was used to call the men together. Another day was begun.

It was a stable lad who ran up to them at midday. He had seen a body in the river. They went back with him. Between one clump of alder and another they found the grass trampled on. There beneath the bank of the river they found the Runner.

V

Now, after fifty years, at the selfsame spot the young men gathered. The grass was deep, drenched with dew. There never was a scene so deep and quiet with pastoral feeling; and the birds were busy in the branches, impudently singing out.

''Tis terrible to think of, what the poor Runner felt when the old shaggy creature rose up before him; maybe he could only half see it in the fog along the river?'

'Maybe he tried to throw it, wrestling with it?'

'Maybe it rushed him in over the edge?'

'And the whole world sleeping quietly. Terrible.'

'The story is finished now for good and all. Callaghan O'Keeffe is gone. A cloud came down on him, and it never lifted for fifty years.'

'God rest them, both of them.'

The young men scattered away to their houses hoping for a couple of hours of sleep before their day's work began. But each of them had his own thought.

VISION

I

Jimmy's mother, sharply, told him once again to keep still; but how could he be expected to do that, ready for the road as he was, dressed up as he was. A thick woollen muffler bound him tightly together from his very lips to halfway down his chest. Within that, again binding him together, was a double-breasted overcoat, while his little legs, sturdy and strong, were bound in also, with gaiters. As he ran about the flagged kitchen his gloved hands seemed to herald his coming, the fingers wide apart. Dressed up like that, how could he keep quiet? Besides, it was only four o'clock in the morning, yet the whole house was up and about. The fire was blazing. His mother was busy at it, or was rinsing the teapot. The lamp on the wall was bright, brighter than he had ever seen it. Whenever the kitchen door opened a gush of cold entered, and he was astonished at the darkness outside, it was so close up against the door. He stared at it frightened; but when their man, Jackie, crossed the haggard with a swinging lantern, and its beams brought out the familiar objects, his terror changed to wonder, they seemed so strange. And there was such silence. The horse rattled his chains in it. The cart was being dragged from the shed. Everything flowed in upon him. To add to the wonder, their man rather noisily once again opened the door from outside and, with his hand on the latch, thrust in his head and said: 'Listen, ma'am,' and saying so turned and stared back into the darkness. The lamplight fell on his round head, his cheek, his shoulder, his hand; he looked like something cut out of paper. Jimmy made towards him, but his mother rapped out: 'Be quiet, can't ye.'

In the silence they heard a distant cart knocking its way down a treacherous hillside. The sounds were faint yet sharp; they widened the night for the boy: that cart, that horse, that man to be out in the middle of all that darkness. He put his gloved fingers against his lips to think of it. But Jackie said: 'That's Miah Sullivan, 'tis no one else.'

'Isn't it early he's stirring?' the mother answered, adding with impatience: 'Tell himself to hurry, I'm after wetting the tea.'

When Jackie had gone Jimmy moved towards the door. His mother raised her voice: 'Look, there's your tea. Sit in. Drink it up or you won't go at all.'

So he sat at the table, and while with his two gloved hands he held the cup dawdling at his lips, his eyes were staring through the doorway, his ears keeping track of the lonely sounds of the distant wheels. His father came from the haggard, and at the sight of him comfort and courage returned to him. With his father he would go anywhere. When he saw him cutting the cake he forgot everything except that very soon they would be on the road to the fair at Dunmanway. Besides there was no other fair till after Christmas. His father would buy him something, he didn't know what, he wouldn't tell him. But whatever it was it would be all his own; and he would show it to his cousins when they came from Johnstown.

In the cart with them were six pigs. Only for the old soap-box, which had been put beneath his feet, he could have felt them moving about. He was quite comfortable. They had no light, but his father knew the way; he knew where to duck to avoid the branches that sometimes swished along the cart, unseen.

II

A buyer had come. Jimmy saw him hoist himself on the wheel, bend himself down over the pigs, rouse them: 'They're not much,' he said.

The boy was astonished. He flushed; he looked from the man to his father, but his father was only smiling; he heard him say quietly: 'Now, if you said they were handsome,' and he saw him shrug his shoulders and look away. The buyer turned and made off, immediately came back and faced his father as if he hadn't said anything wrong at all! And his father didn't seem surprised. There was a little quiet talk, and then he saw the buyer grope for his father's hand, and slap his own right hand into it. He knew then the pigs had been sold.

After that his father put the horse, pigs and all, into a yard. The two of them then went into the house. The kitchen was full of people. They were all eating, sitting on long stools. There was noise, confusion, in the place, and he was glad when his father and himself were led into another room, a smaller room. After a while tea and rashers and eggs were brought to them on a tray. His father finished quickly, rose, and told him to sit on the sofa and wait until he came back: 'I'm not forgetting at all, Jim,' he said, and Jimmy knew he was talking about his present. When he reached the door the woman of the house looked in with him and said: 'What fear is of him?' He waited. He was glad he wasn't in the big room where all the people were; you could see the crumbs on their whiskers. But his father wasn't coming. After a long time the landlady again put in her head: 'Are you all right?' she said. He nodded, and was just about to ask where his father was, but she was gone and the door was closed.

He sat quite still: he felt that if he stirred or moved about, somehow his father would not come back so soon. But he listened carefully to the voices outside thinking he might catch his father's voice. The woman once more put her head in. At once he was on his feet. 'Where's my father?' he said.

She seemed surprised; she looked at him sharply. He heard her call out: 'Molly, Molly,' and as the servant girl entered she said: 'Take Jimmy here over to Stephen's.' Without a word, Molly, who was untidy, and flushed from cooking, caught up his hand roughly – he noticed it but it didn't matter – and hastened him across the street towards a very grand-looking doorway with a large round lamp above it.

'Did any of you see Ted Coveney?' she said boldly to the men standing on the steps.

A very tall man answered her: 'He's inside at the meeting.' Another said: 'That's Ted Coveney's little boy,' astonishing Jimmy, who never before had seen him. 'Come on, Sonny,' he said, catching his hand. Jimmy felt himself being led down a long tiled passage; a glass door was opened; he was steered into a crowded room. There was a long polished table with a great many men sitting around it; behind them others were standing along the walls. The man who had brought him in spoke to one of those seated; and Jimmy felt himself being lifted on to the man's knee. 'Look at your daddy,' was whispered in his ear.

At once Jimmy saw him; he was at the other side of the table away down to the right. And his father had seen him too, was smiling at him. He saw him raise a papered-up parcel, a long box it seemed to be. He knew it was his present. As he looked at it he heard a sharp silvery bell ring, ding, ding, ding, ding, ding, and the noise lessened. He heard a man saying something about his father. First he said Mr Coveney, but afterwards he said Ted Coveney, and then again Mr Coveney. And he saw his father looking at the speaker. Then his father began to speak, turning again towards the crowd; he was now looking up along the table, looking almost at himself; but Jimmy soon understood that though his father was looking in his direction he was not looking at him or at anybody else or at anything else. It was queer. And everybody was listening. Jimmy's eyes ranged from face to face. Some of them frightened him: they were cross-looking, they were staring fiercely at his father, their mouths open. But his father wasn't cross-looking at all; he didn't mind them. His head was tilted very much, his brows were fixed, his eyes were intent, he was looking at no one, just talking on and on, and although he was tapping the table with the corner of the box, tapping it very gently, Jimmy felt his father didn't know that he had anything in his hand. Suddenly there was some stir, a chair moved, and Jimmy, terrified, heard some of the men cry out: 'No, no; 'tisn't so; 'tis not,' but the whole roomful cried against them: 'Ye know very well it is, it is; what fools we are.'

His father had taken no notice, kept silent for a moment, then went on talking, the box gently tapping the table. The boy was puzzled. The room was now quite still, listening. Suddenly his father stopped and said: 'That's what I think anyway.' The boy saw him put the box this way and then that way in front of him, staring at it, and at last take his hand from it slowly, carefully, and fold his arms, and sit back. A hubbub of talk began and someone stood up; but to him no one would listen. Some were already leaving the room. Jimmy felt himself being deposited in a vacant chair. 'Your daddy will be over to you in a minute,' someone said to him. There was a crowd pushing through the doorway. Jimmy heard someone else say: 'Ted Coveney is a good judge, none better.' He swung round but he could not pick out who had said it. 'A good judge, none better,' he made his own of the phrase, and he looked intently at his father. He saw him in the midst of a group of men. They were asking him questions. He was answering them. They were looking up at him.

III

The papered-up box contained a toy lorry, a real lorry, because nothing was missing in it. It had a hood with a seat within it; a steering wheel that turned the front wheels; those wheels themselves had rubber tyres, you could smell the rubber. The backboard could be let down. That was how Tim Mason got the churns into his lorry. To note its wonders the boy felt himself trembling all over, his throat smothering. He held it in his two hands broadside to his eyes. He drank it in. He didn't know what to say until suddenly, in a sort of triumph, he found himself breathing out: 'My father is a good judge,' and he trailed his fingers along the toy. He would turn his cap back to front: Tim Mason always had his cap that way. He would race the lorry up the hill; he wouldn't blow his horn going up the hill, she'd make noise enough: Tim Mason had told him that. Coming down was different. He would blow his horn whenever he overtook the other lorries or a churn boy taking his milk to the creamery. You could bring meal in a lorry, a dozen sacks, he had seen them counted. You could take cattle in it, standing up. He'd put the young horse in it, with a halter on him.

As they jogged homewards darkness fell, and he began to feel cold. His father stopped the horse and wrapped an old coat about his son; his gloves he made him put on; and the lorry he stowed away safely beneath the soap-box. That certainly was the right place for it. How well his father had thought of it! Then surfeited with content, in a moment he was sunken in a deep sleep.

IV

When he awoke they were swinging into their own haggard. Familiar sounds had awakened him – the grinding of the wheels on the sloping rocks. Jackie was holding them a lantern, head high. He came forward, put it on a barrel top, took him from his father's grasp, and planted him on the ground. Through Jackie his father handed him his lorry. Jackie then caught the horse's head and led him in. He saw his mother coming from the house. She passed him as he stood there with his lorry in his hands, and made him no greeting. She went straight to the shed. She spoke to his father. He answered, his back to her. And then Jimmy heard her cry out angrily: 'Only twelve pounds for the lot?' He heard no reply. Something else sharp and high she said, and turned, was making for the house. Again she hadn't seen him. He saw his father go into the shed. 'My father is a good judge,' he whispered, in a changed tone, however, as if he were remembering things. He stood there in the darkness puzzled, as still as a stone; his brows were fixed, his eyes intent, his head tilted; as for the toy in his hands, it might as well have been a bit of an old ashplant. He was called twice before he crossed the haggard without a word out of him.

FURTHER READING

Averill, Deborah M. 'Daniel Corkery', in *The Irish Short Story from George Moore to Frank O'Connor* (University Press of America, 1982)

Bonaccorso, Richard 'Tales from the Cork Lanes: Another Daniel Corkery', *Éire-Ireland* 21:4 (Winter 1986)

Carville, Conor 'Becoming Minor: Daniel Corkery and the Expatriated Nation', *Irish Studies Review* 6:2 (August 1998)

Cullen, Louis M. *The Hidden Ireland: Reassessment of a Concept* (Lilliput Press, 1988) [originally published in the journal *Studia Hibernica* IX (1969)]

de Róiste, Séamus *Daniel Corkery 1878-1964* (Cork Arts Society, 1971)

Delaney, Paul 'Becoming National: Daniel Corkery and the Reterritorialised Subject', in Kelly, Aaron & Gillis, Alan A. (eds) *Critical Ireland: New Essays in Literature and Culture* (Four Courts Press, 2001)

Gonzalez, Alexander G. 'A Re-evaluation of Daniel Corkery's Fiction', *Irish University Review* 14:1 (Spring 1984)

Gonzalez, Alexander G. 'Daniel Corkery and the Grotesque', in Stewart, Bruce (ed) *That Other World: The Supernatural and the Fantastic in Irish Literature and its Contexts*, Vol. 2, (Colin Smythe, 1998)

Hutchins, Patricia 'Daniel Corkery, Poet of Weather and Place', *Irish Writing* 25 (December 1953)

Kearney, Colbert 'Daniel Corkery: A Priest and His People', in Genet, Jacqueline (ed) *Rural Ireland, Real Ireland?* (Colin Smythe, 1996)

Kiberd, Declan 'Story-telling: The Gaelic Tradition', in Rafroidi, Patrick & Brown, Terence (eds) *The Irish Short Story* (Colin Smythe, 1979)

Larkin, Emmet 'A Reconsideration: Daniel Corkery and his ideas on Cultural Nationalism', *Éire-Ireland* 8 (Spring 1973)

Lucy, Seán 'Place and People in the Short-Stories of Daniel Corkery', in Rafroidi, Patrick & Brown, Terence (eds) *The Irish Short Story* (Colin Smythe, 1979)

Maume, Patrick *'Life that is Exile': Daniel Corkery and the Search for Irish Ireland* (Institute of Irish Studies, 1993)

McCaffrey, Lawrence J. 'Daniel Corkery and Irish Cultural Nationalism', *Éire-Ireland* 8 (Spring 1973)

McLaverty, Michael *In Quiet Places: Uncollected Stories, Letters and Critical Prose* (Poolbeg, 1989)

O'Faoláin, Seán 'Daniel Corkery', *Dublin Magazine* 11:2 (April/June 1936)

Ó Tuama, Seán 'Daniel Corkery, Cultural Philosopher, Literary Critic: A Memoir', in *Repossessions: Selected Essays on the Irish Literary Heritage* (Cork University Press, 1995)

Saul, George Brandon *Daniel Corkery* (Bucknell University Press, 1973)

Scríobh 4 (Bealtaine 1979) – a special issue of the Irish-language journal, devoted to Daniel Corkery

Also available from
Mercier Press

THE SEA'S REVENGE
& other stories

Séamus Ó Grianna (Máire)

selected & edited by
Nollaig Mac Congáil

Love, matchmaking, storytellers, emigration, feuding and fighting, Séamus Ó Grianna's subject matter revolves around the traditional life and lore of the Gaeltacht of his youth. His aim was never to be a modern, analytic, 'literary' writer but rather, like the seanchaí of old, to relate humorous, engaging stories and anecdotes in the rich, idiomatic Irish language.

Ó Grianna's stories have delighted both readers and language enthusiasts for decades. Here translated into English by the author himself, this collection of stories depicts the ordinary, innocently-portrayed Gaeltacht life – now virtually obliterated – and gives a fascinating insight into the unique life of late nineteenth and early twentieth century Irish-speaking Donegal.

They also convey his despair that his cherished dream of a Gaelic Ireland would never be realised.

Séamus Ó Grianna (1889–1969) was born and reared in Rannafast, Co. Donegal, one of the strongest bastions of the Gaelic language and its oral culture. He was imbued with this rich, oral tradition which greatly informed and influenced his outlook and literary philosophy throughout his life.